WIDOW'S PIQUE

WIDOW'S PIQUE

Marilyn Todd

This first world edition published in Great Britain 2004 by
SEVERN HOUSE PUBLISHERS LTD of
9–15 High Street, Sutton, Surrey SM1 1DF.
This first world edition published in the USA 2004 by
SEVERN HOUSE PUBLISHERS INC of
595 Madison Avenue, New York, N.Y. 10022.

British Library Cataloguing in Publication Data

Todd,   Marilyn
    Widow's pique
    1.   Claudia Seferius (Fictitious character) - Fiction
    2.   Private investigators - Rome - Fiction
    3.   Rome - History - Empire, 30 B.C. – 284 A.D. - Fiction
    4.   Detective and mystery stories
    I.   Title
    823.9'14 [F]

    ISBN 0-7278-6117-4

Typeset by Palimpsest Book Production Ltd.,
Polmont, Stirlingshire, Scotland.
Printed and bound in Great Britain by
MPG Books Ltd., Bodmin, Cornwall.

To Rosie, a small cat with a big personality,
who's now getting her tummy tickled by angels.

One

'Alms! Alms for a poor blinded cripple!'
'Help an old leper, sir, won't you?'

The beggars' pleas carried like midwinter winds – some high-pitched and keening, reminiscent of blizzards, others deeper and low, like the northerlies that keep the earth frozen – and every last one echoed with the bleakness of their existence. Pushing through the huddle of begging bowls and gruel-stained rags, Claudia shielded herself from the April drizzle with her veil. At night, these lined, empty faces would huddle in doorways or seek shelter in the lee of the towering warehouses lining the wharves, but the minute day broke, they swarmed to the approach roads, seeking alms from the multitude who flocked into Rome every day. Merchants, poets, philosophers and sightseers; foreigners, furriers and farmers. The Ostia Gate on the Ides was no exception.

'Can you spare us a copper?'
'Ease an old soldier's war wound!'

Many of the injuries were fake. That amputated leg, for example, would be a lot more convincing if the beggar had put blood on the *inside* of the bandage and tied his ankle higher up the thigh so you didn't see his foot when he hopped. But ribs poking through flesh testified to the authenticity of most of the claims. As did the stench of festering ulcers.

'Clear off, you scabrous scum, you!'

The crack of a bull whip cleared a path for a rich man's litter to pass through.

'Out of the way, you old crone!'

1

A young blade on horseback was equally unimpressed with poverty and destitution.

Claudia stared down at the child sitting cross-legged in front of the gates. When darkness fell, these huge wooden doors would be cranked wide to admit the wheeled traffic that was prohibited during the daytime, the city streets being congested enough. But right now they remained barred and the girl sat in silence, with a resignation far beyond her eight years, her battered bronze bowl held out in front of her, her empty eye sockets fixed patiently upwards.

Claudia pushed on through the crush. Stopped. Then turned back. Girls, she thought. It was always the girls . . .

Vaguely, she was aware of a patrol unit marching beneath the arch in military precision, their breastplates and greaves jangling, the plumes on their helmets bobbing as they splashed left-right-left through the puddles. Of a black stallion pulling up sharply, its booted rider dismounting. Of water-bearers, beasts of burden, a priest in his chariot, of mourners taking flowers to a grave out of town, a flock of geese being herded to market. But these things were a blur. Claudia saw only this little mite's parents deliberately blinding their daughter, that she might keep them for the rest of their lives—

You shouldn't have given the child so much silver, a voice chided. *It only encourages other bastards to mutilate their babies.*

I can't help it, Claudia told the voice inside her head. The kid shouldn't suffer for the brutality of her own parents, the load was heavy enough.

They'll only drink it away, the voice argued. *Then beat her, because she's not bringing home enough money.*

I know, I know. The bruises showing through the rips in her rain-sodden tunic were as angry as they were fresh. But—

'You'd have been better off giving her a good meal.'

Claudia spun round. Since when did the voice of reason start interrupting?

'Here you go.' A warm pie was pressed into the child's tiny hand and was met with a smile as wide as the Tiber.

'Veal and ham, with a honey cake and a couple of figs for afters.'

Dammit, she should have recognized the boots, if not the black stallion.

'Now what, pray, brings the Security Police out on a morning like this?' she asked sweetly. 'Pneumonia?'

Marcus Cornelius Orbilio kept his expression solemn. 'No, I'm saving that for a special occasion.'

His dark, wavy mop nodded in the general direction of the coast.

'I've been sorting out a communications problem with one of our senators.'

The drizzle had eased off and, through a gap in the clouds, the watery sun glinted on the flecks in his hair and she caught a whiff of his sandalwood unguent even above the stench of poverty and destitution, and the acid sweat of his mount. No amount of expensive cologne could disguise the smell of the predator, though.

'It's the Emperor's fault,' he continued. 'He shouldn't have said how he championed large families, citizen numbers being in sharp decline and all that. Sooner or later someone was bound to misunderstand.'

Orbilio grinned wickedly as he held up four fingers.

'And take it to mean wives, instead of children.'

'That situation didn't require intervention on the part of the authorities,' Claudia retorted. 'With four mothers-in-law, your senator would quickly have realized his mistake.'

'Maybe so, but what worried us was that he's got *To Whom It May Concern* inscribed on his marriage contract.'

Good looks, charm, intelligence and wit. Standard issue among the aristocracy, and with Orbilio the only patrician in the Security Police, the combination was exceptionally deadly. But did he really think she was stupid? A serial bigamist stalking the Senate, indeed. Young, dedicated and bitterly ambitious, Marcus Cornelius Orbilio had only one thought in his oh-so-handsome head. Promotion. And how better to grease the rungs of his professional ladder than by a clampdown on smuggling, forgery, tax evasion and – what was that other thing she was involved in? Oh yes, fraud.

'Perhaps I could escort you to wherever you're going?' he asked with deceptive mildness.

'That's terribly sweet of you, but my litter's right behind. I just wanted to stretch my legs for a while.'

'Litter?' he murmured.

'Tch, have they got left behind in the crush? I shall have to sack that head bearer. The man's hopeless.'

'Stretch your legs?'

He wasn't giving up.

'Cramp, you know. Terrible thing. Unfortunately, it runs in the family.'

'Don't you mean *limps*?'

'I—'

'Ahhh.' A well-upholstered Arab with eyes as cold as marble appeared at her elbow. 'Meestress Seferius.'

Damn.

'Punctual, as usual, I notice.'

He performed a sequence of obsequious gestures with automatic correctness, but his hard gaze never left hers.

'You hef my money?'

She'd left it too late and now the long arm of the law was draped nonchalantly over its saddle, with a sly smile on its face.

'Me?' she flashed, twirling her cloak to conceal the stuffing of a fat purse into an even fatter outstretched hand.

With a muffled chink, both disappeared into the folds of his long, flowing robes faster than a bubble could pop.

'I think you have the wrong woman.'

Claudia had nothing against naked ambition. Provided it wasn't at her expense.

'Of course, of course, so sorry to hef troubled you.'

The Arab shot a sharp glance at her companion before backing away with practised unctuousness.

'Wasn't that Anpu the moneylender?' Orbilio murmured, stroking his stallion's muzzle.

'No idea. The fellow was a complete stranger to me.'

'I could have sworn that was the same Anpu who takes on gambling debts, but maybe I'm wrong. After all, everyone knows that gambling's illegal and, in any case, you told me you weren't doing that any more.'

Ah, but I didn't say I'd be doing it any less.

'Yes, well, you needn't worry your pretty head about me,' she told him. 'I'll be leaving Rome for a while.'

'Business or pleasure?' he asked, keeping a close watch on Anpu's oiled curls as they snaked their way through the crowd.

Claudia ignored the implication that Rome had suddenly become too hot to handle.

'Hardly pleasure,' she sniffed.

Instead of settling down to a long, hot, lazy summer stuffed with five lots of games, a dozen festivals and more feasts and processions than you could shake a stick at—

'I'll be stuck in some dire little outpost at the edge of the Empire.'

'Really?'

Yes, she thought. Really. And now maybe he'd find some *real* criminals to chase, instead of hounding innocent widows.

'The King of the Histri wants me to supply him with wine—'

'Wait.'

Orbilio squeezed his eyes shut and massaged the bridge of his nose.

'Wait. You're telling me that the King of Histria . . . wants to *buy your wine?*'

'I'll have you know, my late husband worked long and hard to make Seferius wine synonymous with quality!'

And since no king, not even one ruling over a backward bunch of tribesmen on the furthest confines of the Empire, serves cheap plonk at his banquets, the Histri could do a whole lot worse than import their vintages from what were now *her* Etruscan vineyards.

'Yes. Absolutely. Why wouldn't royalty . . . ?'

He let his voice trail off as he reached into his saddlebag and brought out an apple for his horse. The apple was a bit wrinkly on one side, but the stallion wasn't bothered about that. Its crunching deafened her ears.

'Still,' he murmured, 'I'm wondering whether you mightn't be mistaken in thinking Histria is some dreary little backwater.'

Claudia shot him a condescending smile.

'I might have my faults, Orbilio, but being wrong isn't one of them.'

And she ought to know whether Histria was dire or not! For a start, she'd had trouble finding the bloody place. In fact, it had taken much poring over of a rather smelly leather map from her late husband's account box, not to mention some help from her steward, before she eventually located the horrid little territory, but there it was. That tiny peninsula sticking out into the Adriatic like an insolent tongue.

'You tell me *that* isn't going to be barren and boring, covered in scrub, and with rocks bleached white by a blistering sun!'

'Very well. It isn't barren and boring and covered—'

'Sarcasm is beneath you, Orbilio.'

'Then we're making progress. Previously, you've given the impression that not even the lowliest worm was inferior to me.'

'I believe I said slug slime, but that isn't the point. Histria was dragged kicking and screaming into the Empire, and the pages of their history books are *still* dripping with blood.'

'Strange, but I was under the impression they were our friends.'

'Which only goes to show what kind of company you keep, Marcus Cornelius.'

But the Histri weren't just bloodthirsty, they were stupid as well. After one raid too many on their imperially protected neighbours (and the fact that they would insist on sinking Roman cargo ships), the Senate was left with no option but to declare war. For once, though, superior weaponry and battle-field tactics proved no match for guerilla tactics. The legionaries were trounced in the very first skirmish. Yet instead of giving chase and finishing them off, the tribesmen fell on the wine which had been left behind in the rout. Come the second wave, they were too drunk to lift so much as a fly swat against the invaders. The frontier was pushed out overnight.

What troubled Claudia was that Histrian brutality was ingrained. They could argue until they went hoarse that their motives had been noble, because they had no way of telling what savagery the Roman army might be capable of – but, by Croesus, Claudia would never call throwing innocent women and children over the city walls to their deaths a favour. Not in a million lifetimes.

'Five generations under the eagle,' she said. 'Butchers under the skin.'

'I'll concede their track record in public relations leaves a lot to be desired,' Orbilio said, exchanging three copper quadrans for a bag of raisin-and-cinnamon buns, 'and you can take it from me the Histri are cunning, they're sneaky and they're all double-dealers – but surely, Mistress Seferius, by your standards, those are their plus points?'

Claudia shot him a glare that would have frozen the Sahara, but unfortunately he was bending forward to adjust something on his stallion's harness, with the result that a root cutter from the country took the full force of her scorn. Rhizomes and bulbs bounced over the highway like hailstones, but the cutter was scuttling away far too fast to concern himself with his loss.

Biting into one of the warm, spicy buns, Claudia thought what the hell. Who cares that, until only recently, Histria and piracy were like husband and wife, with little solid evidence that a divorce had gone through? A few weeks of misery was nothing compared to what she'd gain at the end – and let's face it, she'd been on worse trade expeditions!

As sultanas and cinnamon exploded in a fusion of hot, honeyed sweetness, she let her thoughts drift back to last Monday, when a letter bearing the royal seal of a woodpecker encircled by a rainbow was delivered by messenger to her house. The letter was a surprise in itself, but – even more of a shock – it was accompanied by a pair of ivory figurines, three pure white calcite bowls, a bronze mirror whose handle was shaped like a cat, two silver platters engraved with dragons and snakes, half a dozen brightly coloured woven rugs and a counterpane of arguably the finest damask Claudia had ever clapped eyes on. Oh yes. And enough sweetmeats to feed a family of fifty until Saturnalia! Spearing one of the exquisite white truffles preserved in extra virgin olive oil that His Majesty had sent her, she'd broken the seal of the scroll.

To the Lady Claudia, warmest greetings from his Imperial Highness, Ruler of the Forty Capes, Master of the Hundred Islands, King of all the Lands from the Mountains of the . . .

Blah, blah, blah.

. . . son of Dol the Just, grandson of Lijac the Invincible, great-grandson of . . .'

Rhubarb, rhubarb, rhubarb.

. . . begat by Svarog the Sun God, Master of the Heavens, who rides the sky in his chariot of diamonds . . .

She skipped through never-ending sheafs of parchment.

. . . deep regret that, due to personal illness, his Omnipotence is unable to travel to Rome to call upon the Lady Claudia in person . . .

Don't worry about that, chum, the gifts more than compensate.

. . . especially in this most fecund of seasons, when the corn is in full growth and the vines are sprouting . . .

What a windbag. Aha! Here we go! Right at the end.

. . . kindly requests that the Lady honour him with a visit to his Kingdom, in order that a certain contract might be drawn up between His Royal Highness and Herself, binding their two parties in mutual agreement.

Certain – she'd rolled the words around on her tongue with another white truffle – *contract*. Certain contract. Contract certain. That was when she'd reached for that old ox-hide map and found Histria (eventually!) at the junction of Alps, Adriatic and Pannonian plains.

'It's where mountains meet sea, east meets west, civilization meets barbarism,' she told Marcus, through a mouthful of bun. 'Can you seriously think of a better place for a young widow to set out on the road to rebuilding her fortunes?'

'None whatsoever,' he said cheerfully, lifting himself into the saddle and tossing the bag of pastries down to her.

'The challenge of a crossroads is always exciting.'

Her eyes narrowed in deep suspicion. 'You mean that?'

He gave his stallion's neck a firm and reassuring pat.

'I'd have thought you knew me well enough by now to know that Marcus Cornelius always means what he says.'

'Hm.'

'So when he says that whenever Claudia Seferius comes to a crossroads, one road will unquestionably lead to trouble, another to mayhem and the third to chaos and ruin, you can be absolutely sure that he means it.'

He clicked his heels and the horse set off at a trot.

'I just hope you choose the right road this time,' he called over his shoulder.

She threw the buns. Naturally. But he'd timed it so he'd be out of range.

Two

As the last of the seabirds flapped lazily homeward and crickets rasped out their age-old song, Zorya, Goddess of the Night, cast her dark mantle over the Histrian landscape, calming the ocean and cooling the rocks as she tempered the brilliance of the fertile orange soil to terracotta. Bats took to silent wing, moths sipped nectar from the blooms of myrtle and, as Juraj the Moon God rose to meet his gentle lover, soft breezes carried the scent of pine and cypress across the waters from the islands.

In the bowl beside the young girl's pillow, sleep stones wafted their lavender fragrance into the warm night air, and the sound of water lapping against the shore made for a peaceful lullaby. Occasionally, a breath of wind would ruffle the fringes of the tasselled counterpane or lift the edges of the ribbons that hung over the back of the wicker chair beneath the window, ribbons that would tie up her long, black hair in the morning, but for now flittered like pennants from a ship's mast.

Broda didn't know what woke her. A creak, perhaps? The tread of unfamiliar feet? Small ears strained in the darkness for other foreign sounds, but nothing came, and she almost believed that she'd been woken by a dream when she heard the grating noise. As though a table or a stool had been pushed aside.

Swinging her little chubby legs off the bed, she pushed her long, black hair behind her ears and tiptoed across the cool, tiled floor. Pushing aside the curtain that hung across the door, she heard whispering – but who was whispering at this time of night? And why? She oughtn't go any closer (how many times had she been told that eavesdroppers grow ears like asses if they're caught?), but she couldn't help herself. She thought she'd heard her father's name and she was curious. Three tiptoed steps. Four. Five. Then a soft scrape told her that the whisperers had gone outside, closing the house door quietly behind them as they left. Pattering back to her bedroom, Broda climbed up on the wicker chair and was mindful not to catch her nightshift on the windowsill as she wriggled through.

Outside, Juraj had bathed the landscape in his moonlight glow, turning the sea to rolling molten silver and causing everything, from the ancient gnarled olive trees to the little fishing boats lined up along the beach, to cast huge, black pools of shadow across a town which dreamed in silence beneath a million twinkling stars. Keeping close to the stone wall of the house, the child could see the dark line of the deep but narrow channel that separated this hilly island from the mainland and, in the Moon God's clear blue light, the ropes that worked the ferry glistened white, like elephants' tusks.

For a moment, the little girl was tempted to forget about the whisperers and explore Rovin's deserted streets instead. Racing up and down the white stone steps in a way that was never possible in daytime, or skipping down to the water's edge, hoping (who knows?) for a glimpse of those elusive night spirits known as wander-lights, or maybe just lying on the pebbles, staring up at the Milky Way and listening to the croak of the frogs! Then she remembered that she'd heard mention of her father's name. Bare feet padded determinedly on.

The whisperers were in no hurry, but Broda faced some serious distractions. A shiny brass coin on the wayside, which she bit with her back teeth – yes, it was real. An octopus crawling over the pavement – she'd heard they could 'walk' but hadn't ever seen it. A cat rubbing up against her leg. Finally, Broda turned the corner and the coin fell from her hand.

Nosferatu!

She could see the demon's long shadow. Saw his great, bald, lolling head and giant hands that ended in long curved claws black as night against the white stone wall—

'O, Svarog!' she gabbled. 'O, Sun God who sees everything, I'll never be naughty again, never ever, and I'll go to bed when I'm told and I'll stay there, I promise!'

Until now, Nosferatu was just something grown-ups threatened you with. And if you were naughty and didn't obey, then you knew the Shuffling One would come and get you . . .

But Nosferatu was real. All Broda wanted now was to run back to her lavender-scented room and pull the counterpane over her head. *But her little legs wouldn't move.* She wanted to scream for help. *But her jaw was locked solid.* Quivering with terror, the child had no choice as the scene unfolded before her.

In stark silhouette, she watched conversation turning to anger . . . Nosferatu's hands lashing out . . . claws grasping his victim's neck.

With eyes bulging in horror, she watched the terrible bobbing backwards-forwards-backwards-forwards of that grotesque oversized head . . . giant fingers squeezing and squeezing.

Broda closed her eyes, but there was hissing. Grunting. Gurgling. She opened them again and saw shadow arms flailing.

Feet kicking in a dance that never ended . . .

But eventually, as the talons gripped tighter, the struggles grew feebler, until the shadow finally fell limp at the demon's feet. Even then, Nosferatu did not lessen his grip. He kept squeezing and squeezing, and it was only when he'd dragged his lifeless victim out of sight that the little girl's legs finally moved. They buckled beneath her as she fainted.

Three

Under a cloudless cobalt sky and in waters so clear you could almost reach down and stroke the wings of the rays gliding through the turquoise Adriatic, the little galley that had brought Claudia from Rome brailed her red and white striped canvas sails, shipped her polished steering oars and let the tug guide her through the maze of larger merchantmen and warships that were anchored in the bay.

Such was the demand for trade in this new and bustling port of Pula that no sooner had the crew dropped the anchor stones than a swarm of scribes and accountants began positioning their tables and tally stones on the quayside down below, and the poor old gangplank had hardly hit the wharf before the first of the harbour clerks was scampering up, scrolls and ledgers stuffed every which way beneath his arm.

'Ladies first, if you don't mind,' Claudia told him, sweeping down.

Twelve days was quite enough. She had no intention of waiting another second before stretching her legs, and besides . . . That fanfare of trumpets accompanying the long line of rugs being laid across the wharf was obviously in aid of some foreign dignitary's arrival. If she didn't make a break for it now, she'd be stuck aboard this vile floating bucket for another three hours, and dammit, she had an appointment ashore.

'I'll thank you not to use such language in my presence, either,' she added, as the clerk's backwards shuffle consigned two wax tablets and four scrolls to Neptune.

'Wait!' he called after her, manfully juggling the remainder of his scrolls. 'No one's allowed to disembark without registering—'

But the young woman with dark, tousled ringlets had already been swallowed up by the crowd. With a shrug, the clerk tossed his redundant register into the sea and decided he might as well be sacked for a sheep as a lamb.

Dear Diana, did I say stretch my legs?

Between dodging butcher's poles hung with carcases and chased by every mongrel in the neighbourhood and negotiating hawsers, chains and mooring rings while mules brayed and great yellow cheeses were wheeled across the cobbles, it was touch and go whether Claudia's *nose* had room to run, much less her legs. Crossing Pula's wharf was like taking part in some Persian fire dance, leaping this way to avoid amphorae of olive oil and wine that were being rumbled on and off the ships, sidestepping that way to evade the tanks of live fish that thrashed and splashed her dress, and goodness, if that wasn't enough, progress was now blocked by an oak tree in shirt and pantaloons. With his long hair tied back in a leather thong at the nape, he had the air of a man for whom the term wildlife preservation meant pickling badgers in brine.

'Excuse me,' she said.

But when she moved to her right, the human oak stepped to his left and she caught a whiff of strong, leathery scent.

'*Gruzi vol.*'

It didn't matter that he couldn't speak Latin or that she didn't understand a word of his guttural tongue. When she moved to her left, all he had to do was stay put. Instead, he moved to his right. Deliberately.

'*Gruzi vol,*' he insisted, and suddenly daylight dawned.

'Frankly, I'd rather mate with a three-headed gorilla,' she snapped.

Because what kind of ignoramus can't differentiate between dockside scrubbers and women of quality? Only the best, no doubt, only the best, but dammit, the next clod who propositioned her would get a kick on the shins for his trouble.

14

Skirting bales of cotton billowing over the quayside as merchants in bejewelled turbans and bows on their slippers seduced buyers with their rainbow wares, Claudia hoped to blazes that this trip was worth it. It was a long shot, of course, but gambling (as Anpu's bill testified) ran in her blood and in any case, when you're the only female wine merchant in Rome and the Guild is determined to put you out of business, risk-taking becomes daily routine. Ducking sacks of grain and sidestepping a drunken sailor sprawled out on the cobbles, Claudia knew that if she secured this contract to supply the King with her wine, it would put so many feathers in her cap that it'd look like she was wearing the whole damned ostrich. After which, the Guild were equally welcome to stick their heads in the sand. Or anywhere else the sun didn't shine, for that matter.

Of course, there had to be a catch – there always was – and instead of ostrich feathers, there was the distinct possibility that she'd return home smelling more of wild goose. The catch lay in the last paragraph of the King's letter.

. . . requests that the Lady honour him with a visit to his Kingdom, in order that a certain contract might be drawn up between His Royal Highness and Herself, binding their two parties in mutual agreement.

Not the bit about the certain contract, but those two other words, 'mutual agreement'. They suggested that the only reason the King had approached her in the first place was *because* she was the only female wine merchant in Rome. He'd know how tough it would be, a lone woman swimming among sharks, and unless she missed her guess, here was another one, looking to pick up vintage reserve at tavern-quality prices, sending an assortment of gifts to soften her up. What the old duffer couldn't possibly know, of course, was that Claudia Seferius was fighting for survival, not just money. Dammit, the only woman in Rome who'd started out with nothing and still had most of it left!

Decisions, decisions. Suppose she came away from this trip empty-handed, because the old miser was too stingy to stump up for quality wine? She'd be the laughing stock of the industry, her credibility shredded finer than bedstraw. On the other hand, just how low was she prepared to go to secure the King's custom?

If she'd had the funds to commission an agent to negotiate on her behalf, the problem would be solved, but she hadn't dared liquidate His Majesty's gifts immediately or Rome's rumour mill would have gone into overdrive. Juggling creditors whilst maintaining an air of prosperity was crucial to her commercial survival. If so much as one whiff of financial insecurity leaked, she'd be dropped like a hot brick by her clients.

As it happened, the decision had been taken for her.

'There's a foreign gentleman at the front entrance, madam,' her steward announced, 'with two donkeys loaded with fine linens. He requests an audience with you, ma'am. Says it's a follow-up to an earlier communication.'

Front entrance? Foreigner? Follow-up? Bugger. It was that damned Egyptian come for his money and making his demand as public as possible! She'd scrabbled for the note which had arrived the day before, the one threatening seventeen kinds of retribution if his bill didn't get settled—

'Tell him I'm out. Tell him I'm away for the whole of the summer,' she hissed. 'Tell him I'm doing business with the King of the Histri and won't be back until – ooh, tell him October at the earliest, and then, for heaven's sake, man, book me on the first available passage to Pula.'

Of all her outstanding accounts, the linen merchant's was the smallest and a mental picture flashed up of the rest of her creditors forming a leisurely queue back to the Forum. At which point, it didn't matter that Claudia couldn't place Histria on a map or that she risked returning home with egg on her face. Suddenly, hacking this deal seemed a very attractive proposition indeed – although you'd think the King's envoy would at least be on time for the bloody appointment.

Her musings were interrupted by a hesitant tug at her sleeve. 'Mistress Seferius?' Although heavily accented, the voice was little more than a whisper.

'Who wants to know?' She had visions of the harbour clerk exacting revenge through a lengthy process of bureaucracy.

'My name is Raspor and I am – *atchoo*—!'

'The King's envoy?'

Short and chubby, he didn't look much like a regal representative. In fact, in his short, baggy tunic and the ring of dark curls circling his shiny pate like a halo, he looked more like an overgrown cherub. But cherubs don't frown, and their little dark eyes don't keep flashing round as though on the lookout for something.

'No, no, I serve temple of the Thunder God,' he whispered, and as he leaned closer, she noticed a gold chain round his neck hung with flint arrowheads. The odd thing was that he wore it inside his tunic. 'It is imperative that I – *atchoo!* – speak with you.'

'I hate to state the obvious, Raspor, but you already are speaking with me.'

'No, no, must please be private. Is too dangerous here. If I am seen – *atchoo!* – *atchoo*—!'

The snowstorms of dust that were being kicked up from the constant winching ashore of great blocks of limestone were tickling everyone's nostrils, but they seemed to affect Raspor worst of all.

'Let me check that I've got this right.' (Priest indeed.) 'I'm supposed to follow you to some quiet shed round the back of the docks, where my jewels and my virtue will be perfectly safe, since you're really my protector, my life being in terrible danger and all that?'

If he was aware of the sarcasm, he hid it well. 'Not you,' he snuffled, honking into a fine linen handkerchief. 'The King.'

'Oh. The King.'

Bless him, he didn't look like a lunatic. Though in fairness, she hadn't met too many from whom to draw a comparison.

'I must speak out.'

The little cherub began wringing his hands.

'Too many, how you say – innocents? – have died, and the King, he is too trusting. He – *atchoo!* – thinks only good of

17

people, but there are bad people around him. Very bad. You must tell him, Mistress Seferius. You must warn him. You are outsider, please. You are impartial. He will listen. He must.'

Claudia dragged him out of the path of a great tusk of ivory and only narrowly avoided being trampled herself by a string of Spanish racehorses that were proving extremely frisky after their long voyage. In a week or two, the new season's trade would be scenting these docks with spices from India, Arabian incense, pitch from Corsica and Damascan plums, but right now the resinous scent of lumber from the interior predominated, oak, pine, cypress and fir, bound for the shipbuilding yards.

'It's not that I don't believe you, Raspor.' (Ha!) 'But I'm really not the right person—'

'Meet me,' he urged, frantically scanning the crowd. 'Just say you meet, yes? Then I give you names of people who was killed and dates when these accidents-that-were-not-accidents happen. But not here. Not now. Is too open, too dangerous. I am dead man, if I am seen talking to you.'

He was genuinely frightened, she'd give him that. Those beads of sweat out on his forehead weren't from excess heat (April here was pleasant but it was no heatwave) and you can't fake cheeks drained of colour and trembling lips, or the rigidity that comes only from fear. For one ridiculous moment, it crossed her mind that the cherub was serious – that there was indeed substance in his wild allegations – before she realized it was a severe case of wishful thinking. Of wanting to trade deep, dark conspiracies with the Security Police in exchange for getting that human leech, Marcus Cornelius Orbilio, off her back. Fat chance! The authorities would laugh themselves into a collective hernia that Histria could be bubbling this close to treason without so much as a hint of it coming to their ever-vigilant ears!

Besides. She looked down at the overgrown cherub, his little plump hands clutched to his breast, and knew that Greek physicians had a word for his condition. Paranoia, they called it. Insanity characterized by feelings of acute persecution.

'Please, you have King's ear, he will listen. When you give him details of murders, he have no choice but to listen, because Mazares, he will stop at nothing to – *atchooooo*—!'

Recoiling from the mammoth sneeze, Claudia's knees connected with a crate full of peacocks, tipping her backwards. By the time she'd finished giving the delivery man a frank opinion of his navigational skills (a view, incidentally, shared by the peacocks), Raspor's little bald pate was bobbing deep into the crowd.

'Hey!' she called after him. 'Who the hell's this Mazares?'

'I am,' a deep velvety voice drawled in her ear. 'I the hell am this Mazares.'

'Well, about bloody time,' she said, taking in the King's envoy's swirling moustache, the goatee beard that, rather irritatingly, only served to emphasize his strong jaw as his firm grip helped her up. 'I've been hanging around this dock for hours.'

'At least you managed to take the weight off your feet while you were waiting.'

A torque of solid gold hung round his neck, engraved with creatures she didn't recognize. In the Histrian sunshine, it glinted almost as much as the amusement in his lazy, catkin-green eyes.

'However, I am here now, My Lady, at your service.'

The glossy curls dipped in greeting.

'May Rome and Histria find unity in your visit, and may peace and harmony be our guide. This way, please.'

Every inch as tall as the ponytailed oaf who'd propositioned her earlier, Mazares was lean where the oak tree was broad, and his long, dark curls fell to his shoulders in a manner reminiscent of Apollo. On the wrong side of forty, only a smattering of grey at the temples and a deeper-than-usual imprint of crow's feet round his eyes betrayed his age, and his trousers were the tightest she'd ever seen. One careless stoop and he'd be showing more than just his solidarity, she decided.

'I don't think so.'

'My Lady?'

19

'I'm sorry if you've mistaken me for some vacuous little bimbo who follows strangers at the snap of their fingers, but before we proceed further, Mazares, you will show me your master's seal.'

'The lady wishes to inspect my credentials?' The twinkle in his eye clicked up a notch. 'Well, well. Who is Mazares to argue with such a request?'

Slowly, deliberately, and quite uncaring of the nudged ribs among the crowd that had gathered, he untied the drawstring of his crisp white linen shirt. And each time he looped another cross-thread free to reveal more of his broad, tanned, Histrian chest, he made it clear that it was another challenge he was throwing down.

'Feel free to inspect anything you wish,' he rumbled, holding wide his shirt to expose a carpet of dark, springy curls that spiralled towards his belt in a V. His skin smelled of cool mountain forests.

Regal envoy or not, Claudia was damned if she was going to pander to such insufferable arrogance. She grabbed the seal that dangled from the thin gold chain around his neck and yanked, so that, like a dog on a leash, Mazares was forced to jerk forwards with it. Even though she was intent on authenticating the woodpecker overarched by a rainbow, she couldn't miss the change behind his eyes. The grin on his lips didn't falter, though, she'd give him that.

'Satisfied, My Lady?' he purred.

One step too far, my friend. One step too bloody far.

'My dear Mazares,' she trilled, flicking the seal away in a dismissive gesture. 'It takes far more than that to satisfy a red-blooded young woman like me.'

'Aye,' a gravelly Histrian accent muttered behind her, and there was a strong scent of leather about it. 'But unfortunately we're right out of three-headed gorillas.'

She spun round and found herself face to collarbone with the human oak she'd encountered earlier.

'I'm Pavan.' The badger-pickler clicked his heels in crisp military fashion as he bowed, but his steely grey gaze remained locked with hers. 'Commander of the Royal Histrian Guard,' he added, almost as an afterthought.

If there was a worse way to learn that *gruzi vol* meant welcome, Claudia couldn't think of one at the moment.

Four

E ven the most cursory glance beyond the harbour made it obvious why those sneeze-inducing blocks of limestone were being discharged in such quantity. Pula was one huge construction site, with a rash of triumphal arches going up here, the ground being cleared for an amphitheatre there, what looked like a bathhouse going up next to the barracks while, across the way, town houses, shops and tenements stood in varying stages of completion.

This was because Pula had the dubious distinction of being the only city in the Empire to be built twice in thirty years.

What started out as a small fortress to guard Rome's naval base at the head of the Adriatic quickly mushroomed into a thriving trading post that serviced lands far beyond imperial boundaries and provided a crucial, not to mention profitable, link in the Amber Road that ran in an almost straight line to the Baltic.

Pula's mistake lay in backing the wrong side in the civil war after Julius Caesar's assassination. To teach the traitors a lesson, Augustus razed Pula to the ground, but give a chap his due. The Emperor was man enough to admit he'd made a mistake and, before you could say what-the-devil-made-us-think-backing-Mark-Antony-was-a-good-idea, the combination of geography, politics and that lynchpin of the Empire, trade, had the architects' pens scratching, and now Pula was once more poised to take her rightful place on the world's commercial stage.

Claudia wasn't stupid. She knew that if she was to have

any kind of role in this forthcoming drama, rubbing Histrian power brokers up the wrong way wasn't the best way to go about it.

Mazares was one thing. This strutting cockerel had needed taking down a peg or two, but alienating both the King's envoy *and* the head of his personal bodyguard was no way to secure royal contracts. From now on, if anything was to be offensive, it would have to be her charm.

So when Mazares eventually got round to re-tying his shirt at the same leisurely (one might almost say insolent) pace, she simply shot him her most dazzling smile. Even when he asked was there anything else she'd like to look at while she was about it, she merely told him with the utmost graciousness that if there was any sightseeing in Pula, she'd do it on her way home, thanks all the same, because right now her priority was to meet with the King and find out exactly what he had in mind regarding this particular contract.

Maybe it was her imagination, but she thought she caught a swift exchange of glances between the envoy and the general before Mazares said smoothly: 'Naturally, My Lady. This way, please.'

But when he ushered her towards a galley tied up at the far end of the quay, enough was enough.

'I thought we were going to the capital,' she said sharply. 'Which, according to my map, is just one hour's ride.'

'On Pegasus, maybe.' Mazares didn't even break his stride. 'But you need to understand the politics here.'

The trouble with biting one's tongue is the bitter taste it leaves in the mouth. But she bit, and although the teeth marks started to hurt, she refrained from reminding him that, honestly, she would hardly have set out on a trade expedition unless she had a fair grip of the situation, now would she?

'I know the King walks a fine line with his people,' she said smoothly.

Something of an understatement, since half the Histri bitterly resented their Roman overlords and were aggrieved because the King was rolling over before the foreign aggressors. While the other half didn't feel he'd gone far enough in currying favour with the imperialists, not when there was so much trade at stake! Poor old duffer. He must feel like a bone being pulled at both ends by starving jackals.

'Nothing new about that,' Mazares said dismissively. 'And yes, I suppose on the old maps, it would show the capital an hour from here. But Pula's the problem. Pula is new, and Pula is Roman, and many of our people found the proximity intimidating.'

He made it clear that, as far as the Histri were concerned, when their supercilious overlords started laying the foundations of a brand new city within a bow's shot of their historic capital, it was the equivalent of putting a torch to raw naphtha.

'The late King, that was Dol, by the way—'

'He was the invincible one?'

'No, it was Lijac the Invincible. Dol was the just one.' He sidled a glance out of the corner of his eye. 'I take it you find the royal family tree confusing?'

'Let's just say it has more rings than a Persian concubine and leave it at that. What were you saying about the late King?'

'Only that Dol sought permission from Rome to make Gora, in the interior, our new seat of justice.'

'And it was *granted*?'

Rome was celebrated for keeping the closest of tabs on its conquered tribes. How else could they forestall rebellion? A task rendered damn near impossible, surely, if the capital was relocated to the heart of the Histrian interior?

'Not capital. Seat of justice,' Mazares corrected mildly. 'You see, be they from the coastal communities or the interior, there isn't a single Histri who would pledge allegiance to anyone except their own king, and since Rome wishes to maintain order among us barbarians, what better way than to trust the natives to police themselves?'

Provided they toed the imperial line and that taxes were paid in full and on time, foreign rulers were invariably left to their own devices as far as local government was concerned.

The system tended to balance out both ways, since this way Rome steered well clear of the murky waters of local politics. Nevertheless, moving this so-called seat of justice inland showed an almost unprecedented level of faith in the late King Dol. It meant Dol was either exceptionally shrewd or—

They're cunning, they're sneaky and they're all double-dealers, Orbilio had said, and who better placed to know these things than the Security Police . . . ?

'The thing is, madam.' Mazares twirled his moustache in a comical gesture. 'Despite everything you Romans have taught us, we Histri remain a bunch of renegades at heart. The late King, Dol, knew that whatever he counselled, his people would still rise up against this encroachment, same as he knew that, if they rebelled, they'd pay heavily for their stupidity. More than most, our late King understood that, as much as one might wish it, even the gods can't make the sun go backwards.'

Looking at Mazares, Claudia wasn't so certain. Handsome, affable, sure of himself, the King's envoy was as trustworthy as a hooded cobra.

'So, Dol set up a new seat of justice in Gora, where – out of sight and out of mind – the Histri could pretend they were in control of their own destiny, and the King could pretend to let them be?'

'It's wise to know your enemy,' Mazares retorted, grinning. 'But even wiser to know one's self.'

He turned away, looping his thumbs in his gold chain-link belt.

'Needless to say, Dol the Just died suitably young, but the point is, Gora was chosen because it's midway between the east and west shores and equidistant between our northern boundaries and the southernmost cape.'

He ushered her on to the galley, where Claudia's blue-eyed, cross-eyed, dark Egyptian cat, Drusilla, was howling protests between the bars of her wooden crate in a manner that was reducing the crew to jelly, never mind the ship's rats.

'We disembark at Rovin and spend the night, before

travelling inland,' Mazares said, once the galley was clear of the harbour. 'You'll like Rovin. It's a beautiful little island, rising out of the sea like your Venus rising from the foam—'

'Tell me about Dol's successor,' she said, having no interest in overnight pit stops, but a very keen interest in the man signing up for gallons of wine. 'What's he like?'

Mazares rested his back against the red painted handrail as the flautist piped time for the oarsmen, and folded his arms over his chest. Even over the freshness of the ocean and the tarry smell of the ropes, she caught his cool mountain-foresty scent.

'Are you asking about the King or about Dol's successor?' he asked.

High on the yards, the crew were unbrailing the sails. With a roar louder than Jupiter's thunderbolts, the canvas bellied out, the ship bucked, and suddenly there was no longer any need for the oars.

'You see, Dol had three sons,' he said, 'of whom Brac was the oldest. Confident –' he pulled a face – 'some might even say cocky, the elders believed he'd grow into a wise and powerful ruler in the image of his father.'

'But?'

'But.'

Mazares unfolded his arms and concentrated on fiddling with the buckle of his solid-gold belt. It must weigh a ton, yet he wore it as though it was leather.

'Three days before his twentieth birthday, Brac was dead of a fever, leaving the mantle of responsibility to fall on the middle son.'

'Tell me about the middle son, then. The man who wasn't meant to be king. What's *he* like?'

With studied casualness, the King's envoy turned his gaze to a point over Claudia's shoulder.

'Why don't you answer that question, Pavan? Why don't *you* tell Claudia what our illustrious King's like.'

His voice was as smooth and velvety as ever, yet beneath it ran an undercurrent of iron. Or was it ice?

26

The ponytailed general held Mazares's gaze for several long seconds before dropping his hard grey eyes to Claudia.

'That's not for me to comment on,' he growled. 'Ye'd best judge the man for yourself, ma'am.'

And with that, the two men strode off in opposite directions without exchanging another word.

Well, well, well. Claudia leaned her elbows on the rail and watched the prow slice through the glistening waters. Depending on the height of the sun and the tilt of the galley, the sea might be azure, it might be aquamarine, it might be as green as spring wheat after rain. A more perfect mirror of Histrian politics she couldn't imagine. Twisting, turning, constantly metamorphosing, yet all the while the outward picture remained the same. Serene and utterly calm.

She glanced up at the mastheads, where a blaze of flags and pennants fluttered in the mellow breeze. Pavan was annoyed, but was this because he'd been asked to venture his opinion of the King – or pique, at being caught eavesdropping on a private conversation? Also, if Pavan was the King's general, then judging from the deference of the crew, Mazares must be the King's admiral. Which made it moot, just how much piracy this tribe had given up! Sitting low in the water with her single bank of oars, this galley was as fast as she was sleek. Like others of her ilk, her job would be to police these waters on behalf of the imperial navy, but with coast-lines as heavily indented as this, and with hundreds of islands able to provide cover, buccaneering was still a thorn in the Roman side. Claudia considered the wide range of gifts the King had sent, and found her thoughts wandering towards galleys, plundering such luxuries from far and wide – galleys which could be in and out before the alarm had been raised . . .

Were they allies, Pavan and Mazares? Or were they pulling on opposite ends of the political tug-of-war rope? And if so, which of the two was anti-Rome? The General, who controlled an army which had sworn allegiance to the eagle, but had a perfect hothouse for nurturing plots in the new seat of justice in the interior? Or the Admiral, with access to the navy, and thus perfectly placed to burn and sink the Emperor's warships? Equally, a case could be made the other way, though. That trade with Rome would benefit the coastal communities the most, linking isolated towns and villages, generating wealth and lifting social standing to the point where they'd be more Roman than Rome!

Still. If there was a power struggle between Pavan and Mazares, it was no concern of hers. She was here to sign a contract that would make her rich, rich, rich, and not before bloody time, either. She stared into the churning waters. Jupiter alone knew why she'd hung on to the wretched business after Gaius died. True, the Guild of Wine Merchants had acted like vultures, descending almost before his body was cold, in the hope of dividing up his contacts, his client base and his vineyards between them, but so what? She'd only married Gaius for his money, why *not* sell? Why not give in to the Guild, let them have what they wanted? Fighting them at their own dirty game had got her so deep into debt that she'd had to resort to all manner of illegal activities, and it was getting harder and harder to keep that one crucial step ahead of the law. Especially when the law took such long, strong, muscular strides—

'Mazares,' she called. 'This contract with the King.'

'What about it?'

The wind billowed out his white shirt and stirred the aureole of glossy curls that framed his face as he crossed the deck.

'Well, I was wondering how much he'd need per annum.'

The deep crevices around his eyes narrowed into canyons. 'How much what?'

'Wine, of course.'

That irritatingly lazy twinkle returned to his eyes. 'Are you implying our King's a dypsomaniac?'

'Mazares, I don't give a fig whether the old duffer's a drunkard, a dilettante or a down-and-out degenerate. He invited me to Histria to supply him with wine and I—'

'*Wine?*' Mazares threw back his head and laughed. 'WINE?'

In fact, he laughed so long and so hard, that he had to rub a muscle in his side that went into spasm.

'Have you actually stopped to look at the land that we're passing?' he wheezed. 'Because, if not, I suggest you take a look now.'

Something solidified in Claudia's stomach.

'This kingdom, My Lady, is wall-to-wall forests bursting with game and dotted with rivers, lakes and streams that are absolutely chock-full of fish.'

Not barren and scrubby, then . . . ?

'Our bright-orange soil gives us everything we could ever need in terms of grain, cattle, pigs and sheep, and it provides us with more fruit and vegetables than we can eat.'

Not poverty-stricken, either, if they can export.

'The climate is perfect for apples, cherries, figs, pears and plums, for nut trees of every kind, and the boughs of our olive groves sweep the ground because the yield is so heavy.'

Not even a tiny *bit of ferocious summer sun that bleaches the rocks white . . . ?*

'So, naturally, we have vines.'

His hand made a sweeping gesture.

'Miles upon miles of rolling vineyards, Claudia, that produce robust reds on the coast and whites so fine that they are the favourite of a great many high-ranking Romans. Including, I might add, the Lady Livia.'

Who was, as it happened, the Emperor's wife . . .

'Alas, My Lady.' He wiped his streaming eyes. 'The King didn't bring you all this way in order to execute some paltry little commercial deal.'

'He . . .' She cleared her throat and started again. 'He talked about drawing up a contract between us.'

By now, every eye on the ship was on her, though only two seemed to bore straight through. They were hard and they were grey, and she didn't trust herself to return Pavan's gaze. From the recesses of her memory, she recalled how foreign military commanders were forbidden to wear weapons and uniform unless in times of war or for ceremonial occasions.

What a stupid, stupid time to remember. She focussed on a family of dolphins leaping joyfully alongside, and knew that she would always associate them with this terrible moment.

'Yes, but . . .' Mazares composed his face into a mask of politeness. 'I'm sorry if you are under a misapprehension, My Lady, but His Majesty isn't interested in your wine,' he said gravely. 'It is unfortunate that he was too ill to travel to Rome to make his request in person, but . . .'

Dammit, the bastard actually had the nerve to pause for impact.

'. . . but the King invited you to Histria to ask for your hand in marriage.'

Five

The hell he did.

The sun was sinking, and the galley's crew were hauling up the canvas and setting out the oars. The sky, a brilliant sheet of copper, was mirrored on the surface of the Adriatic, fusing the horizon in a blaze of burnished metal. Gulls wheeled lazily overhead, crying out like ghosts to one another, fish darted like quicksilver through the translucent shallow waters, and the broad-chested, weather-beaten, long-haired tiller turned his massive steering oar towards the shore.

The island of Rovin was exactly as Mazares had described it. Part of an otherwise flat green archipelago, her whiteness rose out of the ocean like Venus rising from the foam, only, instead of being surrounded by cherubs and nymphs, fishing boats clustered at her rocky feet, tilted on one side as though asleep, their nets spread wide to dry beside them.

'There was nothing in that letter about marriage,' Claudia told Drusilla.

Mistress and cat were sitting beneath the galley's stern post – which was carved in the shape of an appropriately fire-breathing dragon – eating lobster and scallops and sardines stuffed with herbs.

'Nothing at all.'

'Hrrrr.' Drusilla took time off from a prawn to agree.

'Admittedly, I skipped several large chunks.'

Claudia was nothing if not objective.

'But only because he was such a pompous old windbag.'

Dammit, she wished now she'd brought the letter with her,

rather than leave it for her steward to show to her creditors. But the whole point of that exercise was that no one hustles a supplier to royalty for money. Including Arabian money-lenders!

'Nevertheless, I think I would have noticed a marriage proposal nestling among all those titles and dreary "begats by".'

They're cunning, they're sneaky and they're all double-dealers. Weren't they just.

Drusilla's attention was distracted by the boy responsible for disposing of the ship's slops. Ordinarily, he'd toss them over the stern, but today his task was hampered by a growling, arching, cross-eyed monster as ferocious as anything the Argonauts had had to face.

'Hrrowwwww.'

The boy revealed latent leadership qualities by tossing the contents of his buckets over the starboard wale. A stream of curses from four angry oarsmen didn't discourage him. Backing nervously away, he was more than happy with his decision.

'Have you ever heard of anything more preposterous?' Claudia said, stroking Drusilla's hackles flat. 'The King of the Histri asking the widow of a wine merchant for her hand in marriage – and the widow a pariah at that?'

'Prrrr.'

'Absolutely, my poppet. Jupiter would turn celibate first and the sun would set in the east.'

There was a distinct smell of fish in the air and it wasn't coming from Drusilla's sardine!

So, what was the King's game? That letter was genuine enough, so, could it be a simple case of mistaken identity? That a distance of 300 miles, together with a hiccup in Latin translation, resulted in his request being delivered to the wrong Claudia? Yes, and that ham curing nicely over my kitchen chimney will sprout wings and fly over the Forum! No, no, it was the right Claudia who'd been inveigled into Histria's political tug-of-war, stuck in the middle along with the King. But why her?

'It doesn't make any sense.'

As Drusilla scampered off in search of a nice fat rat to sink her fangs into, or failing that, a nice juicy ankle, Claudia stretched, adjusted the pleats of her pale green cotton robe, and considered her plan of action. Because, whatever the King's game, she had no intention of being the ball!

'Will milady deign to walk on them this time?' Mazares said, grinning wolfishly. 'Or does she intend to swim ashore with her maidservant clamped between her teeth just to prove her independence again?'

He indicated the rolls of carpets lined up on the deck. Somewhere Claudia could hear a grinding sound and had a feeling it wasn't so much the anchor ropes as her own teeth.

She thought back to the last time she'd seen those rugs, when they were being rolled out over Pula's cobbles. That went a long way to explaining Mazares's behaviour, she supposed. First, Histria's honoured guest charges down the gangplank in what could only be perceived as a snub to the fanfare and rugs. Then she insults no less than the Commander of the Royal Histrian Guard. Rounding it off with a hat-trick, she then humiliates the King's envoy in public.

This was probably not the time to ask if Mazares was a man who bore grudges . . .

'I think I'll go for option two,' she breezed, adding that she was sure he'd understand, her being just a shy, retiring girl at heart.

'Yes, I'd noticed.'

She glanced across to the prow, where Pavan stood, hands on hips, his grey eyes fixed on the approaching island, and contrasted his steely remoteness with Mazares's easy charm. Was the lazy sparkle in those catkin-green eyes fired by amusement – or, as she very much suspected, scorn? Derision, with a smidgen of the I-know-something-you-don'ts.

'These islands are some of my favourite places,' he said, and for the first time she actually believed what he said.

And why not? Rocky coves and golden beaches unfolded one after the other, and the scents of cypress, fir and juniper wafted on the warm, early-evening air. From the branches of the fragrant pines that swept down to meet the limpid waters, songbirds proclaimed their nesting territories and crickets throbbed among centuries-old olive groves that had provided shade for countless generations of sheep.

Bathed by the blood-red setting sun, it was hard to see where the hilly outcrop that was Rovin left off and the sea began, but the island appeared to be separated from the mainland by a deep, though narrow, channel across which a ferry operated on ropes. Away from Pula, and thus from overt Roman influence, it was easy to imagine Rovin as a throwback to the wooden shanty-towns inhabited by a rough, backward society who had turned their backs on their foreign masters' customs in favour of the old ways. The island was anything but. The closer they approached, the more it became clear that this was a forward-looking, sophisticated, highly developed community with a group of luminaries waiting at the harbourside to greet them.

'So, this is the lovely Claudia!'

An impossibly handsome individual with liquid dark eyes and hair that was every bit as long, dark and glossy as Mazares's leapt aboard instantly to kiss her hand.

'My brother, Kažan,' Mazares introduced, somewhat unnecessarily. The resemblance was unmistakable.

'Delighted.' The brother was in no hurry to release her as he led her down the gangplank. 'Absolutely delighted.'

Kažan's eyes weren't quite so closely set as Mazares's and his hair was straight, rather than curly, a combination that, coupled with his easy smile, gave him an innocent, almost boyish appearance, even though he was probably straddling forty.

'You've no idea how much we've been looking forward to your visit.'

His voice had the same husky pitch as his brother's, but there was something else in it, too. An adulterer's voice, she decided, matched by the adulterer's light in his eyes.

'And I thought Mazares was the charmer of the family,' she declared. 'Is this your wife?'

She smiled at the sporty creature who'd stepped forward in what was no doubt meant to be some form of Histrian curtsy, but whose lithe athleticism turned it into a full-blown gymnastical manoeuvre. A well-matched couple, indeed. Kažan, the boy who never grew up, married to a sprightly filly who made sure he never had to. All she needed was a quiver on her shoulder and you had a living, breathing Diana of the Hunt. What bet her thighs could crush the juice right out of a melon?

'Vani? Good heavens, no, Vani's my daughter-in-law,' Kažan laughed, 'She's married to my eldest boy, for her sins! No, my—'

'Why, Lady Claudia!'

A booming voice elbowed the ruddy-cheeked Vani out of the way.

'I do so hope that the next time we welcome you to these shores, it will be as Your Majesty.'

'*This* is my wife,' Kažan said, rolling his eyes. 'And will someone please fetch a trowel for her to lay on the flattery?'

'My name's Rosmerta, dear—'

If he was aware of the contemptuous look his wife threw him, it didn't show.

'—and I wish you nothing but happiness and fulfilment during your visit.'

Her Latin was perfect, even though the flat facial features and almond slant to her eyes testified to a heritage on the far side of the Dolomites, but where Kažan was lithe, athletic and shared his brother's dashing dress sense, Rosmerta was something else. Big, of course, can be beautiful, but sadly this adage had bypassed Rosmerta. As tall as her husband, she was at least twice his girth, and in a bid to keep up with the very latest in Roman fashion, a preponderance of pleats and a dearth of flounces simply emphasized her size. Overweight, overdressed and overbearing was bad enough, but who on earth persuaded her that such a ridiculous froth of false blonde curls was becoming?

'These are my sons,' she said, proudly beckoning forward two strapping youths. 'Marek and Mir.'

She didn't specify who was who, nor elaborate on which son was married to Vani, but it didn't really matter, because, having bowed to the newcomer and mumbled a perfunctory greeting, they immediately turned their attentions to where the wine might be stashed on this godforsaken island.

Rosmerta's pinched lips stretched into an indulgent smile, as if to say, *Boys!* and Claudia thought, *Interesting.* Two young men made in their father's image, yet it was from their mother that their characters were drawn.

'This is Drilo, our high priest,' Kažan said.

Bearded and strong-featured, Drilo stepped forward. He smelled of the incense and myrrh that was burned in supplication to his strange gods, and amulets of electrum encircled each wrist.

'You honour us, My Lady,' Drilo said, bowing deeply.

Round his oiled, braided hair he wore a band of gold engraved with the same creatures Claudia had seen on the torque around Mazares's neck.

'On the contrary,' she replied, covering his hand gently with hers. 'It is you who honour me.'

She gazed into his penetrating dark-blue eyes and smiled her most beguiling smile.

Let him think she was hooked. Let them *all* think she was hooked. That she'd been won over by the gifts, by the flattery, by the lure of the big prize at the end, but make no mistake, my cunning, sneaky, double-dealing Histrian friends. You can pay me, because, oh yes, I'll take your money.

It doesn't mean I've been bought.

Six

Marcus Cornelius Orbilio leaned his tall frame against the temple wall and folded his arms across his chest. The sun was setting, but the evening air was quite without chill, despite the gentle breeze that ruffled the hem of his long, patrician tunic. Inside the temple, the priests and scribes were busy cataloguing the day's intake of offerings to Hercules. As patron of commerce as well as leader of the Muses, the gifts covered the broadest spectrum on the religious scale, and from what Orbilio could hear, today's donations included everything from lyres to poetry engraved on bronze tablets right down to humble terracotta goblets and lions carved from sacred wild olive.

Orbilio wasn't interested in the goings-on inside the temple. It was the house along the street that he was watching. It was a fine house, newly built, with red roof tiles and doors of cedarwood, and from the small slits in the walls that faced the road, he could see the bright flickering of lamps, even though the sun had not yet sunk. Reluctantly, he prised himself off the temple wall and sauntered slowly down towards the house, and maybe it was the scent of Hercules's sacred laurel, but there was a bitter taste on the back of his tongue.

He lifted the gleaming bronze panther-head knocker and let it fall. The door opened at once and a naked black girl, her skin oiled and fragrant, bade him welcome. Once inside, the opulence of the mansion exploded from every angle. Pillars of glistening pure-white Parian marble. Fountains with three, and sometimes four, cascades. Exquisite mosaics on the floors, the most superb artistry on the soaring walls. Gilded ceilings emphasized the luxury.

Having removed his sandals and bathed his feet in rose-water, the servant girl handed him a glass of vintage Falernian then offered him a plate of sweetmeats. He took a candied cherry stuffed with almond paste, mainly because he didn't want to offend her, rather than because he was hungry, thanked her with a silver coin and moved on. Rare Arabian resins burned in braziers on the walls. Musicians played on flutes and pipes and drums, acrobats in Eastern dress performed a tumbling act and sword dancers from the Orient leapt across their deadly curving blades with practised ease. The very sort of entertainment, Orbilio reflected, that he was used to seeing at family banquets. Before his family stopped inviting him!

'Is there anything I can do for you?' a voice breathed in his ear.

He cast his glance around the beauties draped across the richly upholstered couches, at the revealing slits in their diaphanous garments and the feathered fans in soft bejewelled hands that made subtle beckoning gestures to the male visitors. Then his eyes lifted to the artfully rouged cheeks, the red pouting lips, the kohled eyes, and he drew a deep breath.

'Another glass of wine would be nice.'

'Of course.'

The voice sounded vaguely disappointed, but the wine appeared almost at once. He resisted the urge to toss it down in a single swallow and forced himself to sip slowly from the green glass goblet as he passed from atrium to dining hall and out into the garden.

'Follow me,' a gorgeous creature whispered, 'and I'll show you paradise.'

'I don't doubt it,' he replied, disentangling his arm and wondering how much the transparent linen fabric shot with gold would cost. 'Give me an hour, though.'

Mingling among the brothel's clientele (foreign merchants mostly, for who else could afford the exorbitant rates?), Orbilio listened to the babble of laughter and this time he didn't ration his drink, but knocked back what was left in his goblet and grimaced. Beneath the joking and the banter, the teasing and the tempting, there ran an undercurrent of desperation and heartache. These were not mosaics that his boots were treading on. He was trampling the remnants of a thousand broken dreams. Crushing the relics of a million shattered promises. For prostitution, even on this exalted level, still exacts a price . . .

And what price am I paying, he wondered? When he joined the Security Police, he genuinely believed he could make a difference. What was the point, he'd argue, in following the family tradition to become a lawyer, when he could be out there, fighting hand to hand on the battlefield in the war between Good and Evil?

He was young then.

An idealist fresh out of the army, and all too painfully he'd discovered that the lines between Good and Evil are frequently blurred. That the enemy isn't always the enemy, and that Good isn't always an advantage – or necessarily right. Furthermore, as the only investigator in the Security Police with blue blood in his veins, he was never fully accepted by the other members of the team, his lower-born boss resented him, and the very nature of his work ostracized him from patrician society. (At least polite patrician society, he qualified wryly, spotting a retired senator sandwiched between two simpering beauties.)

But it was worth it. Half the time he spent traipsing the same old streets, interrogating the same old suspects – little men with big egos or else hotheads with half-baked ideals – and usually all he managed to unearth for his pains was a mixture of bravado and bullshit. Also, the public seemed to be under the impression that once the Empire had rid itself of a few conspirators, that was the end of the matter. It wasn't. Subversion's a weed. A vicious, pernicious, perennial weed, and no matter how often you cut off its blooms or yanked at its stems, the roots of sedition were too deep to dig out. So why did he bother? Why keep beating round the same old dusty bushes?

Simple. If he didn't, the anarchists and assassins would prevail, and imagine if the law of the sword was permitted to win. The seas and the highways would become unsafe to travel; trade would collapse; the Empire would tear itself apart like rabid dogs. It wouldn't happen overnight, of course. Such a downfall would take years. Generations, perhaps. But Rome had seen enough of her own sons' blood spilled. Augustus had single-handedly crushed a hundred years of bitter in-fighting to give the Empire peace and stability, endowing his people with a prosperity and a pride that they had not known before. It was worth the lack of acceptance to keep that flame alive, but there were times – God knows there were times – when Orbilio could use a little human comfort.

He continued to work through the fragrant crush, conscious of fingers sliding against his thigh or brushing his hip. Expert fingers, enticing, inviting; gateways to relief and oblivion.

In the fountain by the rose arbour, a slant-eyed dancing girl, naked apart from a black velvet mask, twisted and writhed to a tune played on a lyre by a blind musician, her long wet hair slapping against her oiled skin with rhythmic provocativeness. He moved on.

'They call me Rapture.' A jangle of bracelets rattled in his ear before a fusion of fine lemon cotton and forget-me-not scent blocked his path.

'I can see why,' Orbilio replied, running his eyes over the transparent flounced gown, the delicate embroidery, the finely tooled kid-skin slippers. 'Unfortunately, Rapture, I've arranged to meet with someone else.'

'Pity.' Black-rimmed eyes at a level with his flickered with practised coquettishness. 'Maybe next time . . . ?'

'Definitely,' he lied, watching Rapture sashay seductively down the path.

Too tall, he thought, far too tall, and his heart lurched for the woman who only came up to here on him. The woman who was not forced by law to wear the dyed yellow wig of the prostitute, but one with hair piled high in tempestuous curls and eyes that flashed like twin forest fires – and a tongue

The gasp was pure terror.

'My father?' Tears began to well up. 'Does he know about . . . about this?'

Orbilio wished he'd had the courage to follow his desires and walk out that front door a few minutes ago. Why did he have to be so bloody tied to his duties? Family duties, in this particular instance, but none the less binding for that. And how bloody ironic that his uncle so disapproved of his role in the Security Police, until he needed his help . . .

'He'd been hearing rumours,' he explained patiently, because, heaven knows, it wasn't the first time his little cousin had been caught whoring. 'He asked me to investigate.'

Translation, hush it up.

'Marcus, I beg you on my life, don't let my father find out! I'll be ruined. Oh, for pity's sake, Marcus. I'm married.'

The sobbing was pitiful.

'I've two boys and – sweet Jupiter, you know the law. What I'm doing isn't just adultery. It's – it's – Oh please, if word gets back, they'll take my kids away, I'll never see them again.'

'Pity you didn't think of the consequences beforehand,' he snapped. 'After all, it's not as though you needed the money.'

He'd checked. But no, this was for kicks.

The kohl was making ugly black stripes down the rouge. 'I can't help what I do, Marcus. I genuinely can't help it.'

He drew a deep breath. Held it. Let it out slowly. 'I know,' he whispered.

His cousin wasn't alone. There were plenty of people, wealthy people at that, who had the same problem. Addicted to sex. Addicted to selling their bodies. That was the reason he hadn't walked out earlier. The poor sods just couldn't help it.

'But you can't go on prostituting yourself like this,' he said gently. 'You have to stop, for your own sake as well as your family's.'

This was probably *not* the time to bring up the subject of diseases. Or blackmail. Or beatings. Or what happened when good looks started to fade . . .

'Marcus, oh, Marcus, what am I going to do?'

Orbilio spiked weary fingers through his hair. 'For a start, you're going to dry your eyes, patch up your make-up and put that ridiculous wig back on. Then, my dear cousin, you and I are going to walk out of here as though I'm taking my little playmate home for the night.'

He felt a hundred years old, not just twenty-eight, and a vice was crushing the life from his ribs.

'When we're far enough away from this place,' he continued, 'you're going to wash your face, change into a tunic that isn't see-through and slit to the crotch, then you're going to go home to your poor bloody wife, tell her you spent a wonderful evening with your cousin Marcus and then tomorrow morning, Horatio, you're going to sit on the magistrate's bench as usual. Is that clear?'

Silence.

'Horatio, I said, is that clear?'

Unable to speak, Horatio nodded dumbly.

Seven

As much as Claudia would have liked to think the islanders' searing scrutiny was centred on Mazares's skin-tight pants, she knew it was curiosity at a possible future Queen that had their eyes drinking in everything from the straightness of her back to the gilding on her sandals, the childbearing potential of her hips to the shining silver tiara that stopped her curls from tangling in the breeze. Darkness had encompassed the archipelago, but she could feel the women contrasting her elaborate coiffure with their own simple braids and comparing her fashionably pleated (and hideously expensive) embroidered gown with their own plain and practical tunics. Ah, but when they weighed up the stiff gold girdle beneath her bust, how did that rate against the comfort of a soft woven belt tied loosely round the waist?

Kažan had shouted, 'Drinks all round!' to everyone who'd turned out to welcome the King's bride, an offer seized upon with alacrity by his two sons. The ponytailed Pavan had strode off into the night, presumably to find some more badgers to pickle, Drilo had led his priestly entourage off to make sacrifice for Claudia and the ship's safe arrival, heaven knows where Vani had disappeared to, probably arm-wrestling with the crew if those muscles were anything to go by! So, with Rosmerta barking orders for the disembarkation of Claudia's luggage with an efficiency that many a centurion could learn from, it was left to Mazares to lead Histria's honoured guest through the labyrinth of winding streets to the King's house.

Any preconceptions of this being a nation of backward, warring pirates who needed to be kept in check by their Roman vanquishers had long gone. Between the late King, Dol, and his successor, a culture had been created that was as sophisticated as it was autonomous, and although the Histri worshipped different gods and retained their own traditions, theirs was as vibrant and progressive a society as any within the boundaries of the Empire.

Equally, though, Histria was a land of opposites. Half the kingdom comprised a string of isolated coastal communities who made their living from the sea and were defended by a fleet of fast, sleek galleys. The other half was made up of the hunters and farmers of the peninsula's interior and was policed by an army officially classified as Roman auxiliaries. Light and shade, she thought. Light and shade . . .

'The person who can successfully juggle the needs of two such diverse factions must be quite a man,' Claudia said.

She saw no need to add that there was no way such a hero would seek out a low-born, impecunious widow for his wife.

'Not for someone born among the two communities,' Mazares replied, holding the torch high, so she wouldn't miss her footing on the steps. 'To us, it's no different from having a man and a woman as parents. Separately, they're chalk and cheese; together, they make the perfect team.'

An interesting analogy, because, in Claudia's experience, most domestic murders were committed by the spouse . . .

'I don't think the King's general approves of me,' she said, as they climbed yet another flight of steps cut in the rock.

Mazares let out a soft, velvety laugh. 'Don't mind Pavan. He's a soldier through to his marrow and sees no point in using three words when none will do.'

Hardly an answer.

'And what about you?' she said cheerfully. 'Why don't *you* want me to marry the King?'

She expected to hear a frantic fluttering of wings as half a dozen cats were dropped among the pigeons. Instead, there was an imperceptible stiffening of back muscles and, when Mazares turned, his expression was diplomacy personified.

'I cannot imagine . . .'

For good measure, she lobbed in a couple more moggies. 'Is it because I'm a foreigner? A widow, perhaps? Or is it because I'm in trade?'

'My Lady.'

With Histrian solemnity, he clicked his heels and dipped his head towards his chest without the slightest hint of obsequiousness.

'My Lady, nothing would please me more, believe me, than for you to contract an alliance with the King.'

He was lying. There was nothing in his eyes, in his voice, in his mannerisms to betray him. But Mazares was lying through his strong white teeth.

'Good. Then you can advise me on the wedding ceremony.'

Catkin eyes held hers for a beat of perhaps three.

'An honour,' he murmured, and as he set off up the slope, she could feel emotion pulsing off him like raindrops on parched earth. Though, for the life of her, she didn't know what.

'Like all Histrian marriage rites,' he said, 'it would take place under the watchful eye of the Sun God, for it is Svarog who governs our happiness.'

He didn't say it will take place. Only that it *would* . . .

'Governs happiness, because he lives in a palace of gold and rides the sky in a diamond chariot?' she asked brightly.

See! Some parts of the King's long-winded introduction had stuck!

'Actually, I think it has more to do with Svarog keeping two nubile wives, Dawn and Dusk, and having his youth restored to him every morning.'

'Is that the same youth every morning, or do they take turns?'

'No idea,' he laughed, 'but I'm – *oof!*'

Turning the corner, the breath was knocked out of him by a figure coming the other way. In the light of his spluttering torch, Claudia could see that the woman was nearly as tall as he was, with a mane of dark red hair tied back in a pale grey ribbon. Her skin bore the deep, healthy tan of the outdoors, yet there was something about her long nose and finely chiselled cheekbones that suggested she wasn't of Histrian ancestry.

'Salome!'

'Mazares.'

Like an eel through water, something passed between them and just as quickly it was gone.

'How are you?' Salome asked quietly.

Mazares ignored her concern for his health. 'I'd like you to meet Claudia, Salome.'

Green eyes widened in surprise – and perhaps with something else. 'Well, congratulations, my dear!'

She put down her basket laden with herbs and opened both arms to embrace the newcomer, but Mazares held up his hand.

'Whoa! Claudia hasn't accepted the King's proposal. She's merely checking out the lie of the land.' He turned dancing eyes on Claudia. 'Or have I read the lady wrong?'

Frankly, she doubted Mazares read any lady wrong. Out across the water, a flock of late seabirds made their way home, their wings almost skimming the dark heaving ocean, and the air was fragrant with oleander and myrtle.

'And since she knows very little about his illustrious majesty,' Mazares put in before she could come up with a suitable retort, 'Claudia is also keen to find out as much about him as possible.' His grin widened to something a wolf would be proud of. 'I feel sure you'd be only too pleased to enlighten her.'

Salome's eyes moved slowly from Mazares to Claudia and back again.

'I appreciate the compliment, but I really don't feel a lowly Syrian farm widow is qualified to comment.'

'I beg to disagree, but . . .' Mazares stroked his goatee beard pensively. 'That's your prerogative, I suppose. The King still intends for you to change your practices, you know.'

48

'The King –' Salome turned the word into a cross between a laugh and a sneer – 'can intend all he likes. He has no jurisdiction over me.'

She turned to Claudia and took both her hands in hers.

'I do hope you enjoy your stay on Rovin, my dear. There's lots to explore in the area and I know Mazares will ensure you have a wonderful time here, but if you'll both excuse me, there's a little girl I need to see before the ferryman closes up for the night, leaving me unable to get back to the mainland.'

'Nothing serious?' Mazares asked, indicating Salome's basket, which also contained several phials among the lavender, yarrow, chamomile and mint.

Salome's expression changed. Became sad. 'Poor child,' she sighed. 'For the last couple of weeks, she's been unable to sleep. The little mite's convinced she's seen Nosferatu.'

'Nosferatu?' Claudia asked.

'It's nothing,' Salome said, with a shake of her head. 'Nothing at all. Little ears pick up tales of shroud-eaters who suck blood from human veins, men who transform themselves into wolves and fire-breathing, serpent-tailed giants, and their childish imagination runs riot.'

Mazares laughed. 'Even if there were such an arch-ghoul on the prowl, I'm sure the ferryman would have picked Nosferatu out of a crowd of passengers. I mean, we're an ugly bunch, us Histri, but we're not *that* ugly!'

Ghouls? Vampires? Werewolves? This was yet another example of the diametrically opposing faces of this little kingdom, with Histria selling itself as the home of the Nymphs of the West, whose sweet songs lulled folk to sleep. But then, under the circumstances, promoting the gentle offspring of Night and the Evening Star, who lived in the Gardens of the Hesperides, which had been walled by mighty Atlas and were washed by the waters of purity *would* be preferable to owning up to home-grown nocturnal monsters!

'Whether Nosferatu exists or not,' Salome said, looping her basket over her arm, 'he's real enough to the shipwright's little niece. I only pray my remedies can help.'

With a broad smile of farewell, she turned and marched confidently down the narrow steps, even though they were pitch-black and in shadow.

'What practices?' Claudia asked.

Mazares stared down the hill for several seconds. Far in the distance, a dog began to bark.

'I beg your pardon?' he said.

'What practices does the King intend Salome to change? She doesn't look the sort to use her herbalism to practise the black arts, but then again, if you told me she was five hundred and eighty-two last birthday, I might be prepared to revise my opinion.'

Mazares didn't laugh.

'This is Salome's thirtieth summer,' he murmured. 'Ten years ago, she came here with her husband. He was newly retired from your army and you don't need me to explain how the Histrian mainland is being parcelled up by your illustrious Emperor and our land distributed among your war veterans, now do you?'

The bitterness in his voice was raw, and he regretted it. Ever the diplomat, he apologized at once, but not before Claudia had glimpsed how differently people viewed things from the opposite side of the imperial fence.

In Rome, it all seemed so expedient. The reward for twenty years' hard slog was to allocate fertile plots of land to retiring soldiers, shipping in slaves to work the fields and bring home the harvest. Such was the efficiency of these agricultural practices that high yields were guaranteed, thus increasing the retired warrior's profits as the surplus was sold on, and Augustus had been lauded to the heavens for introducing the scheme; a win-win situation as the Senate liked to say. Win-win for everyone, it would seem, except the poor sod whose land had been taken from him.

'You still haven't said what practices the King is against.'

For the first time since Salome left them, Mazares laughed. 'Try all of them! Do you know the locals' nickname for her farm? Amazonia!'

'Amazonia?'

'Land of the Amazons,' he said, rubbing his jaw. 'Claudia, I swear that woman flies in the face of every convention you can think of and then half a dozen on top. You see, not only does our Salome have strong views on women not being treated as chattels, she rejects the concept of slavery on every level. The first thing she did after inheriting the farm from her husband was to free his slaves, then before you know it, women started to appear on her farm from all over, calling it a refuge—'

'Is that so bad?

'Of course it bloody is!' The anger in his voice surprised her. 'I told you before, you can't make the sun travel backwards, but equally you cannot force its progress.'

He ran his fingers through his glossy curls.

'The Histri have had to cope with a lot of change in a very short space of time. New laws, new practices, new rulers – these things don't come easy, but they're adjusting the best that they can.'

'Your King seems to be making a pretty good stab of the merger.'

Mazares shrugged the King's good deeds aside. 'It's his job. The point is, for the last decade our people have seen land that's been in their families since the dawn of time snatched away and given to strangers.'

There was no question of holding the passion back now.

'Then along comes Salome and suddenly their *principles* are eroded, as well as their security. You have to understand, Claudia, that in a Histrian's eyes, women need the protection of men. To them, anything else flies in the face of nature and it's quite beyond their understanding how battered wives might need a refuge. To put it bluntly, they view Salome's farm as a lesbian commune, and unfortunately there's always an element that wants to teach Sappho a lesson by trampling her crops, or . . .'

Just as quickly as the heat had flared up, it died down, to be replaced by a weariness she hadn't imagined.

'Or else they view the women as a ready supply of whores and, quite frankly, Claudia, we're sick and tired of burning rapists around here.'

'Did you say *burning*?'

'Oh, don't look so shocked. No one forces a man to commit rape and ultimately it's their choice whether they die that way, they could always leave the women in peace! But I'm telling you straight. Amazonia has stirred up a lot of trouble round here and, if Salome doesn't change her ways, and soon, something terrible is going to happen. I know it.'

Looking at the anguish behind his eyes, Claudia almost felt guilty about what she was about to do next.

'Let's talk about Rovin,' she said sweetly.

What was it Salome had said? Much to explore in the area? And that Mazares would make sure she had a wonderful time here . . . ?

'Because I was under the impression that this was an overnight stop.'

'If that's what you want, then of course it can be one night,' he said smoothly. 'Only, it's so beautiful here, all these rocky coves, pinewoods and golden, sandy beaches, that I thought you might prefer to relax for a day or so before moving on. Take a boat round the islands, swim in the lagoons—'

'Beat around the bush? No, thank you, Mazares. Tomorrow we head for Gora.'

'If that's your wish, then—'

But he was talking to himself. Claudia had spun on her heel and was marching purposefully down the street. She could hear him yelling behind her, but he could shout all he liked, she didn't trust him *or* this place; as his pace stretched to catch up, so her pace quickened with it. Lit by his own torchlight, she could see his arms waving and now he'd broken into a run. Sooner or later, she'd let him catch up, but right now, cutting that smarmy snake down to size by having him chase after her seemed a good idea.

Except she'd forgotten about the steps on this island and too late she realized that what he'd been yelling at her had, in fact, been a warning. That he'd been trying, goddammit, to save her from breaking her neck. Running too fast and with nothing to grab hold of, Claudia pitched forwards into nothingness.

Nosferatu, huh?

The reflection staring back from the mirror couldn't decide whether to be pleased or insulted at this allusion to Histria's shuffling demon of the night, the bastard son of a bastard son who was supposed to drink human blood and feast off the warm, dripping flesh of his victims.

Insulted, because the figure in the mirror was no ghoul, no monster, no killer for pleasure, and the suggestion of having an oversized head, long curved claws and a fat, lolling tongue could not be further removed from the well-groomed figure reflected in the flickering lamplight. Ogre indeed!

All the same . . .

Where better to hide than under the umbrella of a mythical monster? In which case, could any description be *more* pleasing?

The reflection turned this way then that, admiring what it saw, until, satisfied with the result from every angle, it smiled. Very well. Nosferatu it is!

But what to do about the little witness, that was the question. By all accounts, the child hadn't actually *seen* the ghoul, only its shadow, where a full moon would account for the physical distortions that she'd seen played out on the wall. That, and a child's overactive imagination!

'Nosferatu' paced the room – up and down, up and down – then finally came to a decision. The girl could be safely left to her demons. Superstitious though the islanders were, no one believed her when she said she'd seen Nosferatu, not even her mother, and since no evidence of slaughter was left behind, it was probably wise to leave well alone and not start tempting providence at this stage.

The plan was going well and according to schedule. Let it be. Right now, there were more pressing matters to deal with.

Nosferatu picked up the blade from the table, tested its edge, then slipped the knife back in its sheath. The dagger was carried for protection, not harm. For tonight's work, Nosferatu needed a noose.

Eight

Through an explosion of fireballs, Claudia was distantly aware of being asked to count fingers. Since the fingers that were being held up were dancing like fireflies, she could not see the point and closed her eyes again.

The next time she awoke, it was to an orchestra of tone-deaf percussionists and she could smell comfrey and catnip, elder and borage, and thought, dear me, some poor soul must have an awful lot of bruises to warrant that lot, but then something warm and scented was sloshed down her throat and she promptly lapsed back into unconsciousness.

She dreamed.

She dreamed the Nymphs of the West were singing lullabies to her in the Gardens of the Hesperides, watched over by Night and the Evening Star. The walls of the garden were made from blocks of pure, white, limestone that kept making her sneeze, but then Atlas came along and laid a cool compress over her forehead and everything in the garden was lovely. Atlas was younger than she'd imagined, with an aureole of glossy dark curls framing his face, but she supposed old men couldn't be expected to hold up the universe, and it was kind of him to use the waters of purity to wash her face, though she hadn't expected purity to smell quite so like hyssop.

Atlas left. Darkness closed over the garden. Juno's golden apples glinted on their tree in the moonlight, and Claudia half-expected to see Hercules sneak in any moment and steal a few for his penultimate labour. She was not disappointed. In he strode, but he was accompanied by Diana of the Hunt, who plucked an arrow from the quiver on her back and fired it over the wall. But this Diana was no virgin goddess. She straddled her muscular thighs over Hercules as he sat, took his impossibly handsome face in both hands and pressed her lips hard to his.

The lullabies faded. Ladon, the hundred-headed dragon set by Juno to guard her golden apples, slithered in and coiled himself round the trunk, breathing fire over the garden. Claudia could feel the heat of his ferocious breath. Cried out at the burning. But neither Atlas, nor Hercules, nor any of the other heroes, not even one attached to the Security Police, came to rescue her from the monster, and she remained trapped in the garden.

Shadows slunk in.

Wolves with human feet. Giants with thick, scaly tails. Then the shroud-eaters clustered round, empty-eyed and stinking of rotted flesh, with blood dripping from their open mouths, and among these shadows moved another, more menacing shape. It had a large, lolling head and hands ending in giant claws, and it answered to the name Nosferatu . . .

She woke bathed in sweat, but the sweat was cold and she was shivering. For a moment, she thought she was still trapped in the nightmare, since many objects in this house had a familiar ring, like the polished oak doors, the white marble floors and the fabulous gold candelabra. But then again, many things hadn't! The paintings on the wall had been exquisitely executed without doubt, but who – and what – did those strange swirls represent? Instead of a Roman-style couch, she was lying on a mattress set high on an intricately carved wooden frame, though the mattress had been stuffed sumptuously with swan's down and the linens scented with oils of jasmine and rose.

When she tried to sit up, daggers drove into her brain, so she lay on her back, staring up at the ceiling, cursing a tantrum that had resulted in that stupid, headlong plunge down the steps. Well, all right, not headlong. Once she'd realized what was happening, she'd launched herself sideways, curling herself into a ball. Ignominious wasn't the word as she bumpity-bumped down the stairs one at a time, but learning how to minimize injury was just one of many tricks her army-orderly father had taught her.

For a moment, she swore she felt the brush of his stubble against her cheek as he whispered *Good girl, you remembered* in her ear. Impossible, of course. She was ten years old when he marched off to war and never came home, and suddenly she longed for Drusilla to be lying alongside her on the bed, her silky, soft fur and reassuring deep rattle a palliative to the throbbing and aches that didn't come from a physical source. But after two weeks' incarceration, Drusilla had sharpened her claws on the elegant bedpost before disappearing into the night to fly the flag for cats everywhere by tormenting the local rodent population.

As ever, Claudia Seferius was alone.

The lamps in the bedroom had been snuffed and no sounds came from the hall, suggesting the hour was late, very late, yet, after her nightmare, Claudia felt far from sleepy. Gradually, she became aware of a white linen compress over her forehead, and as she removed it, she noticed that it had been drenched in an infusion of healing hyssop. So, then. Not everything in that dream was imagined . . .

From under the open window she heard a sneeze, but for all that she'd got off lightly from her tumble, her head was pounding and her eyes felt like lead weights, and all she wanted to do was slide back into the comforting blackness. She reached for one of the sleep stones in the bowl by her pillow and rolled the oil-drenched pebble around in her hand. Lavender. Lavender, to calm and to soothe. Just like hyssop.

'Atchoo!'

The sleep stone fell from Claudia's hand.

'Raspor?'

The very act of sitting up bombarded her with white-hot pokers encased in boiling oil, but when the pain and nausea eventually subsided, she crawled out of bed and staggered across to the window. Slowly – ridiculously slowly – her vision cleared to reveal the light from the waning moon reflecting off the billowing ocean like scales on a fish, silhouetting the islands in the distance. She squinted in concentration, but the only creature abroad at this hour was a night heron swooping silently in to land. She was halfway back to the sanctuary of her bed when the third sneeze floated up from below. There was no mistaking her overgrown cherub now. In the clear blue light of the retreating Moon God, his bald pate shone like a tiny silver platter as he hopped nervously from foot to foot.

'Psst.'

The ring of dark curls spun round at the call from the shadows further out along the shoreline.

'Claudia?' he hissed under his breath. 'Is you, yes?'

'Pssst. Raspor.'

Claudia couldn't see who was calling him, but it sure as hell wasn't her, and a weight inside her flipped over. Something was wrong here. Very wrong. But even before she'd opened her mouth to reply, a dark flash whisked through the air. Raspor jerked sideways as his hands flew to his neck.

'Hey!' she yelled. *'Stop!'*

But her voice was a croak, and he clawed frantically at the ring round his throat.

'Help!' she cried. *'Somebody help!'*

If anything, her croak was weaker and now Raspor's heels were drumming impotently against the rocks. Help him, she prayed to every god on Olympus. Strike his assailant with a thunderbolt, with blindness, with paralysis, with anything! Save him, she prayed. Please step in and save him – *because, forgive me, I can't!* Too weak to run, too weak to throw missiles, too weak to raise the alarm, she could only stare helplessly as the horror unfolded. With every wasted second, more of the little man's breath was being squeezed from his body.

But no thunderbolts flashed.

No divine trident intervened.

Not for the first time, Claudia Seferius had to rely on her own wits.

Picking up the bowl of sleep stones, she dashed it to the floor. Instantly, a stampede of slaves crashed into her bedroom, bringing lights that blinded her from every direction as a hundred voices demanded to know what was wrong.

'Help!' she cried. 'There's a man being murdered out there!'

'*Where?*' '*Who?*' Everyone was shouting at once.

'Hurry!' she screamed. 'Hurry, before it's too—'

It was as far as she got. The oblivion that Claudia had so desperately craved a few minutes earlier was no respecter of changers-of-mind. It claimed her at a maidservant's feet.

The next light to be blinding her eyes didn't come from dozens of hastily lit oil lamps. It came from the sun, shining with inexorable brilliance into the room, and more specifically over Claudia's pillow. From a hundred miles away, she heard someone groan, and had a strange feeling that it might have been her.

'How are ye feeling?' a gravelly voice asked.

'Vile.'

But the cold, solid knot in her stomach had nothing to do with her fall.

'Aye.' Pavan nodded impassively. 'Ye would.'

He was sitting with one massive leg crossed over the other in a high-backed armchair upholstered in damask the colour of ripe Persian plums. His fingers were steepled patiently together.

She drew a deep breath. Willed the shuddering inside to subside.

'Is he dead?' she asked quietly.

Grey eyes stared without emotion for what seemed like an hour, but was probably no more than five seconds.

'When Mazares carried ye up here last night, ye were unconscious and bleeding.'

The seat was large and commodious, but the general made it look like a kid's chair.

'I very much regret, ma'am, that the closest we had to a physician last night was a . . . a mule doctor.'

How comforting.

'Meaning?'

He stroked his ponytail thoughtfully. 'The mule doctor fears his painkilling preparation may have had certain side effects.'

'Name one.'

'Physical weakness.'

'Name two.'

She had a pretty good idea where this was leading, but needed to hear it from Pavan's own lips.

He adjusted his belt. 'We put every available man on that beach—'

'What about Raspor?'

The chair creaked as he rose to his feet. 'D'you feel up to breakfast, ma'am? Would a honeycomb straight from the beehive tempt yer appetite?'

'What – and I'll say this slowly – about Raspor?'

A different voice answered. It was low and velvety, and anyone who didn't know better would have taken his tone to be concerned.

'I'm afraid it's exactly as Pavan says, Claudia. We conducted the most thorough search of the area, but –' Mazares shrugged his very fine shoulders – 'no body, no blood . . .'

'Of course there was no blood,' she retorted. 'The poor sod was strangled.'

Mazares and Pavan exchanged glances.

'The mule doctor has no doubt that what ye saw was real in yer mind,' Pavan rumbled.

'How reassuring to have a diagnosis that comes quite literally from the horse's mouth. No doubt his sick asses tell him what they saw, and he then proceeds to explain to them how they imagined those blue oats and flying cabbages.'

Claudia took advantage of the uncomfortable silence to press on.

'For your information, gentlemen, Raspor was no hallucination.'

Hallucinations don't sneeze.

'He was standing underneath that very window, wringing

his little fat hands, and he was wearing the same single-shoulder tunic that he—'

'My Lady.' Mazares's tone was placating. 'Those who serve the gods also honour them. For a priest not to be wearing his official robes at any time is sacrilege.'

Of course, it could mean the little man had escaped his attacker . . .

'But you do have a priest named Raspor, who serves the Thunder God in Gora?'

'Ye-es,' Mazares said slowly. 'He's Guardian of the Sacrifice and his job is to select and then care for the animals whose lives are forfeit to Perun.'

. . . leaving him too weak and too frightened to seek help on the island . . .

'And would this Raspor be a small, round fellow with a ring of dark curls like a halo, perhaps?'

'Aye,' Pavan said. 'But Raspor is also a dedicated servant of his temple and tomorrow a white ram is due to be sacrificed for the Zeltane.'

Zeltane. Arguably the most important festival in the Histrian calendar . . .

'With all due respect, ma'am,' the general continued, 'it's highly unlikely that, faced with such a solemn obligation, he'd trek out here to Rovin.'

Except when concern for his King's welfare was more compelling than his priestly duties . . .

'Pula,' she corrected. 'He trekked out to Pula – well, you know that.' She turned to Mazares. 'I was talking to him when you arrived.'

'I hate to remind you, My Lady—' even through her fuzzy vision, there was no mistaking that twitching moustache – but when I first saw you, you were sprawled backwards over a crate of peacocks and squawking louder than they were.'

Slimy bastard.

'So, a man's been murdered, yet neither of you intend to take the matter further, because you think I made the story up?'

'It was a nasty fall,' Pavan pointed out.

Claudia snorted. She had not, repeat not, imagined Raspor being strangled, and her stomach lurched when she remembered his sandalled heels drumming impotently against the rocks.

Mazares read her expression. 'Let me ask around,' he said gently. 'Find out whether this was someone's idea of a practical joke.'

Baiting Rome had long been a source of amusement, he added, and if a group of embittered locals thought they could exploit the situation while she was befuddled by drugs . . . ?

'Why only a mule doctor?' she demanded.

Pavan came as close as he would ever come to squirming.

'The royal physician should have been on Rovin a week ago,' he growled. 'There's been no word. No official explanation. But . . .'

His voice trailed off as he found a sudden desire to examine his fingernails.

'Come, come, Pavan. Claudia's a woman of the world.'

That lazy sparkle had returned to Mazares's eyes.

'What the general is too shy to spit out, My Lady, is that the doctor's inclinations differ from the average red-blooded Histrian's, and although he isn't on the island as he was supposed to be, neither is a boat builder of the same persuasion. Now, since we Histri tend to take a, shall we say, more traditional view of family relationships, the general consensus hereabouts is that His Majesty's physician and the boat builder have taken a short vacation.'

He stroked his goatee beard.

'Nevertheless, I think I'll ask Salome to come across and check you over.'

'Tell you what. Why don't *I* visit *her*?'

'If . . . if that's what the Lady Claudia wishes.'

'It is.' Anything to get out of here. Anything. But the mention of Salome had jolted a memory. 'Wasn't she on her way to tend the boat builder's niece yesterday evening? The child

62

who was traumatized after seeing Nosferatu about his grisly business?'

Mazares turned an amused glance on Pavan.

'Good heavens, Claudia's cracked it,' he chuckled. 'Nosferatu! The beast that dares not speak its name!'

'It would explain why the legend's so widespread,' Pavan rumbled back. '*And* why he only comes out at night.'

'Yes, but we can console ourselves, General, that our reviled monster remains a creature of superstition.'

'How so?'

'Oh, Pavan, don't tell me you, of all people, actually believe in fairies?' Mazares forced his expression to become serious. 'I'll arrange transport to Amazonia, My Lady.'

Together the two men strode out of the room, hardly waiting until the door was shut before resurrecting the fairy joke.

Alone once again, Claudia could not control the shakes that gripped her. Raspor had come to her for help and she had dismissed him, an act of disdain that had cost him his life.

Too many, how you say – innocents? – have died, and the King, he is too trusting. He thinks only good of people, but there are bad people around him. Very bad.

She saw again his terrified eyes scanning the crowd.

Just say you'll meet me. Then I give you names of people who was killed and dates when these so-called accidents happen, but not here, not now. Is too open, too dangerous. I am dead man, if I am seen talking to you.

Paranoia, she'd thought at the time. Like Pavan and Mazares, she'd put it down to 'all in the mind'.

Please. You have King's ear. He will listen. When you give him detail of murders, he have no choice but to listen, because Mazares, he will stop at nothing to—

Those were Raspor's last words. Mazares will stop at nothing . . .

Claudia pulled on a gown of soft apricot cotton, fixed her girdle in place. She didn't know why she'd been lured to Histria, only that if Mazares wished her dead, he could have finished the job off last night and no one would have been any the wiser. From that point of view, at least, she was safe. But who else might not be? And how long would her life be protected, once Mazares realized that she was on to him . . . ?

Nosferatu laughed.

Nine

'Oh, there you are, Marcus.'

His aunt breezed along the portico, two slaves trotting at her heels like hunting hounds, as sunlight bounced off the gold-filigree tiara in her hair and dazzled the sapphires dripping from her neck.

'I wanted to thank you, darling, for sorting out that awful business with Horatio. You have no idea what a strain it put on your poor uncle's heart when he heard those rumours. Wicked, absolutely wicked, and frankly, Marcus, I think the people who start them ought to be tied to a post in the Forum and whipped for the anguish it causes.'

'Well, it's settled now,' Orbilio said, mentally crossing his fingers. 'You can both rest easily.'

'D'you know, I can't help thinking that someone must have heard about those unfortunate incidents in the boy's past. I mean, how else could the rumour have started? Between you and I, dear, part of me wondered whether they mightn't have been true, leopards and spots and all that, because, heavens to Hera, I'll never forget the first time I saw my son dressed in women's clothes. Never! The boy was only eleven, but thank goodness, it was just a passing phase that he grew out of. Are you sure I can't persuade you to stay another few days? Your uncle has so enjoyed having you here.'

'I've enjoyed my visit, too,' he lied.

Through a pair of tall double doors opening on to the colonnade, he glimpsed the aftermath of last night's banquet, the Trojan theme mosaic littered with the broken shells of lobsters, mussels, crabs and oysters, and scattered with date, peach and cherry stones, meat bones, pastry crumbs, pools of spilled wine, and a broken lyre that lay in the corner. Oh, and somebody's sandal sitting forlornly under one of the couches. If only his aunt and uncle had talked to their son and listened to what he'd had to say! But no. Night after night, year after year, friends and associates would gather round the table like vultures, gorging on overpriced delicacies, nibbling at the choicest part of the animal, while in the room next door, a lost and lonely child grew into a lost, unhappy man . . .

'Unfortunately, my dear Lucretia, duty calls.'

His aunt sniffed loudly. 'I do wish you'd adopt an appropriate career.'

'Ah, you'd prefer thieves, rapists, fraudsters and killers to remain on the loose. How about anarchists and those planning assassination attempts on the Emperor's life?'

Take the case he'd been assigned to at the moment. A tricky affair by any standards, and gathering the evidence would be a bugger – but then weren't all plots to destabilize the Empire hell?

'Sit down, Marcus.'

It was an order, not an invitation, and therefore he remained standing, arms folded over his chest, his shoulder against the green-veined marble column, and wondered why he felt so ill at ease in this villa where he had often played as a child. The pillars, the paintings, the exquisite mosaics, were exactly the same as he remembered. Likewise the painted marble statues of his forebears, the expensive drapes and awnings, the fountains in the garden. Even the livery of the slaves was the same nauseous pea green. It was him, he supposed. He was the one who had changed.

'Marcus, I don't need to remind you that your father was a highly respected advocate.'

She settled herself on a bench under the shade of a pomegranate tree and clapped her hands. Instantly, a slave appeared and proceeded to waft a fan of ostrich feathers to create a breeze that, like so many things around here, was 100 per cent artificial.

'Both your brothers are in the law, and quite honestly, that's where you should be, my boy.' His aunt's voice grew strident with censure. 'In court.'

'I often am, Lucretia. It's called giving evidence.'

Imperious eyes rolled. 'The Security Police pay you a pittance, Marcus, and snooping is no career for a healthy young man. You're twenty-six and it's high time you married.'

'I'm twenty-eight,' he reminded her, 'and I've been married. She ran off with a sea captain from Lusitania, if you recall.'

'By the lights of Apollo, I swear the whole of Rome still sniggers about that and the fault was entirely yours, you know that. She was your wife, you should have kept tabs on the slut, because, to put it bluntly, Marcus, women of our class oughtn't to be in the position where they're able to fraternize with tattooed types in the first place. I'm not saying it doesn't happen. Occasionally a patrician woman might slip to the point where lust triumphs over common sense, but, good grief, in those instances at least they have the decency to employ discretion. They don't *elope* with the fellow. Tch, you were young, I suppose, and the little bitch fooled us all with her sweet tongue and innocent face, so I can't really blame you for going off the rails and joining the Security Police when she left—'

'Thanks.'

'—even though the disgrace of it drove your poor papa to his tomb.'

'My father drove himself,' Marcus said evenly, 'in the fastest chariot he could find. Riding pillion, you might recollect, were an excess of rich food, far too much wine and more women than most men could cope with.'

His aunt's nose twitched, but only slightly.

'If you had a wife, you would have to settle down,' she assured him, snapping be-ringed fingers for another slave to pour two goblets of wine. 'No wife would tolerate the hours you keep, much less the company you keep them in. She'd see you settled in a more appropriate line of work.'

When Orbilio refused the glass, he wasn't sure whether it

was because it symbolized the shallow lifestyle into which he was born or whether he genuinely wasn't thirsty.

'A wife's job is to provide children, Marcus. Your last one failed to deliver the goods, but you're young, you're good-looking, you can even be witty on occasion, and I happen to know of the perfect match.'

So that's what the lecture was in aid of.

'She's the youngest daughter of one our City Prefects, her name's Camilla and—'

'And she's barely fifteen.'

'See, I knew you'd agree. Like I said, the child's perfect.'

'Child is right, Lucretia. It's obscene.'

'Nonsense! A man needs an heir and many members of your own family have taken young brides. Your second cousin, Cassius, was twice your age. Your grandfather. My grandfather, come to that, and my middle sister was just fourteen when she was contracted, and her groom was in his sixties at the time. Now, Camilla comes with a generous dowry and your uncle has already approved the City Prefect's draft contract.'

Was his aunt cold-blooded by nature, or simply blinded by the prejudice of her class? He studied her. Straight-backed and stiff-lipped, bony, unyielding, and the sad thing was that she was still two years short of fifty.

'What about Camilla?' he asked. 'Has anyone consulted her views?'

'Women are never consulted in these matters, Marcus, as you well know.'

For the first time Lucretia lifted her face to look into his eyes and her whole attitude softened.

'You really *must* stop trying to change the world, darling. Learn to accept the inevitable and you'll find life so much simpler.'

'It's precisely because nothing in life is inevitable, Lucretia, that I didn't follow my father into law.'

Emotion began to surge in his breast.

'There's no single issue, legal or moral, that cannot, or

should not, be challenged and I'm sorry to disappoint you, but I'm not a sheep to be herded this way and that. When I marry again, indeed if I marry again, it won't be to some vapid, compliant, emotionally docile mouse, who relies on servants to bath her, to dress her, to pin on her brooches—'

'Oh, lord.' His aunt signalled for the little fan-wallah to flap harder. 'You're in love.'

'Hardly!'

Whatever had him by the balls lately, it wasn't love. Love didn't tear a man's liver to pieces and prevent him from sleeping at night. Love wasn't bewildering, terrifying, exhilarating, electrifying, it didn't rip through your gut, claw at your innards and chew your emotions to mush. No. Love was tender and sweet. It was holding hands in the moonlight, strumming tunes on the lyre, gazing deep into each other's eyes. It sure as hell wasn't serpents writhing around in your brain!

'And in any case, my marital status is irrelevant, since I have no intention of resigning from the Security Police.'

If there was one good thing to come out of this sermon, it was to reinforce his belief in his job!

His aunt changed tack.

'Your uncle has spoken to your superiors, you know. They say you have an almost perfect track record for the investigations you've undertaken on behalf of the administration, and despite what you might think, we are proud of you, your uncle and I. Indeed, the whole family is proud of the way you've handled yourself, Marcus.'

He'd like to think his father would have been proud of him, too. But in his heart he knew it wasn't true.

'By breaking with tradition you've shown spirit, and your impartiality does you credit, my boy. However, you know the old saying. Quit while you're ahead, and to have solved virtually all your cases is a commendable achievement. But it's time to rein in that pride, Marcus, and start living up to your obligations.'

'Obligations?' He spiked his hand through his hair. 'Lucretia, if you truly believe that siring sons and defending slander is more worthwhile than quelling insurrection and keeping the Empire stable, then I pity you.'

It would take more than that to ruffle his aunt.

'I don't know what's making you so tetchy this morning, darling, but you'll feel better after a long hot soak in the bath-house.'

She clicked her fingers and more slaves came running.

'I'll get the steam room prepared,' she said, 'and I'll send a girl in, as well.'

'I don't want a girl, thank you.'

His aunt tutted as she clip-clopped down the portico.

'Don't be so silly,' she trilled. 'I'll send Phyllis along. Your uncle's mood always improves after a session with Phyllis.'

He couldn't be hearing this right! His aunt – the same aunt who so staunchly promoted duty and obligation – arranges for slaves to have sex with her husband? Orbilio suddenly had a longing to return to the rough drinking dens and the dark bearpits outside town, where he spent so much of his time tracking down felons. In those places, at least, dishonest people were honest about who they were . . .

'Hello.' A slant-eyed Oriental girl emerged from the main body of the villa. 'Mizz Lucretia tell me you grumpy.'

'Well, I'm not,' he snarled back. 'Bugger off.'

'Mizz Lucretia say woman's touch make you feel better.'

'She wrong.'

'She not wrong. You very grouchy. Phyllis fix that for you, huh?'

A hand had covered his groin before he knew what was happening. Stroking. Fluttering. The same hand that had been over his uncle's groin, and heaven knows how many others . . .

'Look, you're a very pretty girl, Phyllis,' he said, removing the hand and patting it. 'I appreciate what you're doing, but the thing is I – I have an appointment.'

Sod his luggage. Get out of this place ASAP.

But, as he strode down the portico, the thing he hated most

about this morning's conversation with his aunt was that his aunt had been right. He did need a woman.

All night, he'd lain awake in his wide, empty bed with echoes of Horatio's girlish giggles ringing in his ears and the hollow laughter of the whorehouse's clients, so desperate to consume themselves in animal lust. As the stars moved round the sky, Orbilio had prayed to Minerva, goddess of wisdom, that she might confer oblivion on him, but with each hour that was measured by the soft trickle of the sand through the glass on the table, his body had burned for the touch of a woman. For the heat of naked flesh against his. The feel of soft hair in his hands.

God knows, he wasn't alone for lack of availability. A wealthy patrician was always a catch, a single one an added bonus, and Marcus Cornelius was not unaware of his good looks. Indeed, it was something he'd capitalized on many a time, but as he stared vacantly up at the gilded ceiling, he realized that there was only one woman he wanted. A girl with thick, dark curls that tumbled over her shoulders and were streaked with the colours of sunset. A girl whose laugh could fill a whole room yet at other times could barely be heard, and whose dark eyes blazed with passion, and whose breasts, oh dear god, whose breasts heaved like the ocean in winter . . .

In short, Orbilio longed for the only woman in the world who didn't want him.

He wondered whether she'd found out yet that the King of Histria wanted her hand in marriage, not a contract for vintage wine. Perhaps he should have told her at the Ostia Gate? But, stubborn as usual, Claudia wasn't open to listening and he'd let her find out the hard way.

His gut lurched. *What would her answer be?*

She'd married Gaius Seferius for his money, she'd made no bones about that, nor that the arrangement was mutually beneficial. Gaius had wanted a young, witty and beautiful creature to parade in return and even Orbilio had had to admit they'd made a fair pact. Moreover, he was aware of Claudia's, shall we say, indiscretions. Forgery, fraud, tax evasion, smuggling, this was just the tip of the iceberg – Croesus, there was nothing that woman wouldn't do to survive, but he couldn't protect her for ever. Sooner or later, the authorities would get to hear about her illegal exploits – in which case, penniless exile might well be the best that she'd face.

And, tough though she was, and more than capable of handling herself, there were more and more situations of late which had seen her double-crossing characters who would think nothing of slitting a young woman's throat.

Marcus had done the only thing he could think of to protect her.

When the King of Histria asked him whether he could recommend a suitable Roman bride, Orbilio put her name forward.

The King was a good man, he was fair, he was wise, and there was no doubt in Orbilio's mind that Claudia would keep her end of the bargain and give him the heirs that he needed. He ran his hands through his hair. By allying her to the King, he was giving her the life of luxury and wealth, power and influence that she so desperately craved, yet without any loss to her spirit, and she would have safety, security and shelter for the rest of her life. What woman in her right mind *wouldn't* say yes?

Leaning into the gutter, he was violently sick.

Ten

The first thing that struck Claudia about Amazonia wasn't the imbalance of women, hoeing, irrigating and manuring in tunics kilted to mid-calf – which some might say was for ease of working, others flaunting their assets, like the strumpets they were. The first thing that struck Claudia about Amazonia was the colour.

It was as though a rainbow had burst upon the land and hadn't summoned up the energy to move. Sky-blue flax beside white onion flowers, purple lavender adjacent to bright green ears of wheat. Grey geese with orange bills paddled in the margins of a pool fringed with yellow iris, white arabis and blue aubretia, while black donkeys trampled yellow buttercups beneath pale pink apple blossoms, and white goats browsed among the fields of yellow lupins grown for fodder. Every last bit of it exploding out of a bright reddish-orange soil.

The second thing to hit her was the scent. Musky ajuga mingled with spicy basil, understated rosemary competed with blowsy wallflowers, while heliotropes and pinks vied for perfumed attention.

'Welcome, my dear.'

Mazares had arranged for an armed escort to accompany Claudia across the Rovin Channel to Salome's farm, but if the Syrian girl was surprised by the visit, it didn't show as she swept her guest into the house and who knows – maybe every visitor arrived here under armed guard?

'Wild strawberry and rosehips,' she said, handing her visitor a goblet of pale pink liquid. 'You won't find a better tonic, anywhere.'

'News travels fast.'

The drink was sweet, scented and utterly delicious.

'News?'

Salome's puzzled frown was genuine.

'That I didn't sleep a wink last night,' Claudia said quickly. 'Personally, I blame the pillows. I swear they've been stuffed with bricks and old horseshoes.'

'No wonder my geese were eyeing you so warily,' Salome retorted. 'Poor things, they feared themselves featherless. How are you finding Mazares?'

She didn't even break stride and maybe it was the sunlight, but Claudia thought she caught a mischievous twinkle in those cat-like green eyes.

'Which came first,' she asked artlessly, totally ignoring the question, 'the farmer or the healer?'

'My mother, my grandmother and her mother before that were all healers,' Salome replied, smiling. 'With each generation that passes, our skills become richer, each of us adding something from her own bank of knowledge, be it culled from Egyptian, Greek, Indian or Roman medicines.'

How about local, Claudia wondered, thinking about the King's mysterious illness. On a fast horse, Gora was a day's ride from here . . .

'But not richer in the financial sense,' she said aloud, noting the plain whitewashed walls and simple flagged floor.

'No.'

Salome's laugh was as elegant as the woman herself.

'There's no profit in medicine around here, the folk are too poor. Now that Pula's expanding, though, we're gaining quite a reputation for our cosmetic aids and I'm hoping those will generate income.'

'Selling eternal youth to women with more money than sense?'

'There are plenty of those around Pula,' Salome chuckled, 'and every tide washes in a few more.'

74

Washing in more resentment among the locals, too, Claudia mused.

'You're a fine advertisement for your products,' she said, again struck by the young widow's height and angular beauty.

In her thirtieth summer Mazares had said, yet despite so much time spent out of doors, Salome's skin had the bloom of a girl half her age, and the simplicity of her gown only emphasized her foxy red mane and the loveliness of her figure.

A becoming blush suffused the tan. 'Thank you, but it's not only cosmetics we're a dab hand at. With so many talents coming in to our collective pool, we prepare everything from laxatives to love potions to furniture polish that –' she rapped a gleaming door jamb with her knuckles – 'keeps its shine for a year. Did Mazares send you?'

Mazares, Mazares, always Mazares.

'A whole year?' Claudia said, examining the woodwork.

A not uncomfortable silence settled over the room, as Salome laid out a dish of olives and cheese. It gave Claudia a breathing space to assemble her thoughts.

Soldiers weren't allowed to marry until they retired from the army and it was obvious that little had changed in the ten years since Salome's husband built this house for his bride. Constructed of white stone, like everything else around here, it conformed to the standard Roman practice of four wings round a central courtyard, but the accommodation block was small, just three bedrooms and the atrium, which were all sparsely furnished and lacking in the decorative arts that were such a feature of Roman homes. In fact, the only personal artefacts that Claudia could see were a bust of a rather bull-necked individual, presumably the late husband, and an exquisite ivory carving of two racing greyhounds. But there was something else missing from Salome's house. Something Claudia couldn't quite put her finger on . . .

'I can see you love this place,' she said, sweeping her arm round the kitchens, shed, dormitories and workshops that comprised the other three wings and where every craft from weaving wool to weaving chaplets, baking bricks to baking bread was in varying stages of progress.

'Very much.' Salome draped herself over a couch with un-assumed grace. 'Histria is so beautiful, so fertile, so full of *giving*, that you can't help but fall in love with the country.'

Claudia pictured the unforgiving deserts of Salome's Syrian homeland.

'My husband was one of the first to be given a farm here, you know. It's the Emperor's aim to apportion a third of this peninsula to retiring soldiers, although less than half that target has been achieved so far.'

As she spoke, Claudia realized what was so odd about Amazonia. Children! Right across her Etruscan vineyards, the valleys echoed with the shrieks of workers' offspring, so much so, she often wondered the slaves didn't stuff their ears with felt to block out the racket as the little buggers chased one another round vats, played hide and seek in the treading house and hopscotched round the cellars.

'You and your husband weren't blessed with babies?'

'Goodness, is that old lesbian rumour doing the rounds again?'

Salome untied the green ribbon at her nape and combed her long hair with her hands.

'How that starts, I'll never know,' she said, re-tying it. 'Everybody knows I was devastated when Stephanus died.'

Not devastated enough that you didn't free his slaves the very next day.

'But your workers,' Claudia persisted. 'Don't you take on women with children?'

The muscles round Salome's mouth stiffened. 'Most of the girls come alone.'

And most of them were exceptionally young, she might have added. Sixteen, seventeen, Claudia could see how mis-understandings might start to arise, prompting her to take a closer interest in the nubile young Amazons as they bustled about, milking goats, churning cheeses, dyeing cottons and hanging laundry on large circular wooden frames to dry.

In theory, paying hired labourers was not much different from paying slaves. Foreigners had this ludicrous notion that Roman slaves were on a level with dogs – fed, watered, but that's about all. How ridiculous! How could you possibly coax good work from a browbeaten, downtrodden drone? All slaves, regardless of status, received a salary on top of their board and lodgings, a remuneration which naturally varied according to skill. Foreign nobles were always amazed to discover that everyone in Augustus's court, from book-keepers to clerks, was enslaved. That slaves also owned slaves themselves. And that a good many invested their salaries in business, often running a profitable little sideline in barbering or tavern-keeping.

'What was Rome's reaction, when they found out you'd freed all of your husband's slaves?' Claudia asked.

'Since I haven't told them,' Salome said lightly, 'that delight's still in store.'

'They don't *know*?'

She tried not to think of the administration's reaction when it came to their ears that a Syrian widow had undermined one of the driving principles of Roman economy.

'How long ago since you let them go?'

'Six years last autumn.'

Croesus. The Senate would explode.

'I have done nothing wrong,' Salome said steadily. 'When I inherited those people, they were mine to do what I liked with and it just so happened that it pleased me to give them their freedom.'

Technically, perhaps. A master was entitled to free any slave that he chose, and slaves were also entitled to purchase their freedom, providing they had sufficient funds and permission. But to release them all, and at the same time, was to fly in the face of imperial principles – and if there wasn't a law against what Salome had done, there bloody well would be when someone found out. Which they would! As more Histrian soil was claimed by Roman soldiers . . . as Pula expanded . . . as trade and traffic increased . . .

'Salome, it's not too late to own up.'

She was no fool. She must know her actions could not remain secret for ever, why not get in before she found herself arrested for treason – when losing her farm would be the least of her problems! Or had she just been out of the loop for so long that she'd forgotten Rome's attitude towards reprisal?

'What I do with my land and who I employ is my business, not some busybody's in a city, who has never set foot on this peninsula.'

Salome leaned forward and fixed her visitor with her penetrating green eyes.

'I inherited this farm legally, I retain legal title, I pay my taxes, I worship Roman gods and I have a bust of the Emperor on display.'

That? Claudia glanced at the ugly bull-necked image, about as far removed from the handsome, lean, athletic Augustus as a man could get, and thought, hell, he'd have her thrown to the lions just for the insult.

'How did you meet your husband?' she asked, changing the subject.

'Stephanus?'

Something inside Salome seemed to melt.

'Well, the first thing you have to remember is that I was only sixteen at the time and the second thing you need to know is that we Syrian girls aren't anywhere near as worldly as you Romans.'

Her gaze fixed on a point on the wall and many years back in the past.

'Anyway, this particular day, a soldier knocked, wanting to see my mother about a wound he'd sustained on the training ground that hadn't healed. This wasn't unusual. No disrespect, my dear, but your army surgeons can set bones, remove arrowheads and stitch flesh to perfection, but they don't know spit about herbs. However, this day my mother was out delivering a baby, so I offered to lance his festering wound.'

She giggled like a schoolgirl.

'But Stephanus, he starts to back off. Tells me no, no, he'll

78

call back and get my mother to fix it, but in his clumsiness he turns and walks *wham!* into a table. Claudia, I have never heard a yell like it! "So, the wound's high on the front of the thigh," I say, and of course he's squirming with embarrass-ment – I mean, a fully grown man yelping like an infant and in front of a woman as well! – and it doesn't help that I'm laughing. "Oh, come here," I say. "Don't be such a cissy." So I whisk up his tunic, and then it's my turn to turn purple. "Well, it's hot in the desert," Stephanus says lamely. "Wearing a loincloth just makes it worse."'

Salome wiped the tears from her eyes.

'Stephanus always told people how I saw his potential long before I saw his face.'

She blinked rapidly.

'He was a good man, my Stephanus. A good man.'

Who'd have been – what? – thirty-seven when they first met. How would that twenty-year age gap and wide cultural differences affect their relationship, Claudia wondered. And Salome had said *a good man*. Not, I loved him so much, or, I miss him, or, what a tragedy he'd died so young. A good man . . .

'Talking of men,' Claudia said sweetly. 'How come you employ so few?'

On a farm this size there'd be hundreds of tasks that brute strength would sort out in a jiffy, but would tie up two, possibly three women for half a day minimum.

'Sad to say, Claudia, I've found there are very few men who can cope with equality. Even those who *claim* they have no problem feel intimidated once they confront it.'

Salome sighed.

'Men seem to have this constant need to prove themselves. Bragging. Swaggering. Demonstrating their physical super-iority first by chopping wood then by making advances to girls who aren't interested. I don't turn men away, Claudia, but frankly I'm not sorry to see them leave.'

Her voice softened as she glanced out across the rainbow of Amazonia.

'Those who do stay, though, are real treasures. Tobias, for instance, coaxes flowers out of thin air, which means that, when we take our stuff to Pula market to sell, we can offer a much wider range of wreaths and chaplets than our competitors.'

Claudia had noticed the commercial flower beds on the way in. Violet delphiniums beside pale pink gladiolus, deep pink hollyhocks next to pure white lilies, plus a whole painter's palette of roses. She'd noticed, too, the scowling individual who tended them and decided that, rather than coax the plants into producing their magnificent blooms, he most likely threatened the flowers.

'Tobias has a secret weapon,' Salome said, handing over a goblet of golden liquor that was denser than wine, fragrant and sweet, warm on the tongue, hot on the stomach, and which slithered down as smooth as cough syrup.

'He makes it from honey and calls it hydromel, and I'll only blush if I tell you how much we sell *that* for in Pula.'

However much it sold for, it was worth double and if this wasn't the nectar that the gods sipped, then the gods were being short-changed on Olympus.

'You probably saw Silas on your way in,' Salome continued. 'Old man with a white beard? He introduced the art of espaliering to the farm, so now we have apricots, plums, pears and peaches to sell at market, as well.'

Claudia dragged her pleasure zones away from the heavenly nectar and remembered the worker clipping away at the fans trained against a row of trellises, his hands stained orange-red from the soil, and remembered thinking that he looked more like a kindly philosopher than a cross-pollination expert, and that was another odd thing. Unlike the women, who were uniformly young, the men covered all age groups.

But then everything in this country came with two faces.

The sea, sometimes blue, sometimes green, looks serene but has deadly undercurrents.

Politics, in which one side is desperate to get into bed with Rome and the other plots to revolt.

The coastal dwellers who lived off the sea, the hunters and farmers of the hilly interior.

Then there was Mazares. Debonair on the outside, yet devious and cunning as a wolf on the inside . . .

And now Salome. Who portrays herself as the grieving widow doing her patriotic duty and digging for Rome – but where are the statues of the gods she claims to worship? Where are the portraits of her late husband? And why, if she wants to hang on to this farm, doesn't she give the land a legal heir?

As Claudia knew only too well, one of the consequences of a slave population that outnumbered its citizens four to one is that no widow of childbearing age was allowed to remain unmarried for more than two years after her husband's death. For herself, she'd lost count of the tricks she'd had to resort to, to thwart this imperial order, but the law was the law, and even though Rome might not know about Salome's freed slaves, there would be a record of Stephanus's death. Which meant that someone, somewhere, would have followed this up . . . and would keep following it up until Salome remarried.

'Sorry to interrupt.'

An elfin face framed by a cascade of waist-length walnut waves poked itself round the door.

'But the tanner's wife is back.'

'Jarna?' Salome's face dropped. 'Don't tell me he's been beating her again!'

The elf nodded grimly. 'Only this time she's pregnant.'

'Lora assists me in the treatment room,' Salome explained. 'Lora, this is Claudia, who's come all the way from Rome to consider the King's proposal of marriage.'

An unspoken message flashed between the two women before Salome turned to Claudia and tutted over the beaten wife's plight.

'And the Histri still cling to the theory that if a woman has a husband, she's made!'

For someone who believed in equality and freedom herself, there was nothing Claudia could say. Especially since she needed to maintain the pretence of weighing up the King's proposal.

'I'm going to have to see to this poor woman,' Salome said, rising from the couch, 'but you're welcome to come along, if you like.'

Claudia could not have been any closer behind her, had she been Salome's shadow.

Eleven

The treatment room turned out to be a converted cattle shed. At one end, a panopoly of leaves, petals, roots and seeds were in varying stages of being decocted, infused, macerated or pulverized, while at the other end shelves were stacked shoulder to shoulder with jars, bottles, phials and pots, and beneath the shelves stood a table on which ointments and poultices were in the process of being mixed from recipes anchored down at the corners with stones.

It was to these tasks that the elfin Lora returned, pausing only to tickle the ears of a grey kitten snoozing on a pile of cypress or occasionally stroke the plump, black tom curled up on the stool. Indeed, she barely glanced at the bench on which a pale creature sat with her bloodied and swollen head bent, and where two small, frightened children clung to each side.

'Jarna, Jarna, Jarna,' Salome chided softly, kneeling at the woman's feet and taking both hands in her own. 'One of these days that bastard's going to do some serious damage, you know that.'

'As long as iss only me,' Jarna lisped through her cut lip. 'As long as he don't start in on me kids, I can cope.'

'Can you indeed,' Salome replied, tilting the woman's chin to examine the cuts and swellings. 'Show me your ribs, please.'

The children stared at their feet as their mother pulled down her tunic to reveal a torso with barely an inch of undamaged skin.

'He drinks,' Jarna told Claudia, as though that explained everything.

'He wouldn't be able to swallow, if I got hold of the bastard,' Claudia replied, as Salome laid on a compress of decocted dewcup leaves to reduce the inflammation. 'Why don't you leave him?'

The woman indicated the tots sitting white-lipped beside her. 'Where would we go?' she asked wearily.

'You can come here.' Salome rubbed in a cream made from balm of Gilead and calendula to relieve the pain. 'I've told you time and again, Jarna, any time, day or night, my doors are open.' She ruffled the youngest child's head. 'Look, you two. Why don't you go and collect some eggs for your mother?'

Two pale faces looked at each other, then nodded.

Salome called, 'Naim?' and immediately a jolly, big-busted girl with corkscrew curls poked her head round the door.

'That's me,' she quipped to Claudia, with a broad wink. 'A rose by any other Naim.'

The feathers in her hair proclaimed her as Amazonia's poultry queen, and she would have been as plain as a pudding had it not been for the broad smile on her face.

'Now, what can I be doing for you, me lovely?' she asked Salome.

'I was hoping you might help this pair of tots hunt down some eggs for their supper.'

'Sure, me darlings.' Naim scooped a child under each ample arm. 'Sure we can, but if you're wanting to hunt 'em, we'd best find you some bows and arrows first, hadn't we?'

She led her two chuckling charges into the yard.

'Or would you rather be attacking them eggs with a spear?'

Salome waited until the giggles were well clear of the treatment room.

'Right then, Jarna.' She wiped her hands down the side of her gown as though it was an old apron. 'Lora tells me you're pregnant.'

The tanner's wife gulped and stared at her hands.

Salome wasn't a girl to go beating round bushes. 'If you want to keep the baby, Jarna, you're going to have to leave that vicious husband of yours before he kills it with his fists.

84

Assuming –' she proceeded to prod Jarna's stomach with expert fingers – 'he hasn't done so already.'

'He hasn't, has he?' What little colour was left in Jarna's cheeks drained to white.

'No. No, thank Jehovah, he hasn't, but we both know he will. Lora, mix an infusion of cinnamon and ginger, will you, dear? That'll ease any morning sickness and Lora will also give you a supply of marsh-mallow poultices for the swellings.'

'Should I add a phial of hyssop oil for the bruises?' Lora asked over her shoulder.

'Good idea.' Salome helped Jarna back into her clothes. 'Now think about what I've said, my dear, and remember. My house is always open to you.'

'Thank you.' From her purse, Jarna pulled out her only coin.

'Save it,' Salome said, pushing it back. 'Buy some clothes for the children before he drinks it away.'

'You and the tanner have much in common,' Claudia observed after Jarna had gone.

'How so?' Salome didn't seem particularly rattled by the comparison.

'Neither of you pulls your punches,' she said. 'And I get your point about there being no money in medicine around here.'

'We do all right,' Salome assured her. 'As long as I make sufficient to cover my costs, I'm happy, really I am, but listen! That's the lunch horn. Please say you'll stay.'

Tempting . . .

'I can't,' Claudia told her.

'I quite understand.' Salome nodded. 'Mazares is waiting.'

Now why on earth would she think that? Claudia wondered, as she waited for the ferry to take her back to Rovin. That there was something between them was in little doubt, and she couldn't forget the intensity of the surge when they bumped into each other by accident. Both recovered quickly, but Claudia knew that if either Salome or Mazares had been prepared for such a meeting, their reactions would have been very different indeed.

As the ferryman pulled on the ropes, she stared into the dark, oily waters. The very depth of the channel made for currents that were as dangerous as they were unpredictable, and the undertow was deadly in every sense of the word. Next to the landing, a marble shrine, hung with dozens of red mourning ribbons, testified to the fate of those who'd attempted to swim the quarter mile out of folly, drunkenness, necessity or bravado, and a flame burned day and night in supplication to Vinja, the fire-breathing sea monster who protected the island but who also made his home in this channel, devouring any unfortunates who came his way.

A dread feeling in Claudia's stomach told her that Raspor was one of his victims.

How sad that the beauty of Rovin was disfigured by tragedy. Gazing across waters so clear that you could dress yourself in their reflection, to the evergreen archipelago that shimmered under an azure sky, it was hard to imagine heartbreak in this oasis of cypress and cedar. Claudia's eyes followed the necklace of long, curving beaches that encased coral lagoons swarming with turtles and shellfish, then turned her head towards the mainland, to the fertile paradise of vineyards and olive groves, pastures and meadows, which stretched away to serene rolling hills in the distance. Beyond those lay the mountains of Kotar, a region of dense forests and snow-covered peaks which was home to predators such as wolf, bear and lynx. An untamed wilderness of sparkling rivers, deep lakes and rushing cascades, where icy caverns led down to the bowels of the earth and the caves in the hills were patterned with the handprints of men long since dead.

A self-contained kingdom. Magical, beautiful, thick with secrets and primeval wisdom, where jackals prowled, chamois jumped and pinewoods marched down to the edge of the sea.

Right now, their resinous perfume mingled with myrtle and wild oleander, with the smells of fish from the boats, and from cooking, as the island women busily prepared their menfolk's dinners. There was no poverty here, Claudia reflected. In Rome there was poverty. It hit you on every street corner, but here, in this far-flung outpost, there was none. So who would want to undermine what the late King, Dol, and his successor had worked so hard to achieve? Did they believe they could do any better? Or were the motives, as she suspected, venal . . . ?

'I saw him, too,' a small voice piped up alongside. 'I saw Nosferatu, and nobody believes *me*, either. Not even my mother.'

Her hair was as glossy and black as a raven's, and her face was as white as this island's stone.

'I'm Broda,' she said, 'and I'm eight summers old, and my uncle built that boat, and that one, and that one.'

'He must be a very clever man.' Claudia's heart lurched at the hollowed eyes of one so small, at the tunic that billowed around her skeletal frame.

'What about your father?' she asked. 'Is he clever, too?'

Shutters came down over her haunted eyes. 'I have to go now.'

'No, wait!'

Please don't go.

'Why don't we play hopscotch together?'

With a pebble, she scratched squares on the pavement, then numbered them. Troubled eyes widened in wonder.

'You've never played hopscotch, Broda? Then prepare to learn from an expert.'

Claudia threw the pebble and hopped.

'Your turn.'

An hour passed, by which time both of them were wheezing like rusty bellows, though there was colour in Broda's cheeks and a healthy sparkle in her hollow eyes.

'Do you know any other games?' she asked, panting.

'Knucklebones, dice, soldiers, twelve lines – I can show you them all, if you like.'

'I like, I like!'

Proof that you're never too young to pick up a gambling habit.

'Can I come back tomorrow?'

'Whenever you want, Broda. Whenever you want.'

She watched the child skip away, then continued along the shore until she reached the spot where the noose had lashed round Raspor's trusting neck. Knowing Mazares had killed him was one thing. Proving it, quite another. Especially in light of her testimony being dismissed as the unfortunate consequence of a hastily prepared asinine sedative!

Sitting down on the warm rocks, she rested her chin on her knees and concentrated on the azure horizon and the terns that swooped and dived in its translucent waters. A small cat, not dissimilar to the kitten Lora had been tickling this morning, chased its own tail then scampered off in search of meatier prey, and now it was the scent of cypress and juniper that drifted across on the breeze.

Why was it, she wondered, when Salome's heart was so obviously made of gold, that Claudia didn't trust her an inch?

Rising cramped and stiff, as much from the effects of the hopscotch as last night's fall, her eye was caught by a small object glinting in the sun. The glint was dull. Barely noticeable. But a souvenir of paradise was not to be sniffed at, she supposed.

Except . . .

Her stomach lurched. The object in her fingers was no jetsam, no shell, no oddly shaped pebble. It was the unmistakable shape of a flint arrowhead, and her mind flew back to Pula, to the necklace Raspor had worn under his tunic. She'd thought it odd at the time, dismissing it as another aspect of his paranoia, but today, having overheard her escort talking about Perun, the Thunder God, she understood its significance.

The embodiment of victory, justice and peace, Perun protected his people against witches and evil spirits by striking them dead with his spear. In the old days, when Histrian ploughs first started to turn up these flint arrowheads, they'd taken them to be proof of Perun's bolts, carrying these precious thunder stones home to lay under their doorsteps to ensure themselves of his divine protection.

Whatever motives had forced Raspor to abandon his priestly robes, he had not abandoned his god, keeping Perun's holy symbols next to his skin. Obviously dislodged in last night's struggle, this was the first, and possibly only, piece of evidence that Raspor had been attacked, crushing all hope that the little man might still be alive. If Mazares was clever enough to set a trap in which Raspor believed he would be meeting the girl who had the King's ear, and was audacious enough to pull on the noose while the alarm was being raised, then he would not have abandoned his task in the middle!

Oh, Raspor.

Too many, how you say – innocents? – have died and the King, he is too trusting. He thinks only good of people, but there are bad people around him. Very bad.

Another innocent caught up in the struggle, and she had failed him. He'd only wanted to meet her, pass on his information to someone impartial, and through arrogance she had failed him.

I am dead man, if I am seen talking to you.

Can you ever, ever forgive me?

Mazares, he will stop at nothing.

Raspor had been silenced to stop Claudia passing on to the King any details of murders that had been designed to look like accidents. But what killings? What accidents?

She wound her way back to the King's house, barely aware of the sumptuous carvings, the exquisite wall paintings, the elegant rugs on the floor. But once inside her bedroom, she took great care to lock the door and then heave a chest in front for added protection.

First – she ticked them off on her fingers – there was the late King, known as Dol the Just, who had, in Mazares's words, died 'suitably young'.

His successor and oldest son, Brac, was dead a mere three days before his twentieth birthday – but hold on, she owed it to herself and to others to be objective in her appraisal. Fever was no respecter of standing or status, though she made a mental note to find out what had killed Dol and also what exactly ailed the present incumbent of the Histrian throne.

Who else? Well, number three, the King's only son was killed in a hunting accident, and recently, too.

Also, the King was a widower.

Whose only other child, a daughter, drowned not so long ago, when she was twelve.

Then there was the matter of the royal physician. Would a man in such an elevated position really run off with a male lover? The same man, moreover, who was uncle to the child who claimed to have seen Nosferatu? Coincidence could not be ruled out, but there was a limit to how far it stretched, and when you take Dol, Brac, the King's son, the King's wife and his daughter, who had all died before their allotted span, the disappearance of a boat builder and the royal physician seemed highly suspicious. Especially in view of the boat builder's traumatized niece. Add on Raspor's death and, Croesus, we're already up to eight – and these are only the ones I know about!

Like an icy blast from the Arctic, the enormity of the situation slammed home.

No wonder Raspor was terrified. He'd uncovered a campaign to get rid, not just of the King, but to eliminate his entire bloodline.

A campaign so cunning, so stealthy, so utterly cold-blooded in its execution that the conspirators were prepared to wait years to achieve their target, *because this way it would not come to Rome's ears.*

Hugging her arms tight to her chest, Claudia wondered whether Mazares was in this alone or whether he had allies among the others? His dashing younger brother, for example, or the high priest? And what stand did Pavan take in this matter? Also, there was one more possibility. That they were all in it together. Every last one.

In which case . . .

She waited until darkness settled over the island, then dressed in the darkest garment she owned. A tunic of Tyrian purple. It was also the most expensive, but this was no time to worry about snagging or rips. Mazares might be keeping her alive as bait to lure the King, who's to say Pavan was of the same persuasion?

Scooping Drusilla under her arm, Claudia pulled her veil over her head and slipped silently out of the house. No door opened behind her. No footsteps rang out in the blackness. Still, she waited outside in the alley, but the only sounds to echo down Rovin's dark streets were an owl hooting from one of the pines and a snore from an open window above. Keeping to the shadows, she ducked this way then that as she worked her way down to the ferry. Between the gems in her pouch and the knife in her hand, Claudia had every confidence in persuading the ferryman to make an out-of-hours trip to the mainland, where this morning's expedition had revealed the location of Salome's stables.

By tomorrow morning, she would be in Pula.

By tomorrow night, the conspirators would be in irons!

Her heart was thumping louder than Perun's thunderbolts when she finally reached the ferry landing, but she need not have worried.

No one was following.

Nobody cared that she'd slipped out of the house.

The ferry's ropes had been cut.

With a contented smile, Nosferatu turned over in bed.

Twelve

'What a stupendous honour, my dear! Truly, I am so pleased for you!'

Depositing herself with such force that the chair's life expectancy instantly halved, Rosmerta pushed her nose in front of Claudia's. The cosmetics had been applied with a steady, if somewhat generous, hand, but sadly they'd been applied in all the wrong places. She really needed the antimony here, here and here to open her eyes up, and the wine lees on her cheeks should have been extended further along, up and out. As it stood, she resembled a painted doll who'd been running too hard.

'Don't get me wrong, Lady Claudia.'

Rosmerta fluffed out the cuff of her sleeve.

'I've nothing against the way they celebrate Zeltane here, one should always recognize the need for steam to be let off, but I do feel that your being guest of honour will endow the festivities with the dignity and decorum that has been notice-able in the past by its absence.'

Lady Claudia was taking breakfast in the dining hall and trying to come to terms with sitting at a table to eat, rather than reclining sensibly on a couch, when Rosmerta plonked herself down beside her. Lady Claudia pulled off a chunk of warm cheese bread and chewed thoughtfully.

'What's that commotion outside?' she asked.

'Tsk.' Rosmerta helped herself to a honey cake. 'You'd never believe it, but vandals cut our ferry ropes in the night.'

When she shook her head, the wig wobbled so precariously that Claudia primed herself to catch it.

'Mindless it is, absolutely mindless. I mean, what were they *thinking* of, knowing people will be flooding in from all over for the Spring Festival? Who can *possibly* think that is amusing?'

Another honey cake disappeared without trace.

'I blame the parents, you know. Children today aren't disciplined enough, and we're starting to see the result of letting the little buggers run wild.'

Claudia glanced across to the courtyard, where Marek and Mir were tormenting a puppy by tossing it back and forth in the air between them, and mused upon pots calling the kettle black.

'That's a very attractive hairstyle,' she said, lining up a walnut on the table.

'Do you think so?' Rosmerta almost purred in delight. 'My wig maker tells me it's all the fashion in Rome.'

'Your wig maker's right.'

Unfortunately, it was a fashion adopted by far younger women.

'Only, I feel it's terribly important for a woman in my position to be stylish, don't you?'

Distracted by her own flounces and frills, Rosmerta missed the walnut pinging off into the courtyard. She caught only her son's yelp as something hit him hard on the ear, and didn't even notice the puppy drop from his hands and run like the wind for cover.

'Put an onion on it, darling,' she called. 'And get the men to check there isn't a nest nearby, one can never tell with a hornet.'

She turned back and sighed.

'Forgive me, Lady Claudia, but I'd better go. Make sure they get the sting out, and all that. Mustn't have it infecting my baby boy, must we?'

What irony, Claudia thought. The one person she could confide in on this godforsaken island was the last person she ever would . . .

'*Godda margen.*'

Apple cheeks flushed pink from working out in the gymnasium poked themselves round the door.

'Has the old trout gone?' Vani mouthed.

Claudia nodded. 'A hornet made an unprovoked attack on your husband –' (brother-in-law?) – 'and Rosmerta's playing nursemaid.'

'Personally, I can't stand the old cow,' Vani said, perching on the edge of the table and swinging one long, muscular leg. 'But you have to hand it to old Fossil Face there, no one keeps a closer watch on her family. Trust me, cornered vixens couldn't be more protective, and I'm not just talking about her precious cubs.'

She selected a pear from the display on the table, then swapped it for a shiny green apple.

'The slightest sniffle and she's got Kažan wrapped up in bed, and I tell you, if I'd kept all the potions she'd given me to help me conceive, there'd be no room for the bloody bed in the room. Self-defeating or what?'

The sound of Vani's strong teeth crunching into the apple was the only sound in the dining hall and Claudia took advantage of the silence to study the exquisitely executed works of art on the walls, whose significance she was slowly beginning to understand.

Take the scene showing the High Priest hurling a sword into the lake. In this painting, he was surrounded by wailing women and mourners and that's because the spirit of every Histrian warrior is imbued in his weapon while it's being forged. It fell upon Drilo to consign this spirit to the gods after death. Another painting showed the God of the Fields arguing with the god who protects beasts of burden, reflecting the Histri's struggle to balance cruelty with output. But in each of the paintings little fat Varil scampered, either in the form of a goat or, more commonly, as himself. God of Lust and Fertility. In other words, whatever happened in the lives of these people, procreation was paramount.

'You've been trying for babies?' Claudia murmured.

Vani took careful aim before lobbing her apple core into the fountain with a perfect bullseye.

'For that, pumpkin, it takes two, and maybe if my husband spent more time in his wife's bed than with his bloody mastiffs, we'd have a better chance, though frankly, with his miserable performance, I rather doubt it. Mollycoddle them too much and everything goes soft.'

No wonder she found Kažan so attractive. A seasoned womanizer with that oh-so-essential ingredient, charm, he was that archetype of all lovers. The broad hunk with the slow hand. Claudia tried to think of a way to steer Kažan into the conversation.

'It was good of you to look in on me after my fall.'

'Don't be silly, it was the least I could do! I mean, honestly, fit as I am, even *I* don't take stairs twelve at a time. Dammit, woman, you put me to shame!' Vani shot her a sheepish grin. 'Mind, I thought you were asleep. I suppose you . . . well, I suppose you saw me kissing Kažan . . . ?'

'Either that, or I dreamed about limpets.'

Vani eased herself off the table and bridged her back on the floor.

'It's only sex.'

Her back arched like a bow.

'The thing is, I signed up for this marriage and I've no intention of leaving my husband, but – well, Kažan's fun.'

She contorted into another gymnastic position.

'And we do *try* to be discreet. Well, discreet-*ish*! It's not easy when there are so few opportunities, so when that old battleaxe insisted Kažan remained in your room to keep watch—'

'Rosmerta did?'

'I told you.' Vani was in danger of tying herself in a knot. 'She doesn't look the motherly type, but tigresses could learn from that woman. As far as she's concerned, you're Histri now, pumpkin, and even though she's Illyrian born, she's Histri by marriage and that makes her one herself.'

'A dozen more stairs and I would have been history in every sense,' Claudia quipped.

'Another performance like that, my girl, and I'm in danger of losing my crown for the Milk Race!'

'Milk Race?'

'Sorry, pumpkin, I'm forgetting you're a stranger to these shores.' Muscular legs performed the splits. 'See her?'

Vani pointed to a stone cat curled in the corner.

'That's Kikimora, Goddess of Plenty, and on the day of her festival, libations of milk are poured, rather than wine. Also, since Kikimora stands for contentment, her day is a public holiday with foot races, boxing competitions, wrestling, discus, you name it, hence the term Milk Race. Like the Greeks, though, our men compete naked, and the following day, of course, it's the marriage announcements.'

She straightened up and grinned impishly.

'That way, we girls know what we're getting.'

Although principally a fishing community that served every farm and village in the close proximity, the town of Rovin was still that: a town. A thriving, bustling town to be precise, where bankers set up stalls outside the temples, street sweepers kept the cobbles clean and masons hammered dawn till dusk, sculpting the island's bright, white stone. Since the Histri were self-sufficient in every sense, many trades were absent, such as weavers, barrel makers, basket makers, bone whittlers and dyers, and with no funds for luxury goods, there were no ivory carvers on the island, either, no perfume sellers, glassblowers or spice merchants, which would proliferate in the streets of Pula.

Barber shops were missing, too, the Histri having a strong attachment to their hair, whether on the head, on the face or on the body, a sentiment that sadly applied every bit to women as to men. It seemed odd, not having chariots trying to mow people down every ten seconds, for astrologers not to be touting their charts to read your fortune and viper tamers piping over their menacing charges. But Rovin still resounded to the clack of cobblers bent over their lasts, to the grinding of grain and the sawing of timber, and thirsts were still quenched in the many taverns whose stools spilled out into the shade.

Claudia was one such customer, the tavern keeper both flattered and flustered at such illustrious patronage, so that, having already plied her with a jug of his finest red wine at no cost, he was now in the process of inundating his guest with a selection of cheese pastries, ham rissoles and chunks of blood sausage deep fried with garlic. The tavern was nothing like the one she used to dance in, what seemed like a lifetime ago now. That had been smoke-filled and dirty, populated by sailors disembarking after too many long months at sea. She shuddered at the memory.

'It seems my hospitality has been somewhat lacking.'

The shadow that fell across her table smelled of cool mountain forests and his bow was so deep, it was a wonder his pants didn't split. She'd wondered how long it would take him to run her to ground.

'Not a bit,' she replied, tucking into another piece of spicy red sausage.

'But . . .'

A languid boot hooked up a stool and sat down beside her. Wasn't there a nursery rhyme about that?

'. . . I was under the impression that you'd been offered breakfast.'

Claudia reached for another hot pastry. 'And your point?'

Mazares rested his elbows on the table and shook his head slowly. 'None at all, My Lady. None at all.'

People were staring. They were trying to be subtle about it, but they were unable to hide their astonishment. The nobility *don't* eat at streetside taverns! They just don't! It's not done! She'd hoped such indignity would make him squirm, but if it did, he was hiding it well.

'You might be interested to know that the King had invited you to be guest of honour at the Feast of Zeltane tonight.'

'Yes, I know.'

That lifted his eyebrows off their launch pads!

'Rosmerta told me.'

'Did she?' he drawled. 'Anyway, if you wish to travel to Gora instead, and you did say it was your intention to hasten there with all speed, let me know and I'll put the arrangements in hand.'

'Nonsense, I'd love to be guest of honour,' she cooed, returning his artless smile.

So many people milling around. So many opportunities to slip away!

'One thing puzzles me, though, Mazares. This invitation? I understood communications to the mainland were severed.'

'Not all requests come by messenger, My Lady, but in this case the invite is of long standing. And since we Histri can't resist dressing up for our festivities, the King's taken the liberty of having a costume prepared for you in advance.'

Really? How did anyone know exactly which date I'd arrive . . . ?

'How thoughtful.'

'We're a thoughtful race,' Mazares grinned. 'Now, me, since the moon is in Taurus, I shall be wearing the headdress and pelt of a bull.'

'You disappoint me,' she replied. 'At the very least, I expected a wolf.'

'Then I shall make a note to come as a wolf *next* year.' His wrist performed a theatrical flourish. 'But for you, My Lady, and seeing how this festival celebrates the zenith of spring and thus the very flowering of life itself, for you we've had sewn a gown of rainbow colours.'

'I'm sure I'll suit every one.'

'They'll certainly match every bruise,' he tossed back. 'But you see, the rainbow is the Queen of Heaven's sacred emblem, and we Histri believe an iris grows wherever one touches the ground.'

'A nobler notion than the pot of gold we Romans tend to look for.'

'We're a noble race, My Lady.'

'Thoughtful, noble, is there no end to your kingdom's discerning attributes?'

'None whatsoever. Will you walk with me, Claudia?'

Oh, good. He *was* squirming.

She slipped her hand through the proffered arm, encased in its customary crisp white embroidered cotton and, just like any long-time married couple, they strolled leisurely down to the quayside, where fishermen hauled on flax nets across the shimmering lagoon. Thanks to the angle of the sun, one island merged seamlessly into another on the horizon while, behind them, Rovin's white stone buildings retreated up the hill in tidy terraces.

'Zeltane is but one of many festivals,' Mazares said, 'and since you'll be marrying into us, I reckon *somebody* ought to explain about our arcane practices and spooky customs.'

Who better than the werewolf himself?

'How spooky?'

'Ooh . . .' Mazares shrugged his broad shoulders. 'Maybe . . . ?'

As he leaned forward to preen his reflection with both hands in the mirrored calm of the sea, something brushed the nape of Claudia's neck. She shivered, and they both laughed. Amusing, yes. Sleight of hand always is, especially when it's accompanied by comic gestures. But make no mistake, Claudia Seferius was the puppet and Mazares the man jerking the strings. So far, the genial puppet-master had required little of his marionette, but she knew the dance was about to begin, and she shivered again.

'Cold? You're welcome to my shirt.'

'I'd hate to see you go naked.' Though many women would not.

'I wasn't offering to go that far,' he murmured. 'These boots are a sod to take off. Oh, Pavan!'

The general looked up from where his strong arms were assisting a small boat to tie up at the quayside.

'Be a pal, would you, and run through our quaint Histrian ways with our honoured guest? Only, there's going to be a riot soon, unless those ferry ropes are fixed—'

Mazares stopped short, his whole expression changing as a crate was hauled out of the boat and lowered by winch on to the jetty. The latch was flipped and suddenly two enormous Molossan hounds were bounding over the cobbles. Claudia took two paces backwards. These dogs were just one step down from a wolf and, with their heavy grey pelts, amber eyes and pricked ears, she could just picture them roaming the forests of Histria, howling mournfully into the night. Making a rapid calculation on a scale of one to ten at just how tasty these brutes might find her, she put the figure at nine-and-three-quarters.

'Elki! Saber!'

Tails wagging, the dogs lunged straight for Mazares, pressing their muzzles into his hands before rolling over on to their backs for a belly rub.

'Well, this *is* a surprise,' Mazares said.

Friends, she decided, who'd been parted too long. Three wolves together. A pack . . .

Further crates were being lowered on to the quayside, though no one seemed in a hurry to flip these particular latches. Packed with muscle and bigger, even, than the Molossan hounds, their squat, broad muzzles curled in snarls and their wide-set eyes bulged out in hate.

'Why don't you free the mastiffs?' she asked Pavan.

Not that she was ungrateful.

'It seems cruel to keep one lot of pets cooped up in their cages while the others romp free in the open.'

'Them?' Pavan sneered. 'They're not Mazares's. They belong to Kažan and his sons, and they're not pets. They're hunting hounds, vicious brutes, and my advice is to steer well clear of them.'

His grey eyes narrowed.

100

'It was a mastiff like that which killed the King's son. Disembowelled him, when he was out chasing a stag.'

Watching Mazares's white shirt cut through the crowds, his Molossan hounds loping joyfully alongside, Claudia reduced the death toll to seven.

Pavan picked up a handful of pebbles and began skipping them over the water. 'Aye, I suppose an outsider might find one or two of our customs take a bit of getting used to.'

Really? Worshipping in sites made holy by nature, such as in caves, beside springs, or in sacred groves, wasn't so different from Roman devotions. The grandiose temples were simply a way to say thank you. Or was Pavan referring to the Histrian ritual of burying the dead along with all their possessions, and in cemeteries ringed by ditches, rather than cremated and interring them in tombs like the Romans?

'Oh, I don't know,' she breezed back. 'Some practices cross all cultural divides.'

She nodded towards the couple kissing with such ardent concentration in a fishing boat, that they were completely unaware that a combination of passion and current was fetching them ever closer to the shore.

'Or is adultery taken for granted in this particular kingdom?'

Because there was no mistaking Kažan's boyish good looks – or Vani's apple-cheeked athleticism. Diana of the Hunt, still. But chased instead of chaste.

The general made a noise in the back of his throat.

'Hunting, fishing and women – but you have to hand it to the lad, he's bloody good at all three.'

Forty was a bit old to be considered a lad, wasn't it? Especially when Pavan was the same age.

'A bit of a wastrel, is he, then, this Kažan?' she asked in the sort of girly, gossipy tone that tends to draw taciturn types out.

She suddenly sensed Kažan as the conspirators' weak link. Someone to be flattered and teased, slept with if necessary. *Anything to get out of this place alive.*

'More of a dreamer, I'd say.'

Pavan returned to skipping his pebbles.

'The youngest child's always indulged, but being spoiled hasn't spoiled him, if ye get my drift. He's always happy and smiling, everyone likes him, and in turn he's everyone's friend.'

Better and better!

'I suppose when you look at the sourpuss he's married to,' she chirruped, 'you can't blame Kažan for losing himself in his . . . hobbies.'

Down by the ferry landing, Mazares's easy authority was calming the crowd, and progress on fitting the new ropes was improving because of it. Claudia followed the profile of strong, goateed jaw to tight, narrow trousers, taking in the aureole of glossy curls that fell to his shoulders, the crows' feet at his eyes, that preposterous, swirling, drop-dead-sexy moustache.

'Has *he* ever married?' she asked Pavan.

'Aye. Once.' He kept his gaze on a shoal of black fish nibbling at the stone harbour wall.

Odd, Claudia mused, how the Histri have adopted so many of our Roman practices. Construction projects, such as this harbour. Bathhouses, drains, libraries and gymnasia. How seamlessly they've fitted into our rule. Yet remain so emotionally distant . . .

'What happened?'

Several seconds passed before Pavan lifted his steely grey gaze.

'Same thing that happens to us all, ma'am. She died. Now, if ye'll excuse me, I'll lend them a hand with the ferry.'

Claudia watched the general's ponytail bobbing with exertion as he hauled on the ropes, his massive frame towering above the islanders round him. She watched long after the ferry had tested its new connections with a trip to the mainland. She even watched while it fetched back a consignment of wine in oak barrels and game birds hanging from poles for the feast.

Disembowelled by a mastiff? She had instantly scrubbed the King's son off her list, though the difference it made to the death toll was nothing.

It still stood at eight.

Thirteen

Like Greek festivals, Zeltane wasn't due to commence until sundown, and it started with the sacrifice outside the temple of a white ram to Perun. Earlier, in preparation for the celebrations, bonfires had been lit all over the mainland as well as the island, although the types of fire were not restricted. Flames leapt in every hearth in every home, from the grandest to the most humble. Beacons flared, torches spat, sconces flickered and candles guttered, each one symbolizing the sun's rays on earth as, for this one night of the year, night was transformed into day. Bald heads were greased, some had even taken to shaving their long Histrian locks, so they could shine like lanterns during the celebrations. Any glow-worm with sense hid itself deep in the foliage.

Hunters and fishermen in horns and antlers whisked tots up on their shoulders, singing and cavorting as they jollied their way round the plaza. Women in elaborately woven skirts and tasselled scarves chanted happy songs as they garlanded the statues and wreathed flowers in their braids, while the younger girls paraded shyly in chaplets of scented spring blossoms; iris, arabis and pinks. Each celebrant wore at least one amulet depicting mythical creatures that would protect them, although many had taken the spirit of Zeltane a step further by dressing up in full regalia.

Woodpeckers were popular, the men cloaking themselves in green feathers and red hats to emulate the royal totem, and quite a few had come as Perun, painting their faces black, like the god's, to resemble his thunder. Marek and Mir both pretended to be the god of bathing, whitening their hair with flour or chalk and shuffling along like old men, hooting with laughter as they tipped drinks over unsuspecting revellers, forcing them to rush to the bathhouse to clean up.

'My goodness, if the Lady Claudia isn't the spitting image of the goddess Perunika!'

Rosmerta's boom cut through the crackle of the logs, the laughter and the singing, and the hissing of fats dripping from the oxen roasting on spits.

'You will be absolutely perfect, sweeping in after the thunder and leaving a glorious rainbow in your wake.'

'Thank you.'

And thank Mazares. The slimy weasel had neatly ensured that she'd stand out like a sore thumb!

'I see you've come as – oh, remind me again?'

Rosmerta had abandoned high fashion in favour of a closely fitting white garment that highlighted every ounce of corseted flesh. Having also whitened her face with some kind of ash, she'd topped off the ensemble by encasing her head in a white veil as well. Scary enough, without those twiggy things stuck on her cheeks.

'Kikimora,' Rosmerta said proudly.

The twiggy things, then, were supposed to be whiskers. Kikimora, Goddess of the Hearth, was depicted as a cat (for contentment), white (for purity) and invariably a fat cat, because fat equated with plenty. Every household kept a stone or painted wooden sculpture by their fireside.

'*Are* you content?' Claudia asked.

As befits a man who'd taken two wives, even though one of them wasn't his own, Kažan had turned himself into the Sun God for the festivities and was schmoozing his way round the crowd, a vision in saffron, right down to the garland of honey-scented melliot draped over his torque.

'Why wouldn't I be?'

Rosmerta seemed surprised, though not offended, by the question.

'I'm the daughter of an Illyrian chieftain, I've contracted a good marital alliance, I have two strapping sons, a handsome husband, a position of standing – Lady Claudia, I have everything a woman could possibly ask for.'

An appropriately feline smugness settled on her features, but as she waddled off on feet crammed into too-tight white shoes, Claudia couldn't help but steal a glance to where Vani stood, alone but not lonely, and clothed from head to sandalled foot in black. It was a strange choice for such an athletic girl, to come as Zorya, Goddess of the Night. But even stranger was the legend that Zorya's lover was the Moon God, not the Sun.

A moment of silence descended on the square as Drilo made supplication to the gods by throwing incense in the largest fire, the Zeltane fire, which roared with suitable grandeur in the centre of the temple precinct. Tonight, he intoned, was especially sacred. The new moon cast no celestial light. Day would be created by the flames of the Fire God, guardian of Perun's holy bolts, and for this one night of the year, Svarog the Sun God would not need to depart with the dusk.

The high priest was flanked on his right by Mazares, resplendent in a ceremonial torque of a fiendishly complex design, and pants that were lavishly embroidered but no less tight, and over his Apollo-like locks, he wore the headdress of Taurus the bull, complete with gilded horns. Pavan stood on the priest's left, and because this was a formal occasion, he was in full military regalia, the significance of the strong leather scent that accompanied him now apparent, since leather is more flexible than metal for training. The trademark ponytail had been abandoned in favour of the Histrian war knot, looped and tied just above the right ear, and a heavy, double-handed sword, a cubit long, possibly more, hung at his side. The handle of his short stabbing knife was long, to ensure a sound grip, and fluted, that the blood and sweat might run off. But most chilling was that the dagger was human in shape, the outstretched arms forming the hilt.

A fanfare of trumpets signalled the start of the feast.

106

'My Lady?'

Considerably more Minotaur than Taurus, Mazares escorted Claudia to the high table where, as the King's guest, she was seated in the centre. The chair was no different to dozens she had at home. High-backed, well stuffed, finely upholstered, elaborately carved, but there was something wrong with the cushioning. She wriggled as delicately as her gown would permit as liveried slaves set out silver salvers of food on the table, and then wriggled some more.

'Perhaps a throne is not to milady's taste?' a voice murmured in her left ear.

Seated beside her was a stranger. Dressed in silver, as Juraj the Moon God, he wore a silver mask over his face that distorted his voice. To her right, Mazares had taken off his heavy bull headdress and was leaning across Pavan to converse with Drilo, ostensibly unaware that introductions had not been made. On the other side of the stranger, the Sun God was trying his damnedest to run his hand up the Goddess of the Night's thigh. The only thing that prevented him was the presence of a white cat sitting squarely between them. Miaow.

Cheerfully ignoring the stranger's remark, Claudia clapped as a rope-walker balanced his pole and set off above a line of the balefires.

'Or are you perhaps entertaining us with a demonstration of some quaint Roman ritual?' the stranger persisted, seemingly unaware of the crowd's collective gasp as the rope-walker wobbled.

'How strange,' she mused, as a plate of veal seasoned with oil and herbs was brought to the table, 'that human beings possess such a capacity to bore, yet the trait is lacking in all other creatures.'

The eye holes in the mask glittered.

The rope-walker made it safely to the other side. The crowd sighed with relief. Claudia resisted the urge to squirm on the uncomfortable cushion.

Lobster, shrimp, asparagus, truffles, pomegranates, roast

kid and game were passed round, as acrobats began to juggle flaming torches in the air.

'Who's Marcus?' the Moon God asked, applauding the tumblers' daring precision.

The prawn on Claudia's knife slithered into her lap.

'Isn't he the bandy-legged fellow down there dressed as a stag?'

The mask leaned forward and peered. 'And you called out *his* name when they carried you home from your fall?'

This time it was her wine that spilled over.

'I think you'll find I was so grateful at being rescued that I actually said "marvellous".'

'Ah.'

'Long live the King!' someone yelled, as the first slices of roast ox were carved off. Dammit, this seat was uncomfortable.

'Long live the King's bride!' Mazares shouted.

Something deep inside the silver mask growled.

Claudia lifted her own glass. 'Long live Histria!'

The toast was met with thunderous cheers.

'In Rome, we don't celebrate Zeltane,' she proclaimed loudly, 'but we do have our own tradition.'

She rose from her seat and looked down on their upturned, eager faces.

'On the night of the new moon closest to May Day, we down as many cups of wine as years we hope to live.' She raised her goblet to the crowd. '*Salzi vol!*'

There was, of course, a certain irony in toasting the good health of hundreds of people who, because of her, were likely to experience anything but!

'*Salzi vol!*' came the jubilant chorus. '*Salzi vol, Claudinoki! Salzi vol!*'

'I didn't know about that particular custom,' Mazares drawled. 'Did you?'

The question was directed at the Moon God, whose response was to upend his glass.

'Nope,' he replied, leaning back and crossing his soft yellow boots at the ankle. 'But I like it.'

'So do I!' shouted Kažan.

'It has my vote,' said Marek (or was it Mir?).

'Mine, too,' added Mir (or was it Marek?). 'And *I* intend to live to a hundred!'

Claudia sat down again and considered the paradox of this deceptively handsome young lout who wanted to be a long-liver, but whose liver would not live that long.

'*Salzi vol!*'

Mighty Jupiter, King of Olympus, make them all want to be octogenarians, would you – because how could she possibly escape with the conspirators sober?

She fluttered her fingers at a particularly sweet little wood-pecker she'd befriended earlier and felt a warm glow as the woodpecker waved back. But before it was time to pluck his lovely green feathers, she needed to walk a tightrope far more hazardous than the entertainer who'd performed for the crowd earlier. Mazares's cunning was not to be underestimated. So, despite having no appetite to dine among cold-blooded killers, the honoured guest forced herself to eat, even using several tiny flat flour cakes to mop up the mushroom and garlic sauce that her smoked pork had been cooked in.

To Marek and Mir she simpered and tittered. She batted her eyelashes at Kažan, nodded solemnly at Drilo's predic-tions of a fruitful harvest followed by drought, complimented Rosmerta and laughed at Mazares's jokes. In truth, that part wasn't difficult. Mazares was a born raconteur with an easy wit and an ability to win people over.

'. . . so I said to him, look, man, it's better to be mad and not know it than be sane and have your doubts.'

At his feet, the two Molossan wolfhounds alternated between snoozing and stretching, although from time to time they deigned to take snippets of roast ox and other delicacies from their master's hand. The three of them together. A pack, she reflected, that was merely at rest.

'. . . I tell you, the louder that Venetian merchant proclaimed his integrity, the faster we counted our silver.'

'My father told me to beware of only three things in life,'

the Moon God murmured behind his mask, as she applauded yet another of Mazares's witticisms. 'One, the kick of a mule. Two, the tusk of a boar. The third was the smile of a beautiful woman.'

'I'm surprised you've experienced the latter,' she replied, 'but what astonishes me even further is that you actually knew who your father was. Do excuse me.'

He stood as Claudia rose, and dipped his head politely.

'Well, that's one thing my father *didn't* warn me about. To expect all three together.'

Younger than Mazares, and as tall, but a soldier. You could tell by the muscles that bulged through his robes, by the strength and breadth of his hands. The Moon God who, according to his waxing and waning, sees everything, sees part or sees nothing . . .

Among the revellers, the festivities were going well. People passed her barley cakes shaped like wheels to toss into the flames in appeasement of the Fire God and hymns were sung to Perun, to his wife Perunika, to the King, to the Motherland, to Rome, to Svarog the Sun God, to Kikimora the Cat Goddess, in fact to every living creature that moved.

Her toast, god bless it, was working.

Eyes followed her progress. Pavan's seemed especially sharp, but maybe this was merely the reflection of so many fires, though she'd noticed his hand hadn't strayed far from his scabbard tonight. Four, five, six times she returned to the table, flirting and feasting, listening and nodding, only to excuse herself once more in a desire to confer good health and prosperity upon the revellers, throwing more barley wheels into the flames and secure in the knowledge that a combination of music and laughter drowned any whispered words that might be thrown a bashful young woodpecker's way.

'Dance with me, Claudia! Dance with me, and lift my heart with your smile, and sweep me off my feet with your beauty!'

Drink affects people in different ways. It had made Kažan merrier, more effusive, more charming, and as Claudia cavorted between the bonfires, it was difficult to imagine this impossibly handsome creature as a schemer. A dreamer, Pavan had called him. Ah, but what else are dreamers if not idealists – and idealists can be ruthless in pursuit of their goals. What a spoiled child wants, a spoiled child gets, but how far would this liquid-eyed charmer go to get what he wanted, and, more to the point, what would he gain by destroying the King and eliminating his allies and bloodline? She had no time to think. Kažan swept her clean off her feet and danced as though she was an armful of lilies.

'There!' Breathless from laughter, he set her down gently. 'That made my brother's eyes pop.'

Pop was an overstatement, but even from here the catkins could be seen glinting, and there was a set line to Mazares's jaw. No doubt it was the effect of night turned into day, but it seemed to Claudia that the torque round his neck, the one fashioned in such a complex design, flashed in the firelight with menace, and the embroidered creatures on his pants writhed with hatred. She had a sudden urge to throw her arms round the Sun God and kiss him long and hard on the lips, but decided that it was better the focus remain on Kažan.

If the extra wine had affected His Majesty's general, it didn't show, but (dear heart that he was!) the Moon God was swaying at a most alarming angle and Rosmerta's eyes had glazed over as Drilo the Priest, who had become decidedly lofty in his cups, asserted loudly that the *Zeltana*, the play in which Summer triumphed over Winter, ought to be performed tonight instead of tomorrow, and so what if he was the one who'd interpreted the various omens to lay down the schedule; an omen is entitled to a change of heart, is it not? Marek and Mir were growing more and more malicious with each goblet that was tossed down their gullets, taking pleasure not only in drenching the revellers with their own wine, but tipping food over them as well. Psychopaths in the making? Or brothers who had already made the transition . . . ?

Fired by dancing and singing, feasting and laughter, the islanders rejoiced in their history, praising Perun for bestowing peace upon his people, for bringing them victory in war (well, they *were* drunk), for a King who showed justice and wisdom. Drums rolled, horns blew, rattles hissed, trumpets blared, and, in the quieter corners, men plucked strings stretched over huge beech soundboxes. This was the moment Claudia had been waiting for. The moment when the party had reached its peak. So much coming, so much going, such a fusion of colour, that one little rainbow wouldn't be noticed. Gliding between one balefire and another, she followed in the women's ritual of consigning coloured ribbons to the flames until she reached the outer edge of the plaza. The woodpecker was waiting. In the blackness of the shadows, she could almost feel the heat from his blushes as the object of his illicit tryst approached.

'To us.' Her voice was husky as she handed him the goblet.

'Th-thanks.' His was, too. Nerves do that. Though it was hard to say whose hand was shaking the most. 'Gosh, I . . . I—'

The goblet fell from his hands and he slithered to the floor in a heap of feathers. One more hangover among hundreds, and Claudia was already out of her rainbow gown and climbing into his pantaloons and shirt before the first snort emanated from his comatose lips. Grabbing his red felt hat, she pulled the beak low over her face and wrapped the feathered cloak tight about her shoulders. No one gave a second thought to another woodpecker snaking its way through the banquet.

The quay was quiet. Naturally. Who in their right mind would be out here, when the festivities were in full swing in the square? Maybe later a lover or two might escape to its solitude, but not before the feast was finished, and Claudia ran on light feet towards a small rowing boat moored at a ring. Relief swept over her. Whether the governor in Pula believed her story any more than she'd believed Raspor's didn't matter. What mattered was that the conspiracy would be aired. There could be no further 'accidents' now. The King, praise Juno, was safe!

With a gentle splash, the rope disappeared into the water and Claudia sent a brief prayer to Neptune to keep the breeze in her favour. She approached the ladder leading down to the boat. With only a sliver of moon in the sky, precious little light was cast over the quay, so she was surprised when a shadow fell over the cobbles.

'You wouldn't be thinking of leaving us, would you?'

The voice was barely audible through the mask, but there was no mistaking the deer-skin boots as the Moon God stepped in front, blocking her way.

Nosferatu had never had so much fun.

Fourteen

The old man made his way slowly down the hillside, the torch casting unearthly shadows in his palsied hand, and every now and again his arthritic bones jolted painfully thanks to an unseen stone on the path, or maybe a tree root sticking up, or perhaps a fallen branch. He paused for breath. Every Zeltane he made this pilgrimage to the small spring in the valley, but with each passing year the task grew that much harder and took longer to accomplish. The old man was resigned to this, and on he pressed, his wooden clogs making little sound on the springy forest floor.

Once a huntsman with as keen an eye as any true-born Histrian, now it was left to his sons, his grandsons and his great-grandsons to bring home the venison and boar. The most his rheumy eyes could manage was the odd pheasant or hare, but more often than not these days his shot missed, and the leather jerkin that kept out the winter winds and summer rains when he was younger afforded scant protection to frozen bones and parchment-thin skin.

High in the canopy, a blackbird began to sing, always the first line of the chorus, its cadences quickly followed by a woodlark, then a wren. By the time he'd reached the bottom, the valley was a choir of songbirds, finches, tits and warblers, and the Sun God's youngest wife was already rising from her crimson bed. The old man cursed. He must set out earlier next Zeltane. He could not afford to miss the dawn. Dawn was why he came here.

Picking his way across to where a thin trickle of water

seeped from the hillside, he laid down the chaplet of flowers he'd taken such care to carry down, and found comfort on the seat of a soft, mossy rock. This tiny spring was where he and his wife had first plighted their troth. A holy place that was theirs and theirs alone, and for the twelve years since her death he had made this journey to leave flowers in her memory, and here he would sit and he would talk to her, telling her the news of their children, reminding her how much he was missing her, and this year he was able to add that it would not be too many years before he was joining her in the Blessed Realm of the West.

An hour passed, maybe two, until, stiff, he stood up and cast around for a stick to ease his return up the hill.

He recognized it for what it was at once.

His eyesight might be fading and his hands less than steady, but a huntsman still recognizes a kill when he encounters one, even though the kill might be a week or two old and the scavengers of the forest had taken their fill. He could also tell what animal it was, although in this case the kill was human.

Accidents were more common than people imagined. It wasn't just travellers – bead sellers, fortune-tellers, itinerant tradesmen – who lost their footing on a slippery path and fell to their deaths. Native-born Histri perhaps in too much of a hurry, perhaps drunk, fell victim to carelessness and quite often their mount would be found with them. Although not today.

Picking over the scattered remains, the old man searched for the amulet that all Histrians wore. Unique to the wearer, this would provide identification and allow the unburied soul to be claimed by their family and interred as was their right, but the huntsman wasn't prepared for the engravings on this amulet that still encircled the half-eaten bone. Burnishing the metal band with his shirt, his first surprise was that it was gold, and he held it close to his eyes to make certain. The second was the engraving. There was no disguising the wood-pecker, or the rainbow that surrounded the bird, and on either side of the totem, two snakes coiled round a staff – the unmistakable emblems of a healer.

The old man was looking at the corpse of the royal physician.

Fifteen

'**M**y dear Claudia, you never cease to surprise me.'
Mazares was far too polished a statesman to let his expression slip when the Queen of Heaven returned to the table dressed as a woodpecker, but a range of emotions flickered in his catkin-green eyes, including, she could swear, admiration. Quite how much gaining the enemy's respect was important, she didn't know, but her new costume had sure drawn a crowd.

'Astonishing,' Pavan rumbled.

'Ravishing,' Kažan said.

'Refreshing,' said Vani.

'Dashing,' chorused Marek and Mir.

But it was the high priest who voiced the crowd's collective opinion.

'Inspirational, My Lady. Truly inspired.'

With one change of costume, he propounded loudly, the Lady Claudia had made public her loyalty to the King. Indeed, so effusive was he in his praise that, by the end of his speech, even *she* could almost believe that her perception had done her credit!

The royal emblem was, she had to admit, a lucky choice, but when you stack that against the masked stranger blocking her escape, it paled into insignificance.

Rovin was a beautiful island set in a paradise sea . . . but it was still her prison.

Mazares was as dashing and gracious as any man she'd ever met . . . yet he was still her jailer.

117

It crossed her mind that Mazares might be keeping her here for her own safety, but if that was the case, Raspor would still be alive. No, he was keeping her because she was the live goat in the pen. Doubtless it was his intention for the King and his new bride to die in some terrible accident, perhaps the ship taking them to Pula would be attacked by pirates, who knows? But come on. Claudia Seferius a goat? He's the one who had to be kidding!

Daylight had swamped the festivities, revealing just how many spirals of smoke were being carried out to sea on the breeze. Bones and mussel shells littered the pavements, along with battered plates, shattered goblets, and a score of lost or trampled hats, a few broken toys and a baby's painted red rattle. One or two figures slumped in drunken repose, but the party was not due to finish until dusk, and while the sun blazed down upon the token livestock driven through a line of bonfires in ritual purification for the entire herd, Claudia set to plotting a means to escape.

Brac be nimble, Brac be quick, Brac jump over the candlestick.

After the sheep, the goats, the pigs and the cattle, it was the turn of the children to hurdle candles in order to burn off evil spirits.

Brac jump long, Brac jump high, Or Brac fall into a fever and die.

She blocked their chants out, but still plan after plan was thwarted by geography, logistics and the spectre of the masked Moon God by her side. She had just ruled out setting the whole island ablaze on the grounds that it was too problematic, considering all the buildings had been constructed of stone, when Mazares reached for his Taurus mask, adjusted the balance using the gilded horns, and offered his elbow.

'It's our turn next.'

Hurdling a couple of wax candles? No problem. She may have encouraged the whole of Rovin to drink itself stupid, but very little wine had passed her own lips and her co-ordination was—

'We leap the Fire of Life.'

Too late she noticed that the crowd had moved back from the Zeltane fire, which had been banked up since she last noticed, and Claudia knew she had no choice. She'd nailed her colours to the King's mast, there was no going back, she needed to keep the islanders on her side as much as she could.

'Don't be scared.'

'Who s–said I'm s–scared?'

Croesus, the flames were taller than she was!

'Ready?'

The crowd was stamping and cheering them on.

'No.'

By the edge of the fire, a veiled nymph dressed entirely in blue tossed bay leaves, verbena, lemon balm and hyssop into the heart of the flames with studied solemnity. Mazares stared at the nymph and her purifying concoction for what seemed like eternity, then dipped his horns, let out a bellow and pawed the ground with his boot. Everyone laughed, and only Claudia heard him say: 'Really? I rather had you pegged as the type who enjoyed getting her feathers singed.'

He took her hand in his and the grip was firm.

'When I say run, you run like the wind, and when I say jump, you don't jump high, you jump one-two and make the third jump as long as you can. Trust me.'

She wanted to say that she might as well put her head in a lion's mouth, but her tongue had stuck to her palate.

'Run!'

Hand in hand, they hurtled towards the flames.

'Jump!'

One . . . two . . . She had never made such a leap in her life – or found anything more exhilarating.

'Told you.' Panting, Mazares pulled off the bull mask and grinned. 'And only a handful of burnt feathers to show for it!'

To take on fire and win . . .

'Is a charred woodpecker the same as a cooked goose?' she

asked, but whatever retort he intended to make was overtaken by Marek (or was it Mir?).

'Hey! Mazares! Isn't it time you showed the pretty birdie your own wooden pecker?'

Pavan lifted a hand that would have swept him backwards off his feet, but Rosmerta stepped in front of her son.

'You will apologize at *once* for your vulgarity,' she boomed, her white face distorted with anger.

As he voiced his abject contrition, Claudia wondered whether Kažan wasn't the weak link after all, because he'd said nothing. Nothing at all.

'Good boy.'

Rosmerta glanced first to Claudia, then Mazares to establish that no harm had been done and, satisfied, said: 'Now then, who's going to escort me through this year's Fire of Life? Kažan?'

They made an incongruous couple, the Cat and the Sun God, and it struck Claudia how odd it was that, on his own, Kažan radiated confidence and strength, yet beside his wife he appeared weaker and somewhat diminished. Perspective, she mused. By her very size and nature, Rosmerta dominated every scene and Claudia's thoughts flittered back to her own wedding day. Also a marriage of convenience, but whereas Kažan and Rosmerta's was a political alliance, at least she and Gaius had thrashed out a pact for themselves. Did Kažan have any inkling of what he was taking on, when he accepted the Illyrian chieftain's daughter? Were there any hints in the young Rosmerta of the sourness and resentment that lay ahead? Or were those traits born of her husband's relentless profligacy? Neither Cat nor Sun God, Claudia concluded, deserved the other – and she meant it in the kindest sense.

In several places, makeshift bridges had been constructed across the Fires of Life to convey the sick, frail and elderly without risk, though for the majority of Zeltane's celebrants, the leaping was an important part of the ritual, with young couples jostling to race towards the flames. The masked stranger, she noticed, was among them. Hand in hand, he leapt with Vani, their muscular legs scissoring effortlessly across the flames. Vani, dressed as Goddess of the Night. Whose lover was none other than the Moon himself . . .

To the sound of pan-pipes, drums and flutes, the food and wine just kept on coming, with a seemingly endless succession of earthenware pots being pulled out of the logs in which this season's lambs had been slow-roasted during the night. Out in the plaza, a human chain linked hands to weave in and out of the crackling bales, swaying and singing as they danced, their shadows casting a parallel ballet.

'Why do you suppose there are no Romans at this banquet?' the masked stranger murmured.

If Perun was truly God of Justice, he'd have him sweating like a pig under the weight of so much metal, the heat turning it into an oven inside, he'd make it cut into his flesh and rub his skin raw, leaving a rash.

'Remind me to lend you a ruby,' she breezed. 'If you hold it next to your eye, all things become magnified. An excellent aid for short sight.'

'Apart from you, then.'

Easy. The Histri were underhand, they were sneaky, they were all double-dealers. Even without the conspiracy angle, they'd managed to convince Rome that they were perfectly capable of governing themselves without intervention. Doubtless they were right, and although Gora probably bristled with imperial flunkies, such was the propaganda they'd been drip fed for so long that it wouldn't have occurred to any Roman to be on the invitation list for local festivals.

'I have no idea,' she replied, helping herself to a piece of succulent lamb. 'Why don't we ask Mazares?'

The rumble under the mask was reminiscent of the sound Drusilla made when she heard a strange noise in the night. Two minutes passed, in which the Moon God tapped his fingernail on the table.

'I don't suppose you'd care to dance with me, would you?'

He supposed right.

* * *

121

It was only as the sun began to sink again and the exhausted revellers collapsed to watch the *Zeltana* – the play in which Winter (dressed in grey) battled Summer (all in green) – which ended in a comic turn, with Summer setting fire to Winter's tail and Winter running down the island howling at the top of his voice – that Claudia wondered whether she hadn't been looking at this problem the wrong way round.

Clearly, there was no way she could steal away from this island . . . so why try? Why not let them think she'd escaped and lie low until the heat had died down? She couldn't be sure it was 'them' and not 'him', just as she couldn't be sure Mazares was spearheading this campaign, but who else had the patience, drive and grit to execute a plan that would take *years* to come to fruition? As a soldier, Pavan certainly had the ability and tactical knowledge, but no general worth his salt would sit back for that long. Were Pavan the lone orchestrator, he'd have acted swiftly and decisively, and would undoubtedly have come unstuck long ago. Kažan was too self-centred, Drilo too self-important, Marek and Mir too immature and self-absorbed.

She watched as archers fired volley upon volley of flaming arrows at the setting sun in a last-ditch attempt to keep the light alive, and thought, yes indeed. Smoke and mirrors, that was all it was . . . yet it was enough to reverse nature for the duration of the Zeltane Festival. Why not make smoke and mirrors work for her?

All she needed was the right spot in which to go to ground.

Sixteen

'My dear, what a wonderful surprise!'

The tints in Salome's hair glistened like rubies beneath the blazing sun.

'And you've saved me a trip to Rovin, as well.'

Leading Claudia away from her armed escort, she took her to a cool shed packed with a fragrant display of oleanders, pinks, larkspur and hibiscus, orange blossom, lilies and orchids, all arranged with breathtaking artistry.

'The day after Zeltane and in celebration of the Earth Goddess Maija, Histrian women pack flowers into the baskets that they've spent all winter weaving, which they then give away. This tradition is known as the Goodwill Basket and the idea is to distribute luck and good fortune to those who need it the most.'

There were scabious and verbena, sweet periwinkle, heads of fluffy, white peonies . . .

'Tobias's handiwork?'

'That's the beauty of the men who choose to stay on,' Salome said. 'They stay, because they fall in love with this land.'

The thought of the scowling Tobias in love was hard to imagine. Lean and wiry, with a head of thick, springy hair, he struck Claudia as a young man tormented by demons, not angels. But who knows? Perhaps he exorcized them in horticultural perfection?

'Teamwork,' Salome explained. 'Tobias produces these beautiful blooms, Lora fashions them into works of art.'

Lora: the girl with the cascade of waves that fell to her waist, who helped Salome in the treatment room. The same Lora who'd thought to add a remedy for the battered wife's bruises to the preparations she'd been asked to make up. Who'd tickled the chin of a playful grey kitten and stroked a snoozing tomcat. And whose elfin face set like cement when Salome said, *Lora, this is Claudia, who's come all the way from Rome to consider the King's proposal of marriage . . .*

'It's a generous gesture,' Claudia said. 'Perhaps the locals will think better of you after this.'

'Bigots are like leopards, they don't change their spots,' Salome replied. 'But in any case, I can't afford to give them the opportunity. Money's far too tight to simply give away such an expensive crop. No, my dear, these are for you to distribute.'

'Me?'

'Mazares thought you might like to continue the May Day tradition of sending Goodwill Baskets to those who might need them . . .'

'Jarna, for instance?'

Salome smiled. 'You're learning!'

She fixed a chaplet of tight pink rosebuds, pale blue nigella and some feathery white flowers over Claudia's hair, slipped a sprig of myrtle into her own foxy mane, then pursed her lips.

'Just a suggestion, my dear – and this is entirely up to you, of course – but now that you're aware of the custom, have you considered presenting one of these baskets to Mazares?'

'What a splendid idea. Which one contains the poison ivy?'

She diffused her barb with a smile and selected a sumptuous arrangement of yellows and golds with a splash of purple iris thrown in.

'I hope he paid you the full market price,' she added, changing her mind in favour of a display of dazzling blues.

'Better than that. He sent us a pig.'

'Did you say pig?'

'Plump and spotted, not a bit like the crusty old boars you find in the hills, this one's gentle and funny, an absolute darling, and just what I've always wanted. Come along, I'll introduce you.'

'I must be losing my sex appeal,' Claudia grumbled. 'In the past, people introduced me to eligible bachelors.'

'Isn't that the same thing?' Salome giggled.

'It is in Mazares's case,' Lora rasped, stomping in with another basket of blooms under her arm. 'He paid with a pig, because he *is* a pig.'

'Lora, please.' Salome looked as though she'd been kicked.

'What? I can't speak my mind now? You said it yourself, only a few men can handle the concept of equality and Mazares is not one of them.' Elfin features rounded on Claudia. 'A point *you* might want to consider, since you'll be marrying King Chauv—'

'That's quite enough, Lora.'

Salome's tone didn't change, but the steel was unmistakable. The girl shrugged one finely plucked eyebrow, laid down her basket then swept out of the shed. In the silence that followed, dust motes danced in the sunshine and bees, spoilt for choice, buzzed industriously round the fragrant displays.

'I apologize for Lora's outburst,' Salome said at last, 'but there's something you need to understand.'

Outside, an army of young girls milked goats and churned cheeses, spun wool and chopped vegetables, while others drew game birds or plucked poultry, and an old woman ground mustard grains with a pestle and mortar. Salome paused to give orders regarding the preparation of dyes and the sharpening of ploughshares before leading her visitor to a seat on the terrace at the back of the house. Shaded by cool, fragrant pines, a fountain gurgled contentedly, butterflies fluttered between urns of valerian and small birds twittered in the canopy above. Across the way, a bed of commercial lilies wafted their scent on the gentle warm breeze.

'Lora labours under the misapprehension that it's because of *her* that the King's taken against what I do here. It isn't, or, more accurately, it's only part of the problem, but the trouble is –' the Syrian fixed her green eyes on a gap through the trees to where the sun glistened like diamonds on the sea in the distance '– Lora was married to the King's son, his only heir, you remember. After her husband was killed in the hunt, she came here.'

'Ah.'

Imagination didn't need to stretch far to picture the chauvinistic Histri's reaction to their widowed princess labouring in a commune of women!

'In tribal law, just like Roman law, women belong to the men,' Salome continued. 'Lora had become the prince's chattel upon marriage and in her mind the unrest is down to the simple question of the Histri wanting her back.'

'Do they?'

'Of course. Nothing's changed in that respect, but this farm is Roman and they wouldn't dare launch an aggressive action, though you must have noticed by now that the Histri are a boneheaded bunch. Nothing I say makes a scrap of difference to that woman's viewpoint, although –' she dabbled her hand in the fountain – 'having said that, she was mighty glad to see *you.*'

'You could have fooled me.'

'Lora's young, and I can't say her manners have improved since she's been here, hence her outburst. I can promise you that won't happen again, but it's troubled her from the day of the funeral that she might be forced into marriage with the King. It wouldn't be the first time this has happened in this country and, as you know, youth always hides fear with aggression.'

Claudia thought of all the scandals that had wracked Rome and decided that none compared to this tiny kingdom. Square foot for square foot, the city just couldn't compete!

'You see, my dear, even the present incumbent of the throne was forced to marry his dead brother's widow.'

'Brac's wife?'

'Exactly. Delmi was the eldest daughter of the King of the Ispydes, a wealthy tribe who, as you know, are outside the Empire but who are nevertheless allies and an important link on the amber road which runs through here to the Baltic.'

She went on to explain. Delmi had been married to Brac for just over three years when the prince died of a fever, but such was her family's power and influence that Histria dare not break the political alliance. Bereft as he was at the loss of his heir, Dol had no choice but to decree that his second son marry Brac's widow, even though the boy was only fifteen at the time.

'Did he mind?'

And more to the point, how did poor Delmi feel, being passed from pillar to post?

Salome shrugged her elegant shoulders. 'The King has always put his country before himself.'

'There's something I still don't understand,' Claudia said. 'You say Lora believes herself to be the cause of all your rape and pillage, yet she's still here.'

If there was one quality the aristocracy were born with, it was obligation. Duty was the first word they uttered.

'I repeat, boneheaded.' Salome grinned. 'Ultimately, though, it's her choice whether she stays or goes, my doors are open to everyone and, believe me, there's more than enough work to go round!'

The two young widows set off on a slow tour of Amazonia, taking in everything from the spotted pig, snorting happily around her brand-new sty and showing imminent signs of producing piglethood, to the shed where wheat was threshed, to the flock of tiny, dark-brown sheep with arching horns, whose fleeces were in the process of being plucked, not shorn, using special antler combs. Again, the riot of colour on this farm took Claudia's breath away. Yellow lupins, pale blue flax, fields of bright green wheat, but . . .

'No bonfires, I notice.'

Was that a falter in Salome's step, or just a stone beneath her shoe?

'We don't celebrate Zeltane here, since it's purely a Histrian event.'

Claudia's thoughts drifted to Rome, to where the Festival of Flora was being celebrated over seven days, in which theatres and amphitheatres put on non-stop shows. And every one featuring fire and light . . . As they looped back towards the farmhouse, goats with shaggy, raggy coats came skipping from the milking shed, bees buzzed round their woven wicker skeps and cattle raised purely for hides lowed softly in the meadow.

'How about May Day?'

Salome's green eyes danced. 'I told you, my dear, I observe all our Roman festivals. As a matter of fact, we are holding our May Banquet tonight. You'll join us, I trust?'

How smoothly her lies unfolded. Claudia studied the sprig of myrtle in Salome's hair, a herb strictly forbidden on May Day, and said nothing would please her more.

'But you must have joined the celebrations out on Rovin?'

'Regrettably not.' Salome stopped to test the bar on a gate. 'Between sowing the millet and fumigating the byres, we're planting and pruning round the clock, cutting the vetches, heaven knows the weeding is endless, and of course we're still breaking in our new bullock, so rather than embarrass myself by falling asleep before the first sacrifice, I find it simpler to collapse into bed.'

Claudia returned her smile, and remembered the nymph in blue tossing purifying herbs into the Fire of Life. The nymph had been heavily veiled, but there was no mistaking that single, loose strand of hair. It was long, and shining – and unmistakably red. Mazares had noticed the wayward strand, too. He had stood there and watched her, his expression quite blank, then he'd taken Claudia's hand and the grip had been firm.

Harbouring the King's widowed daughter-in-law would

certainly account for the frisson that rippled between Mazares and Salome the night they bumped into each other. But there was something else. Something deeper. Darker. Of words unspoken, of secrets not told . . .

Back on the terrace, Claudia stared out at the glittering Adriatic.

Take one clear, calm sea bordered by golden beaches and rocky coves. Add an island of white stone standing sentry over an evergreen archipelago. Mix in one or two blue lagoons, a smattering of coral, a handful of dolphins, and bake under a cloudless sky. Finally, top with two handsome people, who are both charismatic and kind, and you have the recipe for perfection.

Set on the west coast of the Histrian peninsula, by rights this ought to be the Garden of the Hesperides, peopled by gentle, hard-working folk and protected by the invisible walls of imperial rule. Yet Claudia had never felt so alone and so vulnerable.

Or felt the breath of danger so close on her neck.

Orbilio stared at the parchments laid out before him on the inlaid writing desk, each scroll anchored top and bottom with a weighted wooden rod. To the left of the reports was heaped a pile of statistics compiled assiduously by His Imperial Majesty's bean counters and scribes, and, on the right, a stack of wax tablets containing Orbilio's own calculations, which, for once, didn't differ greatly from official figures.

Damn.

His stylus beat a lethargic tattoo on the desk as he stretched his long legs out beneath the table and leaned back in his chair. He had volunteered for this assignment. He had convinced his superiors that to act on evidence that consisted of little more than tittle-tattle, innuendo, jealousy and spite might well lay the Security Police open to charges of incompetence (or worse) if the charges eventually proved false.

His boss, oily little bastard that he was, saw credit either way in taking his advice and holding back, and Orbilio glanced at the report lying uppermost on the pile, a copy of the original sent to none other than the Emperor himself. Whether Augustus had time to read it, given the amount of guff that came his way, was moot, but the point is, the charge had been raised in sufficiently high places that, if proven, it would shower laurels upon the Head of the Security Police and if not, would still be interpreted as another fine example of his conscientiousness. Naturally, it went without saying that Orbilio's name wasn't mentioned: there's no room for two in the stratosphere of glory. Straightening out the parchment, he read the report through again, his eyes automatically picking out the parts that mattered.

> Allegations have come to my attention concerning a serious and concerted attempt to destabilize the Empire . . . fraud on a totally unacceptable scale . . . undermines the fundamental principles of . . . which, if true, will overturn every value dear to . . . ultimately challenging the whole economy . . .

Unfortunately, his boss was not exaggerating. The numbers didn't lie, and if this case did come to court, it would attract the highest profile of any seen before in Rome. Such would be the passions raised that civil unrest would be unleashed, sweeping through the city, the suburbs, the whole bloody Empire, with unimaginable – and unpredictable – consequences.

It was absolutely right that the matter be drawn to the Emperor's personal attention, just as it was necessary to be absolutely certain before charging in head first, and he was right to volunteer for the job of gathering the evidence. Even his boss agreed, albeit reluctantly, that his patrician blood made him the best man to do it.

But Orbilio had a bad feeling about this case.

A very, very bad feeling about this case.

*   *   *

The body of the royal physician had been carried back to Gora with as much pomp and ceremony as was possible with a corpse that was missing seven fingers, one left foot and half its thigh bone. Despite the ravages of foxes, lynx and crows, identification was made possible by the distinctive gold amulet still wrapped around his arm, and also by the scattering of medical instruments and personal possessions recovered later from the ravine by the army, the operation overseen by a tribune from Rome in his first year of overseas service.

The tribune might have been young, but he was conscientious. He made a thorough inspection of the valley, of the slope, of the slippery scree at the top of the hill, examined the breaks and fractures of the dead man's bones and then made his report.

It was obvious, he concluded, that, while on his way to Rovin, the royal physician had lost his footing, either in the dark or in the rain, and had tumbled down the forested hillside, sustaining injuries that, if they didn't kill him outright, would have rendered it impossible for him to crawl back up for help. Without access to his own medications and without appropriate clothing (the tribune made a special note of the drop in temperature at night in the interior this time of year), the royal physician's death was ruled a tragic accident.

The tribune also took the opportunity to emphasize in a postscript the dangers of people travelling alone.

And that would have been that, had it not been for an equally young, equally conscientious member of the royal physician's team. He, too, concluded that the bone breaks were consistent with a fall down a hillside, and that such injuries could cause coma and death, assuming exposure hadn't claimed the victim first. But the young doctor had a keen eye. He noticed that the distinctive little bone in the throat called the hyoid was broken. There was no reason to suggest this hadn't happened during the physician's tumble. A root or branch slamming into his adam's apple. Equally, though, this injury was consistent with strangulation, and a far more likely scenario, in the young doctor's opinion.

The question is, who could he tell?

Nosferatu couldn't give a stuff.

Seventeen

'**A**re you sure about wearing a simple tunic, my dear?'
Claudia dismissed Salome's concern with a wave of her hand. 'This is fine, really it is.' More accurately, it was perfect!

'Maybe your own robe will be dry in time for the feast?' Though the clouds of concern in her green eyes and the flatness of her tone suggested otherwise.

'Don't worry, Salome.' Claudia gave her arm a reassuring squeeze. 'It was my own fault, falling in the pigsty like that, and you said yourself, these tunics are awfully comfy.'

Question: Where's the best place to hide a pebble?

Answer: On the beach.

Therefore, in order to become one more anonymous Amazon, Claudia needed to ditch her expensive robe for rough work clothes without arousing suspicion, and there was a comforting irony in using her jailer to open the doors of her prison. Unfortunately, Mazares would never know he was the instrument of his own downfall; that it was his pig, his payment for the baskets of flowers, that allowed Claudia to weave her plan. But it had to be the pigsty she 'fell' in, because, yes, a rinsed robe might dry in time for the feast, draped over the circular drying frame. But those stains, bless their hearts, would never come out. My, my, she couldn't sit down to dinner like *that*.

As a tiny freckle-faced creature scrubbed the mucky marks with sage leaves, the sun slowly dipped below the far horizon and the Nymphs of the West trekked home from the fields, their skirts kilted up to their knees, their rakes and bill hooks over their shoulders. Back in Rome, the advent of May was celebrated with gladiatorial games, the bouts interspersed with salacious stripteases performed by state prostitutes in affirmation of the old life-and-death cliché, with the whole event culminating in a torch-lit procession. From the totem dances of the northern tribes, in which they bound winter to a tree with ribbons as they danced to the festival of Zeltane, in which Summer triumphed over Winter, day over night, life over death, such rites were universal. In Amazonia, the only thing that marked the passing of one season to another was that the feast was held at night, rather than during the daytime.

The lovely Salome could protest all she liked, but these were not normal customs. This was not a normal farm.

'You haven't met Mo, have you?'

The soldier's widow wriggled up to allow the little freckle-faced laundress to join the group.

'Her name is Modestina,' she added. 'Mo for short.'

'It is very sorry,' the newcomer told Claudia earnestly, 'but without bleachy it is no rubbing of those stains out.'

She smiled. The last thing she needed was someone to keep plugging away at the stains. Dammit, the whole idea was to persuade some gullible young Amazon to parade round in her Roman robe when it was dry, so that by the time her armed escort realized that it *wasn't* the Lady Claudia they were keeping their eye on, she'd have gone to ground. But no one, not even a girl who'd never felt cotton next to her skin, much less a lavish gown, would want to try on a soggy cold frock!

'Never mind the bleachy,' she told Mo. 'I'll have the robe unpicked and made into a nightshift.'

Mo's freckles warmed to this suggestion, since her laundry expertise lay in eliminating stains from fabrics such as woollens, felt and coarse linens. She haves no experience with them liddle pleaty things, Claudia added to herself, frills and flounces patently a black art to her, and the thought of tangling with the ironing-out of embroidery ruckled by soapy water too dire to even contemplate.

'Yes, yes, is wondergood idea,' Mo said. 'My bleachy only make green dye to run and lovely dress end up even biggy mess.'

'You mean *piggy* mess,' Silas chortled.

Equality had broken down all barriers between gender, age and class, with the result that everyone sat where and with whom they liked, though most of the Amazons spoke little or poor Latin and tended, therefore, to cluster in knots of their own native language speakers. The group seated round Salome's table was different. Silas, the elderly expert in fruit production, had a pronounced Athenian twang. Mo's accent placed her from somewhere in southern Gaul. Scowling Tobias had a rolling Macedonian brogue, Naim she put north of Galatia and Lora's soft Illyrian burr was unmistakable. And now there was another one joining the league of nations round the Syrian's table!

'Sorry I'm late, everyone.'

This Amazon's hair was so fair that it was almost white, her skin as pale and translucent as alabaster. Which probably explained why the black stains on her fingers stood out so clearly.

'Only, that last one was a bugger. I thought I'd *never* get the handwriting—'

'My dear, this is Barribonea,' Salome said, cutting the girl short. 'Except we call her Bonni, and with very good reason, don't you think, Claudia?'

It was the same when she introduced her to Lora. A message, a warning – this time with the stressing of Claudia's name.

'What I wouldn't give to have a waist like yours as slender as the neck of an amphora,' Claudia replied, noting that Bonni's hands, interestingly enough, had already disappeared under the table.

'I know what I wanted to ask you,' Salome said. Attagirl, change the subject. 'How's the restoration of the Marcian aqueduct coming along?'

Claudia brought her up to date, as dishes of mullet in mustard sauce appeared on the table alongside shrimps swimming in garlic, asparagus spears, lobster rissoles with chives and a selection of spicy, smoked sausages.

'I often wonder if that old Nubian sword swallower's still fooling the crowd outside the basilica.' Silas's gnarled but nimble fingers prised a mussel out of its shell. 'By Gannymede, that old fraud must have made a fortune.'

'Tell you who else made a mint, me lovely,' Naim said, and if Silas minded her large breasts pressing against him, he manfully refrained from pointing it out. 'That line walker on the Field of Mars.'

When she pushed her corkscrew curls out of her face, two feathers fluttered gently to the floor.

'Every morning he'd *dance*, I tell you, across a tightrope stretched between two trees, and he'd be there all day, from when the sun rose until it set. Is he still there, me darling?' she asked Claudia.

'Oh yes,' she lied, and she'd been in Rome for eight years and had never seen such a performer. 'Sometimes he dances with a small dog in his arms, as well.'

What colours were in fashion, Bonni wondered, her wide blue eyes drinking in with disbelief their guest's serviceable plain tunic. What hairstyles were in vogue, what style of gowns? Even Tobias stopped glowering long enough to ask whether the old fortune-teller on the corners of Fig and Pepper Street was still going strong, lord alive, she must be eighty-five if she's a day.

So many questions about Rome! Why the sudden interest, she wondered, because most of their queries were distorted by memory or else several years out of date, though the questions suggested they knew the city well. Could it really be that simple? That Rome was the common denominator on this farm? As she brought the group up to date on the latest exotic animals to find their way to the navel of the Empire, creatures like black and white striped horses and fuzzy beasts with two humps on their back and the obnoxious tendency to spit, Claudia was not getting the impression that these were simply reunited friends sitting round a table.

'D'you intend to marry the King, then?' Silas didn't even look up from the chunk of herb bread he was pulling apart.

The sudden switch in conversation caught her completely off her guard, and she wiped an invisible dribble of sauce from her mouth to buy time.

'Much depends on what happens when I meet him, I suppose.'

'Really?' The old man glanced at Salome and frowned. 'I thought it was all cut and dried—'

'More wine, Silas?' Salome asked, silencing him with a smile.

Claudia pretended not to notice. Instead, she rested her elbows on the table and leaned forward.

'What do you make of the King, Silas?'

'Don't have an opinion either way, love.' But the old man refused to meet her gaze. 'I'm too old to concern myself with politics. My job's pruning apple trees and fanning out the peaches, making sure the apricots don't catch the blight.'

'Now, I find that surprising,' she said, spearing a prawn floating in rich garlic sauce. 'Because if the King gets his way and does stamp out Salome's reforms, your job, as indeed everyone else's on this farm, will go. Doesn't that bother you, Silas?' She beamed a sunny smile round the entire group. 'Doesn't it bother any of you?'

'It bothers *me*.'

'Lora, please don't start on that again,' Salome said firmly. 'How many times do I have to tell you, your father-in-law has no jurisdiction over me or my land. My husband was given this farm by the Emperor. I'm a Roman citizen, I inherited it legally, I retain legal title, I pay my taxes, I worship Roman gods, and, dear me, it's no one else's business what I get up to on my own property. Am I correct, Claudia?'

'And you have a bust of the Emperor on display,' she said sweetly.

Salome must be slipping: she'd missed Augustus off the list – or rather, script. Well prepared and well rehearsed, the widow's mistake was to quote it verbatim, which draws more attention, not less. However, the most interesting point was that, last time, she used the same script about Rome!

What I do with my land and who I employ is my business, not some busybody's in a city, who has never set foot on this peninsula.

Now she'd turned it on its head to use it against the Histrian King, and suddenly Claudia realized there was another death to add to her list. Stephanus, Salome's soldier husband, who would have been – what? – just forty-four when he died.

'Excuse me.'

She'd just noticed a creature little more than a child fingering the edge of one of her richly embroidered flounces. The overlap for the girdle would look ridiculous when worn in high society, the girl being at least a handspan shorter than Claudia, but her hair was thick, dark and wavy, and once tied up Roman-style with a few silver brooches to reflect the torchlight, who among the escorts, eating and drinking away happily at the gate, would notice the difference? The girl proved not only a willing accomplice, she was the envy of her young Spanish peers and, seated at the margin of the May Feast, no one at Salome's table had the least interest in what happened to a bit of washing draped over a drying frame, not even freckle-faced Mo. Thus, invisible in her working tunic, Claudia worked her way back to the table.

'Don't you think you're imagining this, me darling?' Naim was saying.

'No, I bloody don't,' she heard Tobias growl. 'That bitch is a spy.'

Spy? Claudia stepped two paces back into the shadows. *Bitch . . . ?*

'Surely she's far too high-status to be a spy?' Bonni countered.

'And that's the beauty of it,' Tobias snapped. 'They think we couldn't possibly suspect the King's would-be bride.'

'Like the Divine Julius's wife, she'd be above reproach, you mean?'

'Exactly, Bonni.'

138

'Sounds a bit far-fetched, lad.' Silas added his voice of reason to the argument. 'If they wanted to send a spy, they'd have put a girl in undercover.'

'They've already tried that once, me lovely.' Naim rested a plump hand on the old man's arm and patted gently. 'Remember that little Cretan girl, the one with the squint?'

Silas buried his head in his hands and groaned. 'We shouldn't have let our guard down there,' he said. 'We should have sent her back.'

The hairs on Claudia's neck started to prickle. There was a cold chill down her spine.

'Well, we didn't and that's one spy they won't be seeing again,' Tobias said with disturbing finality.

'What is you suggesting for Claudia, Tobi?' The little laundress was close to tears.

'What do you bloody think?' Lora snapped back. 'We keep on being nice to her, show her anything and everything the nosy bitch wants to see, and let the blushing bride think we're stupid. And then . . .'

When she snapped her fingers, Claudia's knees turned to aspic. If only she'd had a phial of the sedative she'd slipped the little woodpecker the other night, she'd use it now to drug the guards and make good her escape. Her head began to pound. Croesus, why hadn't she done that in the first place? Why complicate the issue by playing bluff and double-bluff? But this was no time for recriminations. Right now she needed to—

'My dear, I haven't thanked you for the good work you've done helping Broda to recover from the trauma of seeing Nosferatu.'

How long had Salome been standing there, she wondered. And why hadn't she realized before that the Syrian girl was missing from the group around the table?

'It's only jacks and hopscotch,' she said, delighted there was not a hint of quiver in her reply.

'Yes, I know, but her mother tells me that Broda's so exhausted these days, she falls asleep almost at once.' Salome's smile was as ingenuous as they come. 'I can see I'll have to give up dispensing medicines and open a gymnasium instead.'

'You'd still need your remedies,' Claudia retorted. 'Probably more so, after all those wrenched joints and torn muscles.'

'Then we'll have to go into business together. You mix 'em, I'll fix 'em – great Marduk, what's that?'

Her smile had frozen into a death rictus. Claudia followed her horrified gaze, just as screams filled the courtyard.

'It's burning,' someone cried.

'The whole farm's on fire!'

'The bastards!' Salome hissed. 'The absolute bastards. This time they're out to destroy me!'

But even as she spoke, she was racing off to organize chains of leather buckets to douse the flames, issuing orders for the release of the livestock from pens, telling her Amazons to forget the crops in the fields, look to drenching the hives, to protecting the grain store, to making sure they covered their hands to avoid burns, to putting damp cloths over their noses and mouths.

Now was the time. While the Histrian chauvinists told Salome what they thought of her practices once and for all by destroying everything on the farm in one sweep, this was the time to sneak out.

Claudia had already established her hideaway.

The earliest inhabitants of the Histrian peninsula were hunter-gatherers, who'd braved the preponderance of bears, lynx and wolves to make their homes in the hundreds of caverns that pitted the richly forested limestone hills. These caves afforded more than adequate protection from predators and the elements, penetrating the rock by anything from a hundred feet to as much as a mile, where dripping stalactites made strange shapes and the cavernous halls still echoed with the moans of their ghosts.

But as the hunter-gatherers became farmers, so the caves were abandoned as dwellings and used as animal pens or for storage. Over time, the magnificent paintings on the walls faded, pelts over the entrances shredded and fell, bones crumbled to dust, to be blown away on the wind.

But the farmers did not entirely forsake the past. The new homes they built for themselves in the valleys retained many of the hallmarks of their previous existence. They still used stone to protect themselves from the weather and carnivorous marauders. Great flat slabs of stone, laid in small, defensive circles which gradually narrowed as the walls grew until they ended up with a sturdy grey cone with a hole in the roof to let the light in and to let out the smoke from their hearth.

It was in one of these ancient, long-abandoned beehives that Claudia had desposited a basket of food, a couple of thick blankets and one very grumpy cat in a cage. This had necessitated a series of furtive manoeuvres because she'd needed to completely hoodwink her escort, but praise be to Juno, the fires wouldn't touch Drusilla out there.

Amazonia was in chaos. The whole farm had turned into a choking mass of swirling smoke, the flames leaping and dancing in joyful abandon as they crackled and spat and hitch-hiked on the breeze, spreading new fires to new fields, new incendiaries to new buildings. Screams rang into the night, but worse still were the laughter and taunts in the Histrian tongue. Dark figures flitted about with torches, setting fire to whatever they could – goose grass, fodder stores, farm implements. Everything burned.

Amazonia has stirred up a lot of trouble round here, Mazares had said, the night he bumped into Salome. *If she doesn't change her ways soon, something terrible is going to happen. I know it.*

Claudia remembered the anguish behind his velvety eyes, and knew that the anguish was genuine. Bile rose in her throat. Suspicious of Salome and her farm, someone (the King? Pavan?) had sent a young slave girl undercover to learn what went on here. That girl had never returned. The anguish in Mazares's eyes had been genuine, sure – but only for his fellow conspirators. Claudia felt nothing but contempt for them all. Long may Amazonia burn.

She was halfway across the meadow when she noticed the pigsty. No longer fat, calm and contentedly pregnant, the spotted sow was squealing in terror as the thatch on her roof crackled and spat. The pig was new. The Amazons had dealt with situations like this before, although never on such a vicious and co-ordinated scale, and they were attacking the blazes the best that they could. But the pig was a recent arrival. No one, goddammit, had given a thought to the new sty . . .

'Shit!'

Changing tack, Claudia raced across to the smouldering building, the screams of the trapped sow tearing talons into her heart. She could hear her crashing into the walls to escape flames that licked higher and higher, and knew that each collision meant a dead piglet. Terrified of not reaching her in time, Claudia's skin fused with the searing hot metal bolt that fastened the gate. She recoiled in pain and anger, and the pig charged past, shrieking in panic, her snout bloody and raw.

'*Ey!*'

From nowhere, a hand clamped round Claudia's waist. It smelled of cheap wine and stale sweat, tinged with arousal and smoke.

'*Ja bim mir un Amazoni!*'

'Get off me, you fat bastard!'

Too late she remembered Mazares's other complaint. That they were sick of burning rapists round here . . .

'Let go of me, you oaf!'

She thought she could shake him off. She honestly thought that, between her slum heritage and her dancer's training, she could shake her attacker off. Maybe she could. But he was calling out in his thick, guttural tongue words that she remembered from the crew on the galley. Some were what one might call basic. Another was the crew's term for Drusilla. *Vildkatz*. Wildcat. A second figure emerged from the swirling smoke. His laughter was deep as his arms lashed around her, forcing her to her knees.

'*Da! Dom het un vildkatz heer, alfid!*'

His erection pressed into her spine when the first monster

ripped her tunic away with both hands. Squirming, kicking, writhing, twisting, the more Claudia struggled, the more the bulge on her spine jolted in arousal, but she was not giving up. They were not going to take her like this. Never!

'Ayiee!'

A head butt in the first monster's groin sent him retching on his knees into the ditch, but her spunk only fired the second man's hunger.

'*Dom vetta spiel, vildkatzi?*'

You want to play, little wildcat?

Gripping her neck in his elbow, he squeezed.

'*Hetta spiel!*'

Then let's play.

He knew exactly how hard to press. Not hard enough that his victim passed out, there was no pleasure in that. He pressed on her windpipe with exactly the right amount of pressure, while he roared with laughter at her helpless flailing. Around her, screams and shouts filled the bitter night air, and the roof of the pigsty collapsed with a crash. With tears of frustration spurting down her cheeks, she felt him unbuckling his pantaloons. Gagged as his naked erection pressed against her. Smelled the stench of his sweat.

'You'll pay for this, you bastard,' she gurgled.

His reply was to hitch up her skirt.

'I'll find you. I'll hunt you down if it's the last thing I do, and you'll die screaming for mercy.'

'*Da! Spiel, spiel, mir pritti vildkatz!*'

Mighty Mars, Sacker of Cities, hear me! Make him writhe in the Pit of Eternal Fire for this. Make sure he never sails to the Lands of the Blessed to walk with his ancestors in the Elysian Fields. Let the Waters of Forgetfulness never be his to drink.

'*Merr, merr, mir pritti vildkatz!*'

His breath was hot in her ear as his hand yanked at her loin-cloth. Then . . .

'*Dom vetta spiel, huh?*'

Deep and low, the question came through a mouth full of

gravel, and suddenly sweat was overwhelmed by a strong smell of leather.

'*Dom vetta spiel, du bastardo?*'

With a crunch, the grip round her neck loosened as her assailant let out an unearthly yell. As he stumbled past her, she saw his arm hanging at an unnatural angle, with what looked like bone sticking out of his shirt.

'*Dom steel vetta spiel?*'

A punch thudded into his open jaw, spinning him sideways on to the ground, where he landed with a thud on his broken arm. A boot connected to his screaming ribs. The boot was the size of a tree trunk. An oak tree, to be precise.

'I think we'd best get ye home, eh?' Pavan growled, throwing his shirt round Claudia's shoulders.

The war knot had gone, the ponytail was back, and his grey eyes were unreadable as a huge thumb wiped the hair out of her eyes. But there was nothing he could do to stem the sudden flood of tears as he hefted her into his arms.

'Wait,' she blubbed. 'Wait, we need to go into the hills first. I can't leave Drusilla up there alone.'

'Hmm.' The rumble came from deep in the general's throat. 'Ye run round in work clothes, ye risk your life for a pig, ye damn near was raped and now ye want to go looking for cats.'

He nodded thoughtfully as he tucked the shirt tight round her neck.

'I'd say the man who marries ye is gonna have his work cut out, that's for sure.'

Way down in the Ionian Sea, mighty Neptune struck his trident in the seabed and conjured up a tempest. The seas rose obediently, sending great waves to lash the cliffs of the Peloponnese and swamp the coasts as far north as the Gulf of Corinth, but Neptune's rage was short. Having rapped the knuckles of the Greeks for not making sufficient propitiation – who knows, perhaps the bull wasn't black enough? – he banished the winds back to their caves and gave orders for the heaving seas to subside.

Typical of equinox storms, it was over in a matter of hours and could have been far worse. A preposterously clear, calm dawn revealed that only two ships had been dashed against the black rocks in the night, though both had foundered with the loss of all hands on board, and by the time Apollo's golden chariot had begun its slow climb above the horizon, his anger was already being appeased with prayers and offerings in the form of sacrifice, libations and garlands. The ethos of fear and revere was strong in Neptune's book.

Such surges, though, always have repercussions. On the tiny island of Kithira, where Helen of Troy had consummated her adulterous relationship with Paris and sparked off the mother of all wars, a weak roof collapsed, killing the priest who sanctified oaths. Taken as a sign of Neptune's displeasure with a character which, although it appeared on the surface to be completely impeccable, was obviously far from the case. You can fool humanity, the islanders reasoned, but you can't fool the gods. Recent affidavits were instantly rendered null and void, and wailing women prayed for the dead man's wicked soul.

Higher up the coast, another reputation was being tarnished by the storm. A blacksmith in his thirty-seventh year had collapsed from simple heart failure as he fought to batten down the shutters on his forge, but because he was young, strong and supremely fit, none of the villagers could accept death from natural causes. It was obvious to them that he'd been punished by the Furies, those frightful dog-headed creatures with hair like snakes and bat-like wings instead of arms, who hound the consciences of the guilty with relentless passion. His widow ought to count herself lucky she'd found out in time!

The undercurrent left by Neptune's tantrum surged inexorably northwards. It travelled slowly, tempered by the various streams and currents that it met along the way, but it travelled onwards just the same. Eventually it would hit the little peninsula at the very top of the Adriatic, and only a handful of fishermen would grasp the significance of the exceptionally large catch they would be hauling in.

Finally, the swell would impact on the narrow channel separating Rovin from the mainland. Distance, time and nature would have dissipated virtually every ounce of power, but the channel would act as a funnel to the dying surge, swirling up the eddies that comprised the dark and oily realm of the fire-breathing monster, Vinja.

Vinja didn't know it yet, but when that swell hit Rovin, he would be forced to give up several of his grisly secrets, and the corpses of a boat builder and a little priest would be among them.

But, for now, the swell was still gurgling its leisurely way up the Dalmatian coast.

Nosferatu wouldn't have to re-think any plans just yet.

Eighteen

After the exuberance of Zeltane, the mood on Rovin couldn't have been starker. Children still chanted their Latin alphabet under awnings stretched between the streets and parroted their counting, like children everywhere across the Roman Empire, but children are nothing if not little sponges. Rovin children had picked up on the depression that hung over the island, and their recitation was weak. Fishwives, usually so garrulous and bawdy, now filleted the catch in silence, and the expressions of the traders in the plaza where the Zeltane Fire had burned were grim. None of the islanders had been involved in last night's fracas, but they were Histri, and the perpetrators' shame hung around their necks like grinding stones.

Caught off guard by the presence of soldiers at Salome's farm, the attackers had been quickly rounded up, a task made easier by the vigilance of a man with a swirling moustache and hair that fell to his shoulders in a manner reminiscent of Apollo, who'd noticed fires burning on the mainland and knew Salome well enough to realize that these weren't down to any May Day celebrations. It was also thanks to Mazares that much of her livestock, most of the buildings and quite a lot of the crops had been saved, while the prisoners had only their own bloodlust to blame for being caught. If they'd settled for torching the farm and then fleeing, they'd have probably got clean away. Instead, thirteen now awaited His Majesty's justice, five of whom faced execution for rape, including Claudia's attackers.

Attempted rape normally carried the lesser penalty of scorching, whereby a cart was filled with willow sticks over which the gagged prisoner was bound, then the sticks set to smoulder as the oxen plodded slowly round the perpetrator's village, the prisoner's pain and humiliation plain for all to see. But one of Salome's little Amazons had met this pair before – only the Commander of the King's Bodyguard wasn't around to prevent *her* ordeal. The cart carrying this pair of charmers would be filled with sticks that burned properly, and the Amazon had permission to light the fire herself.

'Ever since you arrived, I seem to greet you with the words "How are you feeling?"'

Mazares's expression was grave. Exactly what you'd expect after another predator had tried to muscle in on his tethered goat.

'But how *are* you feeling this morning?'

He'd run her to ground on Rovin's pine-clad tip, where she was looking out across the blue lagoons to the surrounding archipelago, while a white-tailed sea eagle skimmed the water with its talons, eventually flapping off towards an islet, a silver fish writhing in its yellow claws.

The bait shot Mazares her most radiant smile.

'Didn't they warn you that I collect bruises like some men collect art and little boys collect caterpillars?' She didn't miss a beat as she added, 'Have you reconsidered your decision concerning my armed escort?'

Last night, he'd been anxiety personified when Pavan carried her back. But it hadn't stopped him from punishing the escort for dereliction of duty.

His gaze didn't waver. 'No.'

'You don't feel that flogging's too harsh?'

'No.'

'Even though it wasn't their fault?'

She'd tried telling him that it was she who'd insisted they remain at the gate, fearing they'd cast a shadow over Salome's feast. That the men weren't to know she'd fallen into a pigsty and changed her frock. That, when the trouble started, they couldn't possibly have predicted how she'd panic and head for the hills. But Mazares had folded his arms over his broad, stubborn chest, just like he was doing now.

'Their job was to guard you, My Lady. They failed.'

'Only on my instructions.'

'They take their instructions from me.'

'I overruled them.'

'That only makes the men doubly responsible. Once for disobeying orders, and once again for failing to protect you.'

'You won't change your mind?'

'No.'

'Then you leave me no choice. I will petition the King.'

A flash at last behind those impassive catkins.

'On what grounds, exactly?'

'Surely the King's bride is allowed the *odd* indulgence, Mazares?'

The familiar lazy sparkle returned, and he bowed.

'Consider their slate clean, my lady. As of this moment, your escort is free to return to their duties.'

Gotcha, you bastard, and for a split second she considered exploiting the situation by suggesting they set off for Gora at once, but Mazares was wise to her now. He hadn't swallowed that tale about soldiers casting a spectre over the feast and he'd been particularly sceptical when it came to the idea of Claudia panicking. So she simply thanked him for his change of heart.

'My pleasure, and you must let me know if the King's bride has any other . . . odd indulgences.'

Smarmy sod.

'No, no, you've spoiled me enough. I wouldn't want to push my luck, now would I?'

'Wouldn't you?' The twinkle was dangerous now. 'Nevertheless, I think it prudent to post a bodyguard at your door.'

The noose was tightening . . .

'What? And compromise my reputation?'

'I meant outside your bedroom, My Lady, not in,' he said,

affecting a mock swoon. 'And besides. If there's any compromising to be done on that score, I feel it my duty to personally volunteer for the task.'

'I can assure you, Mazares, you would certainly have my first refusal.'

He tipped his head back and laughed, and as the puppet-master retreated through the pines, his laughter echoing above the hammering and sawing from the adjacent boatbuilding yards, she watched the aureole of glossy curls bouncing with every confident step, caught the occasional glint when the sun reflected off the gold torque round his neck, watched the spring in his taut and youthful buttocks. She'd long given up trying to decide whether his galley was crewed by policemen or by pirates, whether the King had genuinely summoned her to Histria or whether it was part of the conspiracy, or even whether Pavan and Mazares were on the same side. Worse, she no longer cared how many people had died on this paradise peninsula, be it from natural causes or otherwise, or what secrets Salome might be hiding. Frankly, who gave a damn that she gave refuge to a score of young, single women, including the King's widowed daughter-in-law, or that Lora's presence on the farm undermined tribal law?

Self-preservation was her only worry now.

She thought of Pula, just one day's sail from Rovin.

So near and yet so far . . .

Kicking off her sandals, she sought out a large, flat, white rock and dangled her feet in the turquoise water. The water was warm, shimmering softly under the Histrian sun as it lapped her ankles, gurgling as it shrank away from the rocks, slapping gently as it hit them again. Terns dived for fish like silent white stones, and the air was scented with the freshness of the oceans and the dense, tangy resins of the pines. She closed her eyes and prayed for a miracle.

'I was under the impression that brides were supposed to be blushing, not washing,' a deep baritone said from behind.

She spun round, and found herself face to face with a pair

of soft yellow Histrian boots that cast a tall, broad shadow over the shoreline. The shadow emitted a faint hint of sandal-wood unguent, which penetrated even the pitch and sawdust of the boatyards.

'And I was under the impression that the Moon God only came out at night,' she replied sweetly.

'That's the beauty of being a divinity,' he drawled, and his pants were every bit as tight as Mazares's. 'We bend the rules to suit. But then that's something you know all about, isn't it? My Lady.'

She tilted her head, half-expecting to see the silver mask. What she saw in its place was far worse.

'*Orbilio?*'

'Marcus Cornelius, international moon of mystery, at your service, ma'am,' he said, clicking his heels together.

'You bastard.'

'Didn't you level that same accusation against me at the banquet? We were both wearing pants, I seem to recall, although yours tended to contain some rather more interesting curves. Unfortunately, you spoiled the fun by concealing them under a cloak of green feathers.'

Six feet and six centuries of aristocratic breeding settled themselves on the warm rock beside her.

'Aren't you curious to know when I arrived?' he asked, pulling off his boots and easing his toes into the water. 'This is nice, although, silly me, I was expecting the temperature to be somewhat warmer.'

The cocked eyebrow suggested he wasn't referring to the heat of the ocean.

'The *when* doesn't interest me, only the why.'

No legionaries, no back-up, just a lone investigator from the Security Police. There was a strong smell of rat in the air, not least from the one sitting beside her.

'The King invited me.'

The world started spinning. 'Why?'

The Security Police grinned. It was the sort of grin leopards make when they're eyeing a kill.

'Who do you think put your name forward as a suitable bride to his old friend?'

Claudia heard a crashing sound, as all her theories fell on the floor and shattered at once.

'Friend,' she repeated flatly.

'More in the sense that he's a good friend of Rome, I suppose, but yes.' Orbilio spiked his thick, wavy hair with his fingers. 'Personal friend all the same.'

She refused to look at him. Wouldn't give him the satisfaction.

'Orbilio, if I had a knife on me, I swear I would face the lions a happy woman. What else have you told him about me?'

'On my mother's eyes, Claudia, your secrets are safe with me.'

'Your mother's dead.'

'A mere technicality.'

That was the problem. You could trust him as far as you could throw an elephant with a rhinoceros tied to its back, yet all the while he charmed you like a snake. And now it seemed the island was infested with the bloody things! Mazares the cobra had gambled, as well. He had gambled on a vivacious young woman being captivated by turquoise seas and sun-drenched sandy beaches, seduced by sheltered coves and the scent of cypress, pine and myrtle. He'd lost the bet, and the irony that the only people she could trust were the louts who'd destroyed Salome's farm wasn't lost on her.

'I suppose you know Mazares?'

'I do.'

'And you'd call him a friend?'

'I would.'

Naturally. Mazares would make damn sure of that.

'What excuse did the King give for inviting you here?' she asked. 'To give the blushing bride away?'

Around her feet, the ocean lapped the hot, bleached rocks and seabirds wheeled overhead.

'Because I have news for you, Marcus Cornelius. You know the job of the Security Police? To root out conspiracies, forgery, fraud and assassins, and all the other nasty hobgoblins that threaten to destabilize the Empire and prevent it from plunging into tyranny, or, worse, into anarchy? Well, while you've been dressing up in silly silver masks, Histria is being brought to its knees, and right beneath your long patrician nose.'

Several seconds passed.

'Honestly?' he asked. 'You thought the mask was silly?'

'Wake up, Orbilio. You've been manipulated every bit as much as I have—'

'Can you hear that?' He pretended to crane his neck. 'The sound of tables turning? Tell me, Claudia, does it hurt *very* much, being on the receiving end for once?'

'At least you accept that I've been manipulated.'

'Only by me, I'm afraid, and I'm sorry about the moon mask. It was just that I wanted to gauge how happy you were—'

'Well, now you know. I'm absolutely delirious, because in the six short days that I've been on this island I've fallen down a flight of stone steps, witnessed a murder that's been swept under the rug, almost got myself raped and now, thanks entirely to you, I'm also a prisoner on this wretched island.'

'Par for the course, then?'

But his voice was a rasp and the laughter in his eyes had been replaced by something resembling anguish.

'Claudia . . .' He cleared his throat and started again. 'Claudia, were you really just one step away from being . . . I mean, Pavan said those men last night—'

'Pavan's exaggerating,' she retorted. She swallowed the guilt of betraying Pavan and fixed her eyes on the horizon.

'He's just making himself more of a hero, by telling everyone how he stepped forward in the nick of time to save the honour of the King's bride.'

'So, those bruises on your arm appeared out of nowhere?'

'A pregnant sow whose sty is on fire can turn pretty nasty, believe me.'

'Well, that's rather the point, isn't it?' He tugged at his earlobe. 'I don't.'

No wonder this man was top of his bloody profession. He had the tenacity of a limpet in a hurricane.

Claudia smiled.

'You forget how protective Histrian men are when it comes to their womenfolk.'

Teeth, teeth, show more teeth.

'They hear a few louts crashing about, then two and two makes five.'

She didn't want him to know.

She didn't want him to know that she'd bawled like a baby for two solid hours. That she'd curled into a ball, shaking with emotions she couldn't identify. That she'd spent the night scrubbing her skin with a sponge until she'd scrubbed herself raw . . .

'You were the one who said you almost got yourself raped.'

'And *you* are the one who's not grasped what's going on here.'

She squared her shoulders and threw back her head.

'Orbilio, so many people have been taking premature ferry boats across the River Styx that Hades is nailing up "Full" signs. You don't realize it, but you've walked straight into a cold-blooded and extremely well-planned campaign to eliminate the King and, trust me, your being here is not coincidence.'

'No. My being here is not coincidence.'

'Nor is your attending the trial of the men who tried to raze Salome's farm to the ground, either. Mazares needs a witness who can confirm to the authorities that justice has been done.'

Oh, Mazares, you're even cleverer than I thought. Not only did you arrange to have Claudia Seferius out here as your

154

bait, you lured the Security Police's most ethical member, so that he could testify to Rome that whatever tragedy befell her and the King, it had truly been an accident!

'He staged that raid last night,' she said.

That's why the soldiers got out there in record time. He wasn't watching. He was waiting . . .

'Mazares planted destruction in those men's minds, stirring up their Histrian prejudices and—'

'Claudia.' The baritone brooked no argument. 'Claudia, I know Mazares. He wouldn't topple a hay cart, much less this government, and, since you ask, I have no intention of being a witness at those men's trial. This is a local issue and Rome would do best to keep its nose out.'

'Bollocks. Salome's a Roman citizen. By attacking her farm, they're effectively attacking Rome.'

'Agreed, but that was not their intent.'

She saw his argument for the dispensing of local justice, but, hell, for the Security Police not to even take notes on the sidelines . . . ? No, no. Orbilio was too shrewd to have been conned completely. There had to be more to this. Something he wasn't telling.

'What is it, piracy?'

'Sorry to disappoint you, but Mazares keeps these coasts pretty damn safe.'

'Same thing,' she sniffed. 'By policing these waters, it's just another way of following the ancestral vocation.'

'I warned you,' he said, and was that a muscle that twitched at the side of his mouth? 'I warned you the Histri were cunning and sneaky and that they were all double-dealers. They've had to be, to survive. The King walks a fine line with his people, but only because he knows them for what they are.'

'We've had this conversation before. Five generations under the eagle, butchers under the skin.'

'Let's just agree that negotiation isn't their instinctive choice.'

He leaned back on the rock, folded his hands under his head and closed his eyes. High in the pines that were shading the cove, flycatchers trilled, brown butterflies danced and squirrels scurried from branch to branch.

'Also, it's not helped by their ignorance,' he continued. 'Histria is a wealthy kingdom in comparison, but virtually all its communities are isolated either by virtue of the sea or by the mountainous terrain of the interior. The coastal communities have a better grasp of the political situation, but for those living in the landlocked villages, they have no comprehension of what the world's like beyond this peninsula.'

Claudia was beginning to understand.

'Specifically, the *size* of the Empire?'

'Exactly.' He splashed his feet languorously in the water. 'All they know is that it's bigger than, say, Illyria, but they can't accept – or perhaps won't – that it's a hundred, a thousand, times more powerful. It's completely beyond the scope of their imagination.'

Explaining why rumblings of sedition were suddenly rearing their head. Pula! While it was still a glorified trading post, nobody minded. No doubt when it was razed to the ground for backing Mark Antony, half of Histria rose up and cheered, but when the city came to be rebuilt, and on such a grand scale, the enormity of the situation sunk in.

'That's why the late King, Dol, moved the seat of justice to Gora,' she said, as much to herself as to Marcus. 'So his people could acclimatize slowly.'

'Histria has never built cities,' he added. 'But the King's seen Rome and he liked what he saw, the running water, paved streets, marble temples, the libraries, bathhouses and gymnasia. You only have to look around Rovin to see his influence, and all of it's good.'

The islanders were approving of these developments, too, but deep in the interior, where villages were merely clusters of single-roomed homesteads, the concept of thousands of people living together in one settlement was incomprehensible. Boiling it down to one basic principle: what you don't understand you either hide from – or you fight it head on.

'Now you tell me what any civilized individual has to gain by inciting his own people to rebel,' Marcus said, 'knowing it will result in Rome crushing this kingdom once and for all.'

Damn.

Claudia chewed her lip as warblers sang, and an adder slithered out from its nest amidst the thick layer of pine needles to bask in the sun. Across the lagoons, fishermen hauled in their nets, emptied their catches into their baskets and cast them again.

'So if it's not piracy or sedition, why *did* you come here?'

'Me?' He plucked a blade of grass and chewed on it. 'I'm looking for a runaway slave.'

'And I'm the Queen of Sheba.'

He closed his eyes again. 'My workload's quiet at the moment.'

'Yes, I can hear it snoring all three hundred miles from Rome.'

He honestly expected her to believe the Security Police were reduced to chasing runaways, the preserve of professional slave catchers, moreover a matter for the civil courts, not the judiciary? It was the equivalent of assigning the architect of a temple to Jupiter to tour the building site picking up litter!

'Orbilio, I don't know whether you've been smoking those hemp seeds again or it's a question of blood being thicker than water and you being thicker than both, but let me spell it out for you. There's a conspiracy here, whether you like it or not, and Mazares is at its heart.'

Ticking the deaths off on her fingers, she started at the beginning.

'Brac, the King's older brother, a young, fit, nineteen-year-old, newly married and with a full life ahead, suddenly dies of a fever.'

'Gosh, you're right. No one's ever died of a fever before.'

'Not when you're the King's son surrounded by physicians and, dare I say it, pretty red-headed herbalists. Did you hear

157

those children at Zeltane the other night? *Brac be nimble, Brac be quick, Brac jump over the candlestick. Brac jump long and Brac jump high, or Brac fall into a fever and die.*'

'Your point?'

'My point is that his death was so sudden that it was instantly absorbed into folklore. Tell me that's a common occurrence! Then we have the King's father, a man called Dol. Dol the Just.'

'Yes, I met him once, when I was small.' Orbilio reached for another blade of grass to gnaw on. 'He did a lot of good things for this country.'

'Apparently so, but he died, to quote your dear friend Mazares, suitably young.'

'Claudia, it was a lung complaint. Pleurisy, pneumonia, I don't know exactly, but hundreds of people die from lung complaints every year.'

'Not when they're a king and surrounded by physicians and, dare I say it, pretty red-headed herbalists. Is a pattern starting to emerge here?'

'You don't seriously believe Salome poisoned Brac and Dol?'

'With Mazares's help, I bloody know she did. Anyway, things settle down for a while. Delmi, Brac's widow, has been palmed off on the new heir to the throne, a situation that suited neither of them, but they put on a brave face and are now the proud parents of two healthy children, a boy and a girl.'

This was the hard part.

'The girl was twelve when *she* died.'

Claudia's knuckles turned white as she recalled the story recounted by Broda's mother.

'The girl is a sickly little thing, prone to bouts of illness that confine her to her bed, but this only binds the relationship between mother and daughter. They become closer than ever.'

She swallowed.

'One day, the family set off from Gora to propitiate the

158

spirits of the lake. I don't have all the details, but it's some-thing to do with creatures like the Sirens—'

'*Ruskali*,' Marcus said. 'Beautiful maidens who inhabit lakes and rivers, but whose loveliness disguises their real purpose, which is to lure victims into the water, where they hold them under until they drown and then feast off their flesh.'

Wherever you turn on this wretched peninsula, there are ghouls, vampires and demons.

'Well, that's what happened to Delmi's daughter,' she said. 'Her body was washed up many weeks later and, superstitious to the end, the Histri still believe the *Ros*—?'

'*Ruskali*.'

'—*Ruskali* got them. As far as Delmi was concerned, it was irrelevant, of course. Her beloved daughter was dead and by all accounts, the mother's spirit died alongside.'

A hand covered her own and squeezed gently.

'Weak lungs are inherited, Claudia.'

She snatched her hand away and wondered why the horizon had blurred.

'Anyway,' she said briskly. 'A couple of years pass and Delmi's son marries an elfin creature called Lora, a beautiful child with waves of walnut hair that cascade down to her waist, and whether Lora reminds Delmi of her dead child I have no idea, but Delmi perks up and the feeling, apparently, is mutual. Lora adores her mother-in-law in return.'

As the sun moved round, lifting the shade from the rocky cove, Claudia turned her face towards it.

'Then, surprise surprise, her only surviving child is out hunting when he's disembowelled by one of his own mastiffs and, racked with grief, Delmi takes her own life by swallowing hemlock. Or so the story goes.'

Orbilio sat up and turned her round to face him.

'Claudia, I'm well aware of all this—'

'Oh, and then the King gets bouts of sickness, as well.'

'Listen to me. Just because one family experiences one tragedy after another doesn't mean it isn't just that. Tragedy.'

He swiped his hands through his unruly mop.

'It happens. It happens all the time, and it happens more often than most people can cope with. Claudia, Delmi isn't alone in ending her own life that way. Hundreds of people beaten down by disaster do the same thing every day, because, like it or not, the gods don't dole out life fairly, and they certainly don't distribute joy and catastrophe evenly. Sometimes one just has to accept the obvious: that an accident is an accident is an accident.'

'It makes me sick to my stomach to agree with you, but for once, my dear Marcus, I do. There are times when one has to accept the inevitable . . .'

She stood up and paddled out to her knees, careless of the salt water saturating her robe.

'. . . but this is not one of those times. Orbilio, I saw a man die. I saw a funny little man who couldn't stop sneezing have a noose thrown round his neck and I watched helplessly while someone throttled the life out of him.'

Every time she closed her eyes at night, she saw his heels drumming impotently against the rocks. Every time she opened her eyes in the morning, she felt the cold thud of failure, that she had not saved his life.

'Raspor would not have been killed if those accidents were just that. He was silenced to prevent the King hearing his evidence, and even though I suspect that evidence was flimsy in the extreme, his killer wasn't prepared to take that chance.'

'Do you seriously think the King can't put two and two together by himself?'

'Maybe he's too close. Maybe it needs someone from outside, someone with objectivity, as a certain little priest lost his life to point out, to see the absurdity of what's happened. Correction, of what's *still* happening. The illness that prevented him from coming to Rome. Has anyone questioned that to his face? Or asked how well he knows Salome, and whether there's a connection between the lovely widow's visits and these inherited weak lungs?'

She waded back to the shore, anger blazing from every pore now.

'Ask yourself, Marcus, who might make that connection – and if the answer is, well, maybe a *doctor* might make that connection, you might find that your next question is, where *is* the royal physician? Followed by, do I actually believe that ridiculous story about him bunking off for a bit of rumpy pumpy with a burly boat builder? The same boat builder, incidentally, who disappeared the night a small girl called Broda was traumatized by the sight of Nosferatu strangling his victim. Oh, and don't forget while you're asking yourself all these questions, Orbilio, that Broda was woken in the first place by the sounds of whispering in her own house. And if you happen to conclude that one of those whisperers was her uncle, the very same boat builder, who lived with them, then you might also conclude that he, too, was silenced to prevent him speaking out.'

'By Mazares?'

Claudia wrung the drips out of her skirt.

'It was a full moon the night Broda caught Nosferatu in action. Admittedly she only saw a play of shadows on the wall – a fluke of fate which I know damn well saved that child's life – but allowing for the distortions from the moon, there's one aspect that Broda's adamant about. The head. Nosferatu's oversized, lolling head.'

In other words, an aureole of thick and glossy curls that fell down to his shoulders, the kind that would mislead the eye in the dark.

'Actually,' he said, his eyes still closed and his hands making what looked like a very comfortable pillow on the rock, 'there are two things Broda was adamant about. The head was one, but the other was the hands. She insists Nosferatu's hands were giant claws, and I'm afraid you can't pass one off as fact and dismiss the other as the product of an overactive imagination.'

Maybe. Maybe not. That wasn't the point.

'You obviously know that Mazares is a widower,' she said, slipping on a pair of pale grey leather sandals. 'Now, whether you believe he's a cold-blooded murdering bastard or not, my advice is not to stand too close to him, Orbilio.'

She marched off up the springy path towards the town.

'People around him have a habit of dying, and that's not an overactive imagination, my investigative friend. That is fact.'

Nineteen

The folk on the mainland had no truck with building houses out of stone. What was the point, with so much timber at their fingertips and the climate so benign? Instead, they built cosy homesteads out of wood, weaving sacred hazel between the structural supports and thatching their roofs with rain-repellent straw. In true Histrian tradition, pine was used for the flooring, from which one trunk was carved into a bear's head, though sometimes a boar or a wolf, from which rose the pedestal for the family table, usually protected by a shaggy, woollen cloth.

Bowl-shaped ovens covered by a terracotta lid sat on grids over the charcoals. Inside, rich stews of hare, boar or pheasant simmered away in metal pots, or maybe a lamb roasted, with little flour cakes baking alongside. Invariably, part of the family pig would end up hanging over the hearth as a smoked ham, rubbing shoulders with lovely, round, village-churned cheeses. Not much taken with fripperies, Histrian homes would still boast a variety of terracotta plaques nailed to their timbers, sometimes painted, sometimes embossed, sometimes both, and rows of fine red beakers, reflective of the Histrian soil, dangled from hooks on the walls.

It was one such longhouse, belonging to the senior village elder, as it happened, that had been converted into a court-house for the day. Seated in one of the wicker chairs arranged around the yard, Nosferatu followed the proceedings with indifference.

In the olden days, soothsayers dispensed justice with bundles

163

of willow rods, interpreting the fall of their willows to determine a man's innocence or guilt. Nowadays, the three soothsayers had been replaced by three elders, who would each form an independent opinion then lay their bundles north to south (guilty) or east to west (not) on the ground. It worked on a majority verdict and, for extreme offences, either the King or his representative would preside. Although serious, these crimes were not considered extreme – the way treason, for example, would be, or indeed any other crimes that impacted upon the kingdom as a whole, such as smuggling, tax evasion and fraud – although the elders felt they'd got the best of both worlds today in inviting officialdom to observe proceedings from the sidelines. Especially since the crime had been perpetrated on Roman soil!

On the other hand, they were enormously relieved that the investigator attached to the Security Police had declined to attend. They'd fully expected this member of their distant, absent and arrogant ruling class to come poking his nose where it didn't belong, and the fact that he hadn't was, the elders felt, entirely of the King's making. Who else could have persuaded Rome to let them get on with it?

'Long live the King!' the senior elder shouted. Quickly remembering to add, 'And long live the Emperor Augustus!' as his gaze alighted on Salome's red locks.

Through the open door of the longhouse, Nosferatu could see beds covered with bright woollen blankets woven by the womenfolk during the long, dark days of winter, and a variety of baskets plaited with multi-coloured withies swung from the ceiling beams. One type was for collecting fruit and berries. Another for winnowing the grain. Yet another for transporting faggots on their backs.

The wicker chair creaked as Nosferatu fought cramp, but people were too engrossed in the trial to notice.

Caught red-handed, the prisoners could only hang their heads in shame as bundle after bundle went down north to south. Their opinions on Amazonia cut no ice with the spectators or the judges. For a farming community, the destruction of another man's harvests and the killing of his livestock was an abomination where neither youth nor drunkenness was accepted as a legitimate excuse, and as their mothers sobbed and their fathers stood white-lipped in silence, sentence was passed upon the arsonists.

'It grieves me to pronounce this particular punishment,' the senior elder said solemnly. 'But the men who stand before us today have been castigated before by this court. They were fined and they were shamed, but clearly they did not learn their lesson, and therefore we, the judges, have no option.'

Silence descended on the yard.

'It is our conclusion that you, sir' – he pointed to the only prisoner who had sneered consistently at the proceedings – 'you are the ringleader in this latest outrage. Your bigoted views have inflamed those with weak characters, influenced their judgement and incited them to commit acts they would previously have held back from. For this, and to set an example that we will not tolerate anarchy, we have no choice but to sentence you to beheading. The execution will take place at midnight. May you make your peace with Perun while you prepare.'

He turned his hard gaze on the others.

'This village does not condone corruption nor will it tolerate the corruptible. I sentence each of you to four years of shunning . . .'

Shunned? A collective gasp rang through the crowd. Thrown out of the village, their names never spoken, for four years it would be as though they'd ceased to exist!

'Four years of shunning,' the senior elder repeated, 'in the hope that you use this time wisely to reflect and repent.'

And how. With no recourse to justice if things went wrong, and banned from sacrifices that would purify their wretched souls, the perpetrators would also be forced to live with the knowledge that anyone caught speaking to them during this time would be cripplingly fined. That meant their wives, their children, their mothers, their brothers, and, with the loss of their breadwinner, at least two families faced penury, resulting

165

in the women being forced to divorce in favour of a husband who could provide and their children being passed to him for adoption.

Nosferatu blotted out the sobbing. Bastards should have bloody well considered the consequences before they started torching everything in sight, not snivelling afterwards, throwing themselves on the court's mercy and begging forgiveness like a bunch of craven cowards. Weren't giving a lot of thought to the word mercy last night, were they? Personally, Nosferatu would have upped the sentence to six years, not four, and beheaded a couple more prisoners, (a) to set an example and (b) to weed out spineless bullies from Histrian society.

When the time for the New Order came – and it was not that far away – there would be none of this are-we-Histri-are-we-Roman bollocks. The New Order would have a strictly no-vacillating policy, and yes, of course it was regrettable that innocent people died in the struggle, but they were sacrificed out of purpose, not mindless, wanton destruction, and let's face it, for most of the victims, the first they knew of what had happened was when they found themselves knocking on the Gates of the Blessed.

Raspor? Well, there was always an exception to every rule, but Raspor brought that on himself, the little blabbermouth, so in that respect his death was not quite so regrettable – and as for that pansy boat builder! All one can say on that subject is that blackmailers get what they deserve. The Nosferatu of legend might kill for pleasure, but not the person whose shadow little Broda had seen. Which was not to say there wasn't a sense of satisfaction in a job well done!

The judges had moved on to trying the rapists, but since four strapping representatives of the King's Bodyguard had taken a great deal of satisfaction in beating a confession out of them earlier, the trial was little more than a formality. Nosferatu tried to look interested as the rhetoric droned on and on.

Murder was child's play. Anyone can kill another human being, provided they have sufficient strength and guts and motive, but it takes a clever person to get away with it and an *exceptionally* clever person to get away with several without arousing suspicion.

On face value, for instance, eliminating the royal physician appeared a simple enough task, but *you* try to make murder appear like an accident. First you have to wheedle his itinerary from some lackey in a way that he won't remember. Then you have to contrive to be in the middle of bloody nowhere without anyone noticing *this* end. And if that's not difficult enough, you have to win the victim's trust. Not the easiest of tasks, considering he already suspects an attempt to destabilize the throne!

However, with the royal physician happily strolling among his ancestors in the Lands of the Blessed, those suspicions had been eradicated and there was nothing now to stand in the way of the New Order. Histria could rise up – become a force to be reckoned with – a powerful nation – wealthy – respected – strong in its own right. *At last, this kingdom was poised to fulfil its true potential.*

Where Nosferatu succeeded was in employing a variety of homicidal techniques, then testing the plans from every angle.

One doesn't take risks when killing a king!

Poor Dol. Lovely fellow, charming, honest, fair and moral, devoted to his kingdom, dear chap, but blind to the obvious, i.e. that bridging the divide within his people only prolonged the country's uncertain future. Dol had to go. Eventually, Nosferatu found the perfect solution, and by coincidence it grew wild in the woods. The humble columbine. Remove the top parts, slip them into a tasty titbit or two and, hey presto, shortness of breath. Nothing fatal, just an uncomfortable couple of days, when the patient is encouraged to eat to keep his strength up and obviously needs his appetite tempted, although his physician is surprised at first that the King doesn't recover more quickly. But, as further bouts lay him low, the physician accepts this as a natural course of the illness, and is not surprised that each bout is worse than the previous and lasts longer, weakening the King's lungs further each time.

Nosferatu sighed. Who would suspect a flower so blue and so beautiful set in a floral display could prove so treacherous? And the columbine's beauty is that, as it dries, so it is rendered harmless.

But then for the big part – and again, the various vases of sumptuous flowers disguise their deadly intent. Lilies, larkspur, roses, foxgloves. Ah, yes, the lovely foxglove. Stately and tall, deep-pink, spotted, it is the leaf which does all the damage. Those beautiful, soft, grey downy leaves bring on nausea, breathing problems . . . and, tragically, cardiac arrest. The nation mourns, but is not surprised. Dol the Just had a weak chest.

A conclusion which was nothing short of inspirational.

Nosferatu hadn't planned it that way, but surely, by default, weakness of the lungs is hereditary? With the King newly crowned and a kingdom divided, one small child's unlucky inheritance aroused no suspicion, not even in the girl's mother. So it was more tasty titbits, more tightness of the chest, more solicitous bedside visits.

Delmi flashed before Nosferatu's memory. Silky blonde hair, wide innocent eyes, breasts as white and smooth as alabaster. Bitch. Publicly, of course, it was all sunny smiles, happy-happy, not a *word* of criticism levelled. Alone? Alone, Delmi didn't even *try* to hide her dislike, and as for holding back with her opinions . . . ! Nosferatu's fists clenched. Slut. I saw you slinking off in the night.

'Your fate is something you have brought upon yourselves,' said the senior elder, as he passed sentence on the rapists, 'for, to let violation pass unpunished is to unleash anarchy. Virginity is sacred in every society, not purely our own, and for you to force yourselves one after the other upon this wretched child . . .'

Supported by a warrior's sympathetic arm, the little Amazon sobbed uncontrollably and Nosferatu's heart went out to her. The girl hadn't been called to give evidence against her attackers, the judges wanting to save her the ordeal, since they had a confession, but she was adamant that the whole community should understand the depths these kinsmen of theirs had plumbed, and she spared the court no detail. Nosferatu resisted an overwhelming urge to reach out and comfort the child.

As the senior elder excused the little Amazon and expounded on the sanctity of marriage and the damage caused by the violation of decent, respectable women, Nosferatu's thoughts were propelled back to Delmi's infidelity. Oh, but how that sunny disposition failed her, fretting over her baby girl! Time and again, Delmi was brought down as her daughter fell ill, only to have her spirits lift each time the youngster recovered. Nosferatu remembered them clearly. Mother and child, each a spitting image of the other, bowling hoops in the courtyard, spinning tops together, braiding hair, laughing and dancing, singing and skipping. Yet all the while Delmi, that most perfect of mothers, that most faultless of wives, was sneaking from bed to bed . . .

Drowning the child as she convalesced after yet another debilitating bout had been hard. Many sleepless nights had been lost contemplating the act, even more afterwards, but if the end justifies the means, what choice is there? A new order had to be created. Histria demanded nothing less. And if this meant terminating the stale bloodline and instituting fresh, then, with the girl in her grave, the New Order was brought another step closer.

No one said it was going to be easy.

The trial ground finally to a close. The prisoners were led away, the villagers dispersed and a smile played at the side of Nosferatu's mouth. Actually, there *were* times when taking life became something of a pleasure. Giving Delmi that hemlock was one.

Twenty

'Are ghosts getting prettier . . . ?'
The voice that took Claudia so completely by surprise was deep and seductively slow.

'. . . or am I the luckiest man alive to find myself suddenly alone with the beautiful Claudia?'

Same husky pitch as his brother's and with hair every bit as glossy and dark, Kažan leapt the ditch that encircled the graveyard with muscular ease. Personally, Claudia found it simpler to cross by the bridge. Dawn was breaking, rosy and warm, and the air was filled with the sound of birdsong and the scent of a million wild herbs. Chamomile, thyme, lemon balm. Today was the Festival of Kikimora and, to honour the Cat Goddess, Histrians everywhere would dress in white and pour libations of milk instead of wine. Later, after a procession, hymns and sacrifice, the races and games would begin, and already stewards were hard at work checking the stadium across the way, straightening wobbly markers and hammering in flags. But Claudia hadn't expected company in the graveyard at such an early hour.

'Are you sure we're alone?' she rejoined. 'You Histri go to a lot of trouble constructing your cemeteries, and it makes me wonder why you're so desperate to keep your dead in.'

Kažan let out a throaty chuckle.

'These moats and banks are designed to keep the shroud-eaters *out*, sweet lady, not fence the tenants *in*, and see those? They're *bajuks*.'

He pointed out four hideous clay masks nailed to the oak

170

trees that surrounded the cemetery, whose faces were painted black, and contorted his features into a comical matching grimace.

'The ferocious guardians of our ancestors,' he said, 'who face north, south, east and west to protect our loved ones spring, summer, autumn and winter through earth, wind, fire and water. In fact, everything inside this graveyard comes in fours. Four is the number of the dead.'

Below the masks, black empty robes flapped menacingly in the breeze.

'I trust you don't bury your people in fours.'

'Only because we have trouble finding three volunteers to go in there with them,' he laughed, falling into step as she strolled round the cemetery.

How different from Rome! In Rome, you died, you were cremated and, according to what you could afford, your ashes were either interred in a marble tomb along one of the approach roads, like Claudia's husband (and dammit, she really must find out which road) or they were laid to rest in little pigeon-hole arrangements, although the really poor had to settle for having their ashes scattered. In the Histri's eyes, burning was the worst punishment that could be inflicted upon the soul – hence the fate of rapists and murderers. So, for their dead, Kažan explained, four-sided pits were dug in the ground and lined with oak planks, in which the deceased was laid to rest on their own bed, dressed in their best clothes along with their worldly possessions, then the grave covered with an unmarked flat rock. The only difference between rich and poor here was the size of the pit that contained their belongings.

'At the risk of sounding stupid,' she said, 'why are you carrying a bird cage?'

It wasn't that the birds weren't pretty. And she was sure they sang like choirs of angels. But Kažan hadn't struck her as the type of chap who made a habit of lugging caged birds round the countryside.

'Well, there's another thing that separates our two cultures,' he said. 'Look around and, yes, you'll see an abundance of floral tributes, but to the Histri, birds represent the souls of the dead. These little creatures,' he patted the cage, 'will provide company for the souls who abide here.'

Claudia tried to imagine every soul as a melodious warbler and failed. She'd encountered far too many hawks on her travels to see them changing their feathers after death. Not to mention quite a few bustards. Kažan stopped by one of the larger top stones to unhook the lid of the cage. Instantly, the birds fluttered off into the trees, but his dark eyes remained on their flight long after they'd disappeared.

'Or, rather, one soul in particular,' he said quietly.

'Your mother?'

'Brother,' he corrected. 'Every year on the anniversary of his death, I come back and release a flock of finches.' His tormented expression was quickly replaced by the more familiar grin. 'Although I can't help wondering whether they're not the same finches I net every year. That I keep recycling the same flock, as it were.'

She tossed back a light riposte, something to do with reincarnation, she thought, but her mind wasn't on jokes. *Because if Kažan's brother was buried here, then so, by default, was Mazares's . . .*

'Since we don't believe in desecrating the top stones with engravings,' Kažan was saying, taking her arm and moving on, 'we resort to other ways to identify the departed.'

He indicated the menagerie of carved creatures that nestled close to the graves.

'The larger beasts denote clan, like those bears, lynx and stags, while the smaller mammals –' he pointed to dormice, pine martens and hedgehogs – 'are the family emblems. The birds, of course, are the true souls of the individual and these denote status within the household.'

An eagle signified patriarch, a dove was the mother, a kite for the first son, an owl for the second and so on and so on.

'The custom harks back to the days when Histria was part of the great Kingdom of Illyria,' he added. 'The days when Jason and the Argonauts sailed these seas in search of the

Golden Fleece and a storm blew Odysseus's ship on to the island of Circe the Enchantress, who promptly turned his crew into swine. See?'

He pointed to a carved boar.

'One clan even claims descent. After she turned them back into humans, of course!'

'I thought you said four was the number for the dead?' Claudia asked. Large mammal, small mammal and bird made three.

'You're not looking hard enough,' Kažan laughed, brushing his hand across the chaplets and wreaths that covered his brother's top stone.

It was only when the butterflies didn't fly off that Claudia realized it was far too early in the day for them to be feeding and that these were, in fact, painted carvings, which had been placed artfully among the blooms. Another example of Histrian sneakiness, but this time the sentiment was at least admirable. As dawn cast her pink cloak over the cemetery, she found an inexplicable lump in her throat at the tranquillity of this enclosure, at the exquisite detail to be found in the carvings and in the loving attention that had been given to the floral tributes laid on the graves. Through the oak trees, she noticed the first trickle of white-clad figures making their way to the stadium, obviously wanting to bag themselves a good seat.

'The butterflies are indicators of age,' Kažan said, clearly in no hurry to join the early birds. 'Holly blues represent one year, brimstones a decade and swallowtails count for fifty.'

Claudia decided to put to the test what seemed like a very clever system for uneducated people. She found the largest top stone in the graveyard and studied the carvings impaled on stakes alongside it. The eagle proclaimed the deceased as the head of the household, a swallowtail and two blues put him at fifty-two when he died. But, of course, she had no idea whose family carried the squirrel totem, much less whose clan belonged to the dragon. But wait. Why were there *five* groups beside this particular grave? She peered closer and saw that two of the carvings were birds. The eagle, and a woodpecker, unmistakable with its long, pecking bill. Two people in the same grave? Or . . . ?

'*Dol?*'

'Indeed,' Kažan replied, a sparkle lighting his liquid-brown eyes. 'His Royal Majesty rests here in full military armour, together with his rings, cloak pins, ceremonial torque and his amulets, plus his scissors and knives, a quiver of arrows, his finest yew bow, his shield, his axe, an assortment of gold salvers, three silver finger bowls, ten pells of parchment plus, I am reliably informed, the sword and helmet of a Dacian warrior, although officially, you understand, such an ambush never took place.'

It was when Kažan smiled like that, with the same self-deprecating grin as his brother's, that the family resemblance really struck home. Even with eyes wider apart than Mazares's and straight hair that he restrained in a soft leather headband, there was no mistaking the blood that ran through the men's veins, and although Kažan's good looks exuded boyish innocence, how much of that was actually heredity, she wondered? Her eyes rested on the gold torque round his neck, engraved with creatures she was beginning to recognize now – dragons, *bajuks* and serpent-tailed giants – and wondered how close the brothers might be in other ways, too.

Drum beats rolled in the distance, signalling the start of the procession, but through the trees, though on the opposite side of the cemetery to the stadium, she noticed Marek and Mir leading their mastiffs on leads. Unlike Kažan, they weren't dressed in festival white, but wore the short kilts of the hunter, and in their hands they carried spears.

'I'm afraid that, to my sons, local events such as these games are a waste of their time,' their father explained, perhaps in response to Claudia's raised eyebrows, perhaps justifying it to himself. 'Rosmerta goes blue in the face telling them how they ought to compete in the spirit of politics, but the very mention of that word bores the boys rigid, and no matter how much their mother bends their ears, they won't budge.'

'Have you tried fatherly persuasion?'

'Me?' An impish grin twisted his lips. 'I leave that kind of stuff to Rosmerta, she's far better at it, and anyway, after the executions yesterday, can you blame the lads for preferring the smell of a good spoor to roasted man meat?'

It wasn't often that Claudia Seferius was stuck for words, but this seemed to be one of those moments.

'Anyway,' he chortled, 'it would be a bit rich, wouldn't it? Me telling them to hang around . . .'

He pulled his white robe at one shoulder to reveal the hunting tunic beneath.

'Last year, Mazares roped me in for the boxing contest followed by three bouts of wrestling, and I swear the bruises lasted a month. This time I've made a bet with my sons that it'll be me drawing the first blood in those woods! Me that brings home the tusker! And though they usually do that – sneak off to get a start on their old man, I mean – and I'm sure that one day they'll beat me, you can take it from me –' he turned to Claudia and winked – 'that day won't be today.'

'I'm guessing politics holds the same appeal for you as for Marek and Mir?'

'Less.'

Damn.

'You see, I happen to believe that it's every man's right to be happy, and if you look at the King, see how he's sacrificed his own happiness in the name of duty, you can see why I steer clear.'

Unfortunately, he appeared completely genuine.

'You'll never find me married to any job, Claudia.'

'For a man who wasn't born to run this country, your King seems to be making a pretty good stab at it.'

'Brilliant, if the truth be told, but ask yourself, what freedom does the poor sod have? I think back to the days of our misspent youth, when we'd take off into the high alpine forests whenever we liked, or set off sailing the wide, open seas, but he can't do any of those things now, poor old bugger. Me, I reckon if a man is content within himself,' he continued, 'and I mean truly content, then that happiness radiates out and spreads to everyone it comes into contact with.'

'Would that radius include Rosmerta?'

'Impudent minx!'

Kažan tapped her lightly on the tip of her nose as he laughed.

'But yes, as it happens, it does include Rosmerta. She and I have everything we need from this marriage, and by that, frankly, I mean separate lives. It wouldn't suit me having a wife who clings like a wet loincloth, or a sickly woman I'd feel guilty about leaving when I take off on long hunting trips, and certainly not one who'd make scenes over my occasional philandering.'

'Only occasional . . . ?'

'Vani's a good girl.'

Kažan replaced one of the graveside carvings that had toppled sideways.

'And I'm very fond of her, as you know, but – well, this might sound odd – but I care for her more as a father-in-law than a lover. Can you understand that?'

Protective, even though they're having an affair? Yes, Claudia could identify with that sentiment. Might not agree with it. But she could see how someone like Kažan might think it could work.

'Besides,' he breezed, 'Vani needs kids.'

'You're all heart.'

'Well, *obviously*, I'd rather they were her husband's,' he said, with a roll of his seducer's eyes. 'But don't beat me up about this, Claudia. I'm not the one pushing for bouncing grandchildren. It's Vani who wants them and –' a look of deep affection flooded his face – 'can't you just see her, whirling them round in the air, romping and rolling over the meadows, teaching the little ankle-biters to swim?'

Selfish and shallow to his drop-dead-handsome core. Pavan was right, though. There *was* something endearing about this boy who wouldn't – perhaps couldn't – grow up, because, for all his blinkered, self-serving persona, Kažan was quite without ego. And yet . . . And yet . . .

'Is that how you felt about Broda's mother?' Claudia asked.
He stiffened. 'Come again?'

'Playing the artless ingénu doesn't suit you, Kažan.'

Raven-black hair, just like her father's, same liquid, dark
eyes. Claudia remembered the child's reaction when she'd
enquired after her father. The shutters had immediately come
down over her eight-year-old haunted eyes.

I have to go now, she'd said dully.

Claudia had talked her out of leaving by teaching the girl
hopscotch, but the message was clear. She wasn't prepared to
discuss her father, and for an eight-year-old, that meant only
one thing. She'd been forbidden to.

'All right, Broda's mine, I admit it,' Kažan said. 'But she
was an accident, if you like. Her mother and I – well, it was
just an affair, Claudia. Long, hot summer. Pretty boat builder's
sister. Both of us with time on our hands . . . come on, you
know how it is.'

Actually, no.

'I support them, of course I do, but – well, let's say I'd
appreciate you respecting the confidence.'

'If you mean you don't want Rosmerta finding out, I suspect
you're eight years too late.'

Hell, if an outsider can see the resemblance, it wouldn't
have escaped Rosmerta's sharp eye.

'So? My wife and I sleep in separate wings of the house.'
Kažan shrugged.

'I've performed my patriotic duty, Claudia, I've sired two
sons, and to be honest with you, if I never sleep next to her
ugly, snoring face again it's too soon. I have no problem finding
pleasure elsewhere.'

Claudia didn't doubt that.

'And how does Rosmerta feel, do you think?' she asked
sweetly. 'Or haven't you thought that it's just a teeny bit of
a coincidence that it was exactly eight years ago she began
piling on weight? Took to wearing the very latest in Roman
fashions?'

'That was *Pula*, for heaven's sake!'

Kažan was rattled, and about bloody time.

'Dammit, the minute that city started to boom, that woman was all over the trade boats, raking over exotic delicacies, digging out the best foreign fabrics!'

'So, either way, it's acceptable?'

'Sorry?' He frowned. 'Don't think I quite follow.'

'Then let me spell it out for you, Kažan.'

Claudia resisted the urge to slap the smugness off his handsome face.

'Whether your wife overeats out of comfort or because she's addicted to gourmet foods, that's all right, and the fact that she chooses to dress like a teenager doesn't concern you either, because if it's in a bid to make her attractive it won't work, and if it's to improve her social standing, she's on a loser there as well, because status doesn't concern you. Just hunting, fishing and, remind me again, oh yes, women.'

'Well, I wouldn't put it quite like that,' he blustered. 'I mean, you're making me out to sound a bit of a scoundrel.'

'Really? Well, maybe it's me who's out of kilter,' she snapped. 'Maybe fathering a child on another woman is the perfect way to cement a failing marriage.'

'Claudia, please.' His voice was filled with anguish. 'I'm not the bastard you make me out to be . . .'

'Probably not,' she conceded, 'but your daughter is.' And it's Broda who's caught in the middle of all this. Broda who saw Nosferatu at work. *Broda who heard people whispering her father's name, and went wandering the streets to learn more.*

To be honest, Nosferatu didn't give a toss about Broda.

Twenty-One

Marek and Mir had it all wrong, Claudia thought. They could take off into the forests any old time, chasing after their wild boar and stags. The games were only held once a year, with the winners fêted with olive crowns and ribbons and given a Victory Banquet in their honour. The very act of participation was considered a mark of distinction, and whereas Kažan had baled out from laziness and bitter experience, she suspected that his sons cocked their snooks at the games out of fear.

Fear that, when competing naked and oiled like the rest of the male athletes, their youthful paunches would not compare well.

Fear that, when pitted against men who had been training for weeks, their skills would be shown to be lacking.

Had Marek and Mir been truly unconcerned about the games, she reflected, they would not be sneaking away during the drum roll that summoned people for the start of the procession.

The stadium lay in the bowl of a ring of low hills, at the confluence of the two rivers that fed the fertile red plain that in turn swept down to the Adriatic half a mile distant. In true Histrian tradition, the joining of these waters was marked with an ancient oakwood shrine, overflowing with gifts and donations to the cat goddess, from offerings of food to ornate, painted terracotta plaques. In addition, the spirits of the rivers were appeased with chaplets of wildflowers, though those who could afford it consigned more precious objects to the rushing waters and the river beds glistened with silver and bronze.

After prayers had been sung to Kikimora, including one eardrum-piercer by a group of children whose faces had been painted to resemble cats, it was time for the competitors to take their oaths beneath the sacred oak tree, holding a flint arrowhead in each outstretched hand as they swore on Perun's thunderbolts that they'd play fair.

'Too jolly right!' Rosmerta muttered in Claudia's ear, as she shook the drips off her pudgy hands after sacrificing an amulet to the waters. 'This society can't afford to tolerate cheating, that's why the fines are so hefty, and if the rogues don't cough up, tough. The onus falls on their family.' Rosmerta grinned. 'That fear alone keeps them honest.'

Can't afford to tolerate cheating? How did that square with Kažan and Vani, then, because, overweight, overdressed and overbearing she might be, but Rosmerta was no fool.

As the athletes drew lots for their starting positions, Drilo the High Priest beckoned Claudia over.

'Place of honour, my dear,' he said, patting the seat between Mazares and himself.

It was interesting that on Mazares's left sat a certain patrician investigator. You'd think, wouldn't you, that when you're trapped on an island in the middle of nowhere, the arrival of the Security Police would have been reassuring? Instead, Orbilio didn't believe a single word of what Claudia told him, despite the evidence to back up her story – and that was Mazares for you. He'd used friendship and charm to suck Marcus Cornelius into becoming a pawn in his conspiracy, and the only thing she could hope for now was that Orbilio hadn't passed her opinions on to Mazares.

'Thank you.'

Claudia smiled deep into Drilo's penetrating blue eyes, inhaling the heady scents of incense and myrrh that emanated from his strong, bearded features. White robes didn't suit him half as much as the rich colours he usually wore, but they accentuated the gold headband round his braided, oiled curls, and the amulets of electrum that encircled each wrist. There would, she decided, be no half measures with Drilo.

The first race of the day was the women's, and Claudia wasn't the only person to be taken by surprise when several Amazons stepped up to the starting slabs and slotted their toes into the grooves.

'I don't believe it!' Mazares shook his head in despair. 'That bloody woman is going to be the death of me,' he said, fixing his astonished gaze on Salome, who was standing shoulder to shoulder with Vani on the starting line.

Her skirt had been kilted up to her thighs, her red mane was tied in a bun at the nape of her neck and, cheering her on from the sidelines were Mo, Naim, Tobias and Silas.

'One minute she tells me there's too much work to get away, now she's wasting whole days at a time on bloody foot races!'

'Thank your lucky stars Lora isn't running as well,' Pavan growled from Orbilio's other side, and Claudia's interest in track events suddenly clicked up a notch.

After the fires, Mazares had despatched men to help repair the damage, but Salome refused to allow them to set foot on her land. Why? Thieves falling out? And what exactly *had* brought Orbilio all this way from Rome . . . ? To complicate matters further, it was obvious that the Amazons were late entries to the competition, because Vani won the race by a comfortable margin. The crowd roared and stamped when she cartwheeled over to accept her crown of olive cut from Kikimora's own sacred grove. When she cartwheeled off again, the spectators nearly went wild.

'Not like Rome,' Mazares murmured, watching Salome's friends bestowing consolatory pats on her back.

'Not quite, no,' Orbilio agreed, shooting a sly smile to Claudia, who categorically refused to meet his eye.

Dammit, she'd petitioned the Senate a dozen times that women should be allowed to hold their own competitions, but the notion was jeered every time. A woman's place, the Senate insists, is to organize her household and raise her children, and Claudia wished now she'd put her own name to those damned petitions. Show them that women were perfectly capable of succeeding in whatever walk of life they damn well chose, but, of course, that would only get the authorities poking about in her affairs – and she wasn't sure that being arrested on joint charges of fraud, tax evasion and those other little misdemeanours would be beneficial to the sisterhood's cause.

After a couple of other races, it was time for a break and, as the heat of the day became trapped in the valley, people took the opportunity to shift seats in search of shade and fill jugs of refreshing water from the rivers. Claudia thought it was time she took an opportunity herself.

'Tell me about the King,' she said to Drilo, as the pentathlon began. 'Tell me everything you know about the man I'm going to marry.'

Because a theory was beginning to form.

It had started last night, when, lying in bed and unable to sleep, Claudia realized there were two separate parts to this puzzle and that she was no closer to understanding either. Until now, she'd only considered the puzzle from the conspiracy angle, simply because of its immediacy factor. As a result, she had ignored the other side. The side with the King's head on it.

All right, let's start from the beginning. The King needs an heir and the King is a friend of Orbilio's, who promptly puts her name forward as a potential candidate.

The reason for Orbilio's actions had yet to be established, but she was damn sure it was unscrupulous. Dammit, when promotion hinges on halting a one-woman crime wave, she's the very *last* person you recommend to royalty. Especially when Orbilio was aware of her slum-dwelling past, and knew her to be the very antithesis of Histrian values! Claudia's personal belief was that it was a trap. Something he and the King had cooked up between them, hoping to catch her in the act of stealing valuable artefacts from the palace or palming him off with table wine when it was billed as vintage.

In which case, everything after made sense.

But! What if the King was dead?

Suppose he'd been taken ill, like he and everyone said, too ill to travel to Rome, but suppose he then died? His only son had been disembowelled by a mastiff on a recent hunt and his daughter was also cold in her grave. That left the King with no heir. Exactly what the conspirators had contrived – except now they'd been gifted a heaven-sent opportunity. The King's letter requesting the hand of a wine merchant's widow in marriage!

With Histria prospering under its imperial patronage, why should the people question their widowed King taking a bride to unite his country with Rome? In their eyes, this would be no worse than any other inter-tribal marriage, and thus, having sold that lie publicly, all Mazares needed now was someone he could pass off to Claudia as the King. Of course, this would take some organizing, but it explained why he'd isolated her out here on Rovin, and who better to help his plan run smoothly than a free-spirited Roman girl with no ties? No family to chaperone her, no friends to counsel her, no one to whisper caution in her ear, he must have thought it was his bloody birthday.

Last night, as her thoughts drifted on the mellow night air, the notion had seemed far-fetched. But *how* implausible was it, exactly? As she'd taken that early-morning stroll round the cemetery, she was again struck by the extraordinary lengths that had been taken to eliminate the King's blood-line over the course of many years. Such coldness and deliberation had to be for a purpose other than greed or revenge. Some kind of insurrection, she suspected. The establishment of a new regime, since there were no contenders left for the old one.

Inheritance, then, by default . . .

As the pentathletes raced down the stadium, she set her mind to thinking as Mazares might think. It was all very well palming her off with an impostor, but he'd also taken great pains to invite Orbilio to Histria – and more precisely to Rovin

– therefore it was imperative to his plans that his 'good friend' continued to believe the King was alive and well. Right now, people in Rovin thought their King was in Gora and people in Gora no doubt thought he was on Rovin, but there was only so long Mazares could keep up this pretence! This suggested that he intended to separate his two Roman visitors, for how else could he hope to engineer whatever terrible accident was about to befall the 'King' and his bride and still have Rome accept it on trust?

The problem was, Claudia still had no idea of exactly who the conspirators were. Salome, certainly, but just how deeply, Claudia couldn't be sure. Was she in it for love, for money, for land or for principle? And how was Claudia supposed to weed out an impostor? Mazares would be sure to find someone who matched his physical description, so the solution lay in understanding the soul of the man. Which is why, now that the pentathletes had raced a full length of the stadium and were brushing the sand off their feet, she set out to bleed the high priest dry.

'Tell me about the King's strengths,' she urged prettily. 'His weaknesses, his aims, his ambitions.' She smiled artlessly into Drilo's blue eyes. 'Tell me about his inner demons.'

'His strengths?' The high priest stroked one of his oiled braids thoughtfully as the competitors drew lots for the long jump. 'Well, I suppose the King's greatest strength is that he trusts people, My Lady, and perversely, his greatest weakness is also that he trusts people.'

Accompanied by flute players, the athletes lined up one after the other, each holding a stone weight in his hands to add impetus to the jump.

'I see.'

At the last moment, each competitor threw back his hands for the final thrust.

'He must be a very dull stick, if those are his only virtues and faults.'

Drilo inclined his head forty degrees towards her as the athletes moved on to the discus, weighing up the heavy bronze plate, which they swung before throwing.

'My apologies if I gave the wrong impression, My Lady. I assumed you were just making small talk.'

So the high priest was not without sting! And she wondered how Raspor had coped. Did the Master's barbs pass over his little bald head? Or did Drilo not need them for those who served the thunder god? Only uppity Romans? Claudia pasted on an expression of wide-eyed earnestness, the one that had never failed in the past, and Drilo was no exception.

'His Majesty possesses many strengths,' he informed her, 'and although some might not see cunning as a virtue, trust me, it is a strength.'

They're cunning, they're sneaky and they're all double-dealers, Orbilio had said. *But, by your standards, Mistress Seferius, those are surely their plus points.* She pursed her lips as Drilo continued.

'His Royal Highness also possesses an innate sense of justice, a high level of integrity and a sense of responsibility, which, I regret, weighs heavy on him. As a result, he tends not to delegate, endeavouring to do everything himself.'

There was a flicker of emotion in his strong features, but it was quickly mastered.

'It's wearing him out,' he said sombrely. 'Slowly, his pride is killing him.'

Pride be damned, Claudia thought. Salome's the one who's doing (*has done?*) that – and on Mazares's orders!

There was no use in labouring this point to Orbilio, of course, Mazares had him eating out of his hand, but today had shown that all was not well in the Salome-Mazares camp. She had run in the women's race purely to annoy him and, clever girl that she was, her tactics had worked. Maybe he wasn't paying her enough? Or maybe she was just getting greedy? Either way, Claudia had seen a chink to exploit.

And dammit, a neatly plotted conspiracy laid flat on the table with the culprits held bang to rights, as they doubtless said all the time in the Security Police, would be an excellent trade for a pardon . . . !

'What about the King's ambitions? His hopes for the future? His fears?' she asked, as the athletes slipped the first two fingers of their right hands into the leather thong positioned halfway along the shaft of their javelins.

'His Majesty has only one aim, and that is for his people to prosper,' Drilo said crisply. 'As for fears, he has none, My Lady. None at all.'

The javelins stood the height of a man, but each competitor threw them as though they were sticks for dogs to chase after, though the slight twisting movement carried the spears far down the field.

'That could be construed as arrogance,' she said sweetly.

'I wouldn't disagree,' the priest replied dryly. 'But if it's your future husband's temperament you're enquiring about, then you probably need to know that he is slow to anger, but implacable when roused. On the other hand, he is patient, extremely patient, and one might liken this aspect of his character to the art of the hunter – stalking his quarry with persistence, and refusing to give up.'

'You obviously know my husband well,' Claudia commented, as the javelins were paced out on the field.

'Men who drink together, think together.'

Really? Somehow she couldn't picture this stuffy individual knocking back goblets of wine with the boys! But then, if the King was as Drilo had described him – and indeed as she'd gathered from others – then he was very much a man of the people, and would encourage those around him to be, as well. Drilo, she concluded as the distances were announced, was not part of the conspiracy. He had been brought here to observe and testify. A man whose word could not be besmirched.

Claudia turned to Mazares and squeezed his upper arm.

'This is such fun, isn't it?'

With irritating slowness his aureole of dark curls turned towards her, the lazy catkins dancing with amusement.

'*I* think so,' he agreed.

Out on the field, it was the final event of the pentathlon. The wrestling.

'Of course you do,' she replied. 'In fact, we both seem to enjoy games in which no holds are barred, people get hurt and accidental death is not uncommon. But you know what I like most about this particular game?'

'I'm pretty sure it isn't watching grown men knocking one another's teeth down their throat or pulling their opponent's cauliflower ears off.'

'Quite right. What I find most attractive about this partic- ular sport, Mazares, is watching the contestants trying to trip each other up. Round and round they go, see? Feinting and dodging, testing and parrying, sizing strengths and weighing movements, until one of them starts to get cocky.'

'Overreach himself, you mean? Think he's invincible?'

'Oh, yes,' she breathed, 'and that's where the real skill lies. Not in brute strength or endurance, but in guile. In getting inside the other man's head.'

His smoky eyes danced as he rubbed his goatee beard slowly in thought. 'Tripping your opponent through his own conceit, in other words?'

'We each choose our weapons, Mazares. The knack is to beat the enemy with his own.'

'In which case, My Lady –' he rose from his seat, turned and bowed deeply – 'you must excuse me while I retire to the training ground to sharpen my tongue.'

The sun was starting to sink over the Gardens of the Hesperides, turning the rolling countryside a deep heather- pink. Crickets throbbed in the lush green grass, cattle lowed from the meadows, fat brown trout nibbled at flies and, far across the valley, Marek and Mir's mastiffs howled.

The games had wound up with a comic race featuring soldiers in full armour carrying other soldiers piggyback down the running track, swapping over at the bottom and then lumbering back up. Two hundred yards is a long way at the best of times, but on a warm day and encased in metal sheeting, it was surprising just how close the contest was. But then, in Histrian society, coming second counted for nothing.

After the race, hymns had been sung to the Cat Goddess, Kikimora. More libations of milk poured in her honour. And now white-robed spectators trooped slowly home through the woods. Their mood was one of happiness and contentment, just as Kikimora intended, and tomorrow afforded them another event to look forward to, since it was the one day in the year when marriages could be announced.

Nosferatu wondered whether the Roman girl realized the significance of this. From her behaviour, it seemed she'd forgotten. Excellent. The little madam thought she was clever, and no doubt she was – only, Nosferatu was smarter!

It would not be long now before the New Order was established. Everything was going according to plan, and soon there would be no more of this ridiculous business of trying to keep both parties happy. Histria could only move forward if it jumped one way or the other, and just as there would be no vacillating in the New Order, no half-heartedness, certainly there was no room for any of the shilly-shallying that was so prevalent in the current administration.

The King is dead, long live the King!

Nosferatu practised the chant – silently, of course.

The King is dead, long live the King!

But it wouldn't be long before those cries rang out round Rovin, round Gora, round Pula.

The King is dead, long live the King!

Yes, indeed, Nosferatu had everything mapped out according to schedule, a schedule that had seen no mistakes so far and would see no mistakes in the future.

Being a perfectionist isn't easy, of course. But it does bring incredible rewards.

Back on Rovin, three things happened at once.

Firstly, a young man arrived tired and weary after a hard ride from the interior. The young man was more used to wielding scalpels and forceps than bridles and reins, and his soft hands were bleeding from where the leather had rubbed. Also, he was more used to bending over patients than intractable brutes with a mind of their own, and his thighs were chafed raw, his buttocks were bruised and he doubted his knees would ever close together again. For this reason, he decided to soak his aching bones in the bathhouse before dropping his bombshell about the royal physician.

Since there had been no one in Gora he could trust with the news, he'd decided that, really, the best person to confide in was the King. The King was honest and fair, not swayed by emotion, and the King would listen objectively to how the hyoid bone in the royal physician's throat had been broken by manual strangulation. So, the young medic had hired a horse and put himself through hell and back to ride all the way out here to Rovin for an audience with the King.

But, according to the sign posted outside, the bathhouse closed one hour after dusk, and there was only half that time left. The young medic had no intention of wasting another minute.

He kicked off his sandals and dived into the hot, scented waters.

The second thing was that the undercurrent from the storm that had wracked the Pelopponese two days before had finally made its way to Rovin. As previously mentioned, the swell was only slight, but, funnelled into the deep channel that separated island from mainland, it was sufficient to dislodge a lot of the debris that had collected in the fire-breathing monster's domain over the past year or so. Raspor's bloated corpse and that of the boat builder were just some of the gruesome objects which were about to float to the surface.

And thirdly . . .

Salome, returning from checking up on little Broda, came across the Lady Rosmerta stumbling along one of the alleys, with blood pouring from a wound on her forehead.

A tile, it appeared, had slipped from a roof and only narrowly avoided a tragedy.

Nosferatu was furious. Mistakes do not happen. Repeat, mistakes do not happen.
They just do not bloody well happen.

Twenty-Two

Night had coiled herself over the landscape, carrying pine-scented vapours into the houses and echoing the soft hoots of owls round the islands. Foxes skulked on the edge of the middens, pipistrelles squeaked on the wing and moths diced with death round the flickering flames of torches set high on the gleaming white walls. Down on the foreshore, feral cats sniffed the slumbering fishing boats as gentle waves gurgled and slurped, and in Claudia's bedroom, a familiar wedge-shaped face pressed itself against hers and began rattling.

'Frrr.'

'I know, poppet.'

She unhooked a claw that had snagged in her gown.

'First Raspor, now Rosmerta, and don't tell *me* that was an accident.'

'Prrrrr.'

A mass of warm, silky fur curled round Claudia's neck and gently butted her chin with its head.

'Exactly!'

It was here, beneath this very window, that the little priest had stood wringing his hands.

'Raspor risked everything,' she told Drusilla, 'so that someone objective would listen.'

'Hrrrow.'

'Except someone objective laughed him out of town and her disdain cost him his life.'

Beads of sweat trickled down Claudia's breastbone, soaking

the cotton of her whale-grey gown, and each droplet had the word 'guilt' written all over it.

'I failed him, Drusilla. I failed him and, thanks to me, Rosmerta was this close to becoming another of that bastard's victims.'

She screwed tight her eyes and pinched the bridge of her nose, but the dam couldn't prevent something salty and wet dribbling over her cheeks.

'Brrrp?'

Dammit, it was only because of Rosmerta's insufferable vanity that the ferryman wasn't rowing her across the River Styx at this very minute!

'Rrrow.'

'Too true, poppet.'

Claudia scrubbed the tears away with the back of her hand.

'There are some things a killer just can't legislate for.'

In this case, it was that ridiculous froth of Roman-style curls. The wig was so thick it had saved Rosmerta's life!

'But enough is enough,' she said, stroking Drusilla's ears.

Too many people had died, or else, like little Broda, had been scarred from this ruthless campaign. She was no longer prepared to wait while more innocents suffered, simply to gather evidence in exchange for a free pardon.

'It means we'll have to find other ways of getting the Security Police off our back,' she sighed, setting the cat on to a chair. 'But honestly, what choice do I have?'

The only path open to Claudia now was to voice her suspicions loudly and often – and to everyone within earshot. Then pray to every god on Olympus to protect her, because although the 'accidents' would be forced to stop, she suspected this would only be after an attempt on her own life . . .

Outraged that she had been dumped like a sack of stale parsnips, Drusilla promptly exercised her claws on the lushly embroidered upholstery, then, in one fluid movement, bounded over the windowsill. Claudia's heart stopped. The drop – twenty feet – it was far too far for a cat . . .

She ran to the window, her nails gouging the woodwork as her eyes scanned the darkness for a small, lifeless body. But Drusilla was too shrewd to have misjudged her descent. She'd used the fig that grew against the wall as a climbing frame, and her dark fur had already fused with the night. Claudia's heart thumped with relief as she sank against the frame of the window, and now she realized what had sent Drusilla diving into the void. The sound of trumpets and drums would have been picked up by feline ears a lot earlier, as the victory procession wound its way through the town. The noise had sent Drusilla to ground. As Claudia watched the approach of the torchlit snake, she heard angry voices approaching below.

'. . . you could have bloody well told me that this Marcus character was attached to the Security Police!'

'Dammit, Salome, I know what I'm—'

'No, really, Mazares. How hard would it have been, to actually *talk* to me first?'

His white shirt stood out like a beacon in the blackness as he stepped in front to block her way. With no lamp burning up in Claudia's bedroom, there was no reason for either of them to suppose that their conversation would be overheard and, invisible in her dark-grey cotton robe, Claudia leaned over the windowsill for a better snoop.

'Is that why you entered the foot race this morning?' Mazares asked quietly.

'And wasn't it a good thing that I did?' Salome retorted. 'Otherwise I'd never have known your . . . your *friend* was a—'

Dammit, the clashing of cymbals drowned out the rest of her words and much of his reply, too.

'—god knows, I've warned you enough times, Salome—' clatter, clang, crash '—and believe me, Marcus isn't stupid—' batter, bang, boom.

'—well, you're a fine one to dish out advice about Rome—' now it was the drums and the trumpets again '—and what about Lora, eh? What about her?'

'For heaven's sake, don't you think I've thought about that? Good god, Salome, all I'm asking is that you—'

Claudia would never know what Mazares was asking. At that moment, a mighty cheer rose up from the crowd, calling the victors' names over and over, but in any case, Salome seemed to be in no mood for discussion, storming off just a few minutes later, leaving Mazares tossing exasperated hands in the air. The same hands, Claudia reflected miserably, that had thrown a noose round Raspor's neck and throttled the life out of the priest . . .

The same hands that had killed Broda's uncle, drowned a twelve-year-old child and callously murdered his way to his goal.

Nosferatu.

Demon, ghoul, fiend in human form.

Ah, yes, my friend. Claudia stared into the blackness. But no one said you were immortal.

They were all there, clustered around Rosmerta's bedframe. Drilo, the high priest, in rich flowing robes scented with incense, stood on the far side, his dark blue eyes narrowed in thought. He was flanked by her sons, and although their handsome faces registered concern, one tapped his foot and the other drummed his fingers against the wall. Behind them stood Vani, and Pavan towered impassively in the corner, his arms folded over his massive chest, each corded muscle bulging the fabric of his shirt. There was, of course, one noticeable absence, but the puppet-master needed time to plaster the right expression on his face. No doubt he would be along shortly.

However, it was Kažan who surprised Claudia. For once, the little-boy-lost expression had been overtaken by Kažan the man. By Kažan the husband, Kažan the father, Kažan the head of the household. In turn anxious, devastated and shocked, he paced the room, his face drawn and white as a stranger placed a poultice of mouldy bread over the head wound.

'How is she?' Claudia whispered, but she needn't have bothered.

'I could have *died*, you know,' Rosmerta boomed. 'I could have been *killed* with that wretched masonry tile!'

Claudia couldn't help smiling. Some things, she thought, never change. This woman, dammit, was bulletproof.

'If it hadn't been for Salome, I would have bled to death, too!'

'Not at all,' the young stranger reassured her, bandaging over the poultice. 'Head wounds invariably gush.'

His patient's snort reflected her opinion of that.

'I tell you, Lady Claudia.' Rosmerta even managed a feeble wag of her finger. 'If that girl hadn't been on hand to staunch the blood with a decoction of yarrow and dead nettle, they'd be embalming my corpse at this moment!'

Without the usual preponderance of make-up and flounces, Rosmerta looked like every other piece of mutton who tries to pass herself off as lamb. She looked *younger*, and for the first time it was actually possible to view Rosmerta as her husband's contemporary, rather than a bossy older sister or (sometimes) even his mother. On the other side of the bed, Marek, or perhaps Mir, opened his mouth in a yawn. Kažan's glower cut it short.

'Well, I hear the Lands of the Blessed get a lot of rain this time of year,' Claudia quipped. 'You're far better off with us here, on Rovin.'

She glanced at the box on the chair by the stranger's side and noticed a grisly array of scalpels, retractors, catheters and probes poking out. Hardly the instruments of a mule doctor, then, but it seemed the curiosity was mutual. It was the first time, she realized, that he'd appreciated the newcomer was Roman, but the minute he noticed, his eyes narrowed in hostility.

'I'd prefer visits were kept to the immediate family,' he said brusquely, pinning his patient's bandage in place.

A ripple of glances were exchanged round the room, but it was Pavan who stepped forward to answer.

'The Lady Claudia is contracted to marry the King, lad,' he rumbled.

The physician's hostility evaporated at once.

'Good,' he decided. 'Excellent, in fact, because I was just about to go looking for him, before I was summoned up here.'

This time the glances were sharper, longer, and Claudia felt a ripple of alarm run up her backbone.

'Listen, laddie—' Pavan began.

'The thing is,' the doctor said, checking Rosmerta's pulse with one hand, as the other packed instruments back in their box. 'When I was called to examine the body of the royal physician, I discovered—'

Everybody began exclaiming at once.

'Good heavens, man, what are you saying?' (Drilo.)

'The King's physician is *dead*?' (Kažan.)

'We thought he was a poof run off with his lover.' (Marek.) (Or Mir.)

'Ah!' It finally occurred to the young man that no one had actually told these people that the royal physician had died. 'I – uh – I'm really sorry, but yes. The fact is, his body was found at the bottom of a valley halfway between here and Gora.'

Embarrassment at his gaffe had turned his face and neck as red as a turkey-cock's wattle, and he tried to cover it by rearranging instruments which didn't need rearranging.

'He'd fallen, obviously?' (Vani this time.)

'Well, no, that's the odd thing,' he stammered, clicking the clasp on his instrument chest. 'I can't help feeling the accident had been staged – oh, shit. I shouldn't have said that, should I? Not before I'd talked with the King.'

'No, lad, ye shouldna,' Pavan growled, and his grey eyes rested on Claudia for a very, very long time. 'Look, son, why don't ye and I take a stroll?'

'Well, I really think I ought to stay with—'

'A stroll, lad,' Pavan insisted, laying a huge paw on the young doctor's shoulder and pushing him out of the door. 'And as for the rest of ye – I reckon we should let the patient rest.'

'Absolutely,' Vani said, patting her mother-in-law's hand.

'But first, I have some thrilling news that I know will make you very happy, Rosmerta.'

She patted her tummy, delight sparkling in her eyes.

'Well done, girl. Jolly well done!' Rosmerta winced as she grabbed Vani's hand, but her joy was plain for all to see. 'I told you rubbing bear's fat on your womb would do the trick.' She sank back on her pillows and sighed happily. 'Just think, Kažan! We're going to be grandparents at last! Isn't this just *so* exciting?'

'Indeed.' Kažan's smile was as broad and proud as his wife's, but his was without surprise. 'I'm so happy for you, Vani, I really am.'

'You must organize a parade,' Rosmerta told Kažan. 'Several! We will need to show the little one off, and when it comes to the Naming Ceremony, I don't think a public feast in Pula would be amiss, either. You'll need to start looking round *now* for a goldsmith to craft the amulet . . .'

Dear me, the baby wasn't born and Rosmerta was taking over, and if she was like this on her sickbed, what on earth would she be like when she was up and running? Vani, who clearly had her own ideas about her child's future, rolled her eyes in the direction of the baby's father, and Kažan responded with a tight, understanding smile.

'. . . our grandchild will have nothing but the best, Kažan, and you must start looking around for a nurse, too. When I'm back on my feet, naturally I will take over the—'

It was difficult to know how far to indulge her, in view of so recent an injury, but high priests must have some in-built knowledge of these things, because, with a flourish of his long robes, Drilo stepped forward and bowed deeply before the mother-to-be.

'Congratulations, my dear, may the gods bless you and keep your child free from harm.'

He laid a gentle kiss on the back of her hand.

'I will draw up the baby's horoscope and pronounce the auspices at once, if you can let me know the midwife's calculation for the birth.'

'Three days after the autumn equinox, My Lord.'

'Perfect.' His oiled braids nodded solemnly. 'A season of bounty and plenty, my dear, of fruitfulness and thanksgiving. You and your husband must be truly overjoyed.'

But when they looked round, the boys had already gone.

'Orbilio, this is no time to be writing love letters,' Claudia announced, marching into his room. 'I have a job for you. Come.'

'Actually, I was writing up my dispatches,' he said, tapping the parchment. 'And frankly, if you think your ridiculous wild goose chase takes precedence over His Imperial Majesty's business – and the case I am working on threatens to affect our entire economy and undermine the very foundations of the Empire – then you are absolutely, one hundred per cent right.'

Look at him, she thought. Funny, solicitous, charming, urbane. Anyone would think we were friends.

'I presume this is the same bee buzzing round in your bonnet about a coup to destabilize Histria?' he asked cheerfully, lengthening his stride to keep up. 'Because, if so, I ought to tell you now, before you go making a complete and utter fool of yourself—'

'Marcus, please.' Claudia stopped and held up her hands. 'When I want your opinion, I'll give it to you.'

'I feared as much.'

'All I require tonight is a witness.'

'Whatever you say, Your Royal Highness.'

'Snide doesn't suit you, Orbilio, any more than black fingers. No chance of it being gangrene, I suppose?'

'Sadly, Your Ladyship, ink isn't terminal, at least not as far as I'm aware, but who knows? It might yet prove to be the ultimate in untraceable murder weapons.'

'When poets tell you the pen is mightier than the sword, you really shouldn't take them literally, you know.'

'You don't think it would catch on in terms of warfare?'

'I didn't say that. Hurling rude letters at one another is what they do in the Senate, why not carry it one stage further and take them into battle? Scrolls are a lot lighter to wield than a sword, and they never need sharpening – ah, so that's where the quarry's been hiding.'

Mazares was, in fact, in the courtyard and was anything but in hiding. The garden was illuminated by scores of torches in cressets, and fragranced by aromatic resins burning in braziers, and Claudia paused in the archway on the pretext of adjusting her sandal. In practice, it was to watch as he scooped a bedraggled kitten out of the fountain into which it had fallen. She watched as he wiped its coat dry on his shirt and as he didn't even flinch when the tiny ingrate shot over his shoulder and down his back, using its little sharp claws to gain purchase. Ah, but there was something about him tonight. Something different. The crow's feet round his eyes were more pronounced, she noticed, his face unusually lined, and there was a stiffness about all of his movements.

A man, she thought, in the grip of emotion.

A man clinging to his temper by a mere thread.

Oh, Nosferatu. A smile twisted one side of her mouth. How the net is closing in on you . . .

'Well, if it isn't two of my favouritest friends,' he said, and she thought, dammit, that man could talk the Ferryman into rowing him to Atlantis instead of Hades and still not pay for the fare. 'Come and join me.'

Ushering them to a table spread with sweetmeats and cakes, he proceeded to pour wine as though it was someone else's sister-in-law who had been brained with a roof tile. Someone else's sister-in-law who had narrowly escaped death. Claudia sipped. The wine was full-bodied and rich, and could match any vintage of hers. Bugger.

'Mazares.'

She folded her hands on the table and noticed that pinpricks of red had begun to show through his white shirt. So Nosferatu bleeds, does he?

'Mazares, I was chatting to your brother in the cemetery

earlier this morning. It appears he was releasing a flock of finches in your brother's memory.'

'He does that every year,' Mazares replied evenly.

'So I gather.'

She glanced at Orbilio, who was suddenly finding something of great interest on his boot. She kicked him on the ankle under the table, which gave him something else to think about, as well as gaining his attention.

'Well, the thing is, Mazares, it occurred to me, I suppose seeing those hideous masks above the black empty robes flapping against the tree trunks, that you do seem to have a history of tragedy in your family.'

His skin had a strange pallor tonight, too. That row with Salome had cut deep – oh, and right on top of his victim escaping, the poor little moustachioed lamb . . .

'Yes,' he agreed. 'Death does tend to shadow me.'

Actually, chum, it's the other way round. But this was not the time to mention Raspor, Rosmerta, the royal physician, the King, the King's son, his daughter, his brother, his wife and Uncle Tom Cobley and all. Confine it to his immediate family for now. God knows, there was still enough to go round!

'Tragic,' she simpered. 'I mean, your wife dies, then your brother—'

'To be pedantic, My Lady, the order is reversed.' His smoky green eyes locked with hers. 'My older brother indeed lies in the cemetery, but his bones have lain there for many long years.'

'I hate to rake over old wounds, but would you mind telling me – us –' she slanted a glance at Orbilio and thought, this'll damn well make the Security Police sit up – 'how your brother came to meet his untimely end?'

'How?'

Mazares leaned back in his chair, stretched out his legs on the table and crossed his booted ankles.

'I thought you already knew,' he said slowly. 'It was three days before his twentieth birthday. Of a fever, if you recall.

And, since you seem to be taking such a close interest in my family, the name engraved on his amulet was Brac.'

Aargh.

Twenty-Three

Orbilio unbuckled his belt, pulled off his soft deer-skin boots and groaned. Anyone else suddenly confronted by royalty would have dropped to her knees and apologized. Not this woman. Claudia Seferius stomps off along the colonnade without a backward glance, and before Marcus could apologize on her behalf, Mazares had also stalked off, but in the opposite direction.

He didn't know what hurt the most.

Seeing his friend wounded by her assumptions.

Or witnessing the passion with which their marriage bonds would be woven.

He dunked his head in a bowl of cold water until he could hold his breath no more, and when he came up for air, he couldn't be certain at first that it wasn't his imagination that picked up footsteps in the corridor. But they were real. They were light, fast, confident footsteps, the step, no less, of a dancer, and there was an ache inside as they passed by. Orbilio towelled his hair dry. He often forgot that was how Claudia used to scrape a living, performing in dingy, backstreet naval taverns, and a muscle tweaked at the side of his mouth. That was in a previous lifetime, of *course*! Before she'd forged a new identity for herself and enveigled her way into a prosperous marriage. The twitch gave way to a fully fledged grin.

Poor Claudia. When she took Gaius for better or worse, she never expected to face problems like . . . well, like having the man she had pegged as a murderer turn out to be a king, for one thing.

Or having a conscience, for another.

He dipped a sponge in the water and ran it over his arms and chest. As much as Claudia Seferius would have people believe that scruples were the dangly bits at the back of her throat, she had a strong taste for ethics – though if she'd only face up to the fact, her life would be a whole lot less complex.

He wrung out the sponge and re-soaked it, knowing that he would never be the one to tell her.

Scrubbing his shoulderblades, he pictured her preparing for tonight's banquet. He imagined her taking a brush to the thick tumble of curls that cascaded over her shoulders. Drizzling her spicy Judaean perfume into the dips of her collarbones.

His gut wrenched. Mother of Tarquin, it would never happen! It would be Mazares, not him, who'd be privy to such intimate moments. The King who'd watch Claudia unpin the clips that held her tunic in place and gaze as the soft cotton fluttered down to make a pool at her feet. Suddenly, he couldn't bear it. He couldn't bear the thought of her untying her breast band—

The burning behind his eyes halted abruptly as he reached for a towel and caught sight of his bronze powder box on the table. He'd picked up the idea from athletes. Discus throwers always smother their hands with powdered chalk to keep their palms free from sweat on the field. Orbilio had merely taken the concept a stage further, by dusting powder over his skin after a bath. The powder kept him fresher for longer. Only, someone, it seemed, had been poking around in his box. He knew this, because the level was too even, suggesting fingers had searched for something hidden in the powder then shaken it flat. To prove his point, he noticed a light snowfall of particles over the bronze lid as dusty fingers replaced it.

A professional gaze swept the room, taking in the clothes chest that was ever so slightly askew, the counterpane that was ever so slightly ruffled from someone feeling under his mattress. Taking a deep breath, he reached for his satchel and unhooked the clasp. The contents remained in exactly the same order – his letter of authority, for instance, and his other credentials – except the parchments were overly neat. As though they had been patted together before being replaced. The scrolls re-rolled with their ends tucked tidily in.

A woman's touch, experience concluded. This was a woman's doing, and—

'You dirty, double-dealing, low-down skunk!'

His bedroom door almost flew off its hinges.

'Why the hell didn't you tell me Mazares was the King?'

Marcus made a dart for the towel. Claudia whisked it out of his reach and brandished it like a weapon.

'Why did you leave me to make a fool of myself?'

'I didn't leave you,' he said, snatching a shirt to cover his embarrassment. 'You insisted I stayed on, remember? You wanted a witness, you said.'

'Bastard.'

'Am I to conclude that you didn't find Mazares's joke funny . . . ?'

'Oh, absolutely bloody hilarious. No wonder people wouldn't tell me what the King's like . . . he's standing right in front of their faces, and – what a hoot! – everyone in on the joke except the poor bitch who's marrying him. Now honestly. What bride could *fail* to be tickled by that?'

'I did try to warn you,' he said.

The first time was at the Ostia Gate. He'd even tried to tell her tonight, but no. Modom just wouldn't be told.

'The Divine Julius said no man could do his dying for him. In your case, Mistress Seferius, no man can do your letter-reading for you. Because, if you'd read it through properly, instead of cutting your usual corners, you'd have saved yourself a whole lot of grief.'

'So this is *my* fault?'

Marcus managed to turn a laugh into a respectable cough.

'Dammit, Orbilio, that slimy snake was winding me up from the start.'

She looked like she was about to burst a blood vessel. Unfortunately, it looked like one of his she was after.

'From the minute I demanded to check his credentials in Pula—'

Orbilio couldn't help himself. 'Yes, I've heard that women find them impressive.'

Bad move. She balled up his only towel and lobbed it out of the window.

'—right up to the point where I cornered him tonight in the courtyard—'

'—Or perhaps right up to the point when Mazares decided the joke had gone on long enough? Don't forget, Claudia, tomorrow's the day when marriage announcements are finalized and—'

'Orbilio, who's talking here, you or me?'

'It's my bedroom. Don't I get to decide?'

Her response was a look that scorched timber.

Orbilio belted his shirt round his waist and poured her a goblet of wine. 'Claudia, calm down. Please. Just calm down a moment.'

If there was one thing the aristocracy was good at, it was oiling, he supposed. It wasn't a tactic he resorted to very often, going totally against the personal grain, and admittedly, when it came to stoppering up volcanoes, this wasn't going to be the easiest of tasks . . . but after slinking four goblets of vintage red down her throat, followed by two of fruity chilled white, he managed to reduce the eruption to just a few spurts of lava, interspersed with the occasional showering of hot coals.

'You said it yourself, Claudia, and though you didn't realize it was Mazares you were talking about, the King's a good man. Nothing's changed in that respect, and that's why I insisted it couldn't possibly be him who was responsible for the killings.'

'But you do believe there are killings?'

Hmm.

'I believe that a lot of tragedy has befallen his family,' he said carefully, then added swiftly, before she could cut in, 'Look, if you intend changing your gown for the victory banquet, there isn't much time.'

205

'Sod the victory banquet. Just tell me what you're doing on Rovin.'

'I already have. I'm following up on a runaway slave, remember?'

'Yes, and when we discussed the matter before, I believe we also agreed that I'm the Queen of Sheba. Dammit, Orbilio, you've cooked something up with Mazares, haven't you? And don't play the innocent with me. I can smell your lies three miles away!'

Personally, Marcus would put the distance at a hundred times more (at the least), so perhaps it was time to come clean with her, after all? He rested his back against the wall and tried to look as dignified as any man can, when he's wearing nothing but a tribal shirt wrapped round his waist.

'Mazares came to see me in Rome,' he told her. 'Not in any official capacity, but as a friend. A man he could talk to.'

It had come to his attention via the tribal elders, Mazares said, that something odd was happening at Salome's farm. The elders reported seeing women coming and going at an unusual rate, and since the women were uniformly young, foreign-looking and spoke precious little Latin, the elders feared Salome was running some kind of slave trade. Mazares had reassured them that, if that was the case, then the girls would only be coming, not going, and that there would be ships anchored nearby to take them away, or at the very least wagons. The elders knew this wasn't happening, of course, and accepted the King's explanation that freeborn women travel without restraint in the Empire, that visiting friends and relatives was commonplace, blah-blah-blah, but lying to his people didn't sit easily on Mazares's conscience.

'He couldn't raise the matter with the tribunes in Gora for risk of legionaries raiding the farm. This would prove him a liar in the eyes of the tribal elders, he'd alienate himself from Rome if there turned out to be some perfectly innocent explanation, and you must remember that his daughter-in-law, Lora, is also living up at the commune.'

'So he decided to have a quiet word with his old friend, Marcus, instead?'

Orbilio nodded. Having listened to Mazares's concerns, he explained, he realized this was connected to the disproportionate number of runaways who were disappearing so effectively from the city that not even professional slave catchers could trace them.

'With this case bearing all the hallmarks of an organized gang, it was already under investigation by the Security Police.'

Slavery was the lynchpin of the imperial economy. Anything that threatened to undermine it was naturally classed as treason.

'Salome inherited her husband's slaves,' Claudia retorted. 'She was quite within her rights to give them their freedom.'

'This isn't about what she did six years ago, it's about what's been going on *since*, and I have to tell you, we're talking serious numbers here.'

'Pfft.' She dismissed the notion with a wave of her hand. 'Show me a bureaucrat who doesn't exaggerate and I'll show you a day tripper in Hades.'

Orbilio spiked his hands through his hair.

'If only it was as simple as that,' he replied, and wondered whether he'd been adequately able to disguise the weariness in his voice. 'But, hell, even if it was only half the number being mooted in the corridors of power, can you imagine what would happen if word of these escapees got out?'

Right across the Empire, slaves would revolt. There would be anarchy and dissent, murder and chaos. Streets would run red with blood.

'I didn't tell my boss about my meeting with Mazares, I just convinced him to let me take over the case and—'

'Came to Histria to investigate. I see.'

'No,' he said quietly. 'No, Claudia, you don't see.'

He had a sudden urge to bury his face in her hair.

To close his eyes.

To forget . . .

'From what Mazares had told me about Salome, it seemed inconceivable that she could be running a racket for venal motives,' he said. 'She's a herbalist, a healer, a nurturer, a nurse, and he and I both felt that – well, if anything untoward was going on at the farm, then Salome had to be doing it out of misguided goodness.'

He swallowed the lump in his throat.

'To prove my point, I decided to send a girl undercover.'

'Sweet Janus, not a little Cretan girl with a squint?'

Hope leapt in his breast. 'You've seen her?'

The look of pity he received in reply dashed his hopes.

'They knew right from the outset that she was a spy,' Claudia replied hoarsely. 'I overheard Silas and the others talking. It was the night of the fire and they . . . they said – and god forgive me, I'll never forget it – Tobias said –' she swallowed – 'he said, "That's one spy they won't be seeing again."'

Something congealed in Orbilio's stomach. Every night when he closed his eyes, he'd see the girl's wide trusting face in front of his, and every morning when he awoke it was still there. Now, he realized, it was her ghost looking at him . . .

'There's more,' Claudia said. 'I'm afraid Lora is part of this scam.'

'Yes, and tonight I come back to discover that Salome has been searching my room.'

She was on to him, but that didn't matter. He hadn't committed anything to paper that she wouldn't have suspected already. No. What mattered was how he was going to break the news to Mazares that the woman he looked upon as a trusted friend was a murderess – and the daughter-in-law whom he cherished was in it up to her neck.

Mazares.

The King who prided himself on justice and right.

Twenty-Four

A nestful of hornets was buzzing inside Claudia's head. She couldn't hear. She couldn't think. She didn't know which way was up.

One minute Mazares is the leader of the wolf pack, Nosferatu, a ghoul, the arch fiend, her jailer. His description fits what Broda saw to a tee. A lot of people around him have died. Who better placed to organize a conspiracy? Suddenly, though, the tables have turned. Mazares isn't the bad guy after all, he's the King. The King is a good man, everyone says so, and Claudia herself knows it to be true. Raspor gave his life to protect him and, for all his assumed arrogance, underneath he's just a big soppy dog, not a wolf. A deliverer of justice, not a fiend. Claudia's protector rather than jailer.

The clues were all there, of course. The way people looked at him on the quayside, the deference of the crew on board ship, the elaborately engraved gold torque. Then there was the passion with which he spoke of his people, his country, and the depth of his understanding. The way the islanders reacted at the Feast of Zeltane; the way he led his 'bride' through the Fire of Life; the way he'd responded to all of her questions. With hindsight, she ought to have asked herself *why* Mazares had been so astonished when she'd demanded to check his credentials on the dockside, and who could blame His Majesty for taking revenge by stringing the arrogant bitch along? (Dammit, to think she'd been worried about offending the King's general, as well!)

But recriminations were pointless. For his part, Mazares had taken great pains to ensure that no one in his circle gave the game away – hence the silly word games with the likes of Pavan and Salome, and the ridiculous farce that ensued – but in the end, the facts hadn't changed.

Only the perspective.

The King's father, his brother, his wife and his children had all met untimely deaths. Now the royal physician had been confirmed dead, Broda had seen her own uncle murdered, so . . .

So, if it wasn't Mazares, who the hell was Nosferatu?

Claudia paced her room, up and down, up and down, up and down, the exquisite frescoes on the wall no more than a blur. There was no way she could twist her mouth into a smile and sit through the victory banquet tonight. Rosmerta's brush with death had made sure of that, because the roof tile slipping was no accident, she was convinced. Had the attempt been made on Kažan, she could understand it, but how on earth did Rosmerta's death fit the plan? She pulled up short in her pacing. Plan? *What bloody plan?* If she was wrong about Mazares, surely she was wrong about the conspiracy, too? Kettledrums pounded behind her eyes, cymbals clashed inside her temples. Janus, if only she could think straight . . .

Could they really have been simple accidents? His father's weak chest, his daughter's drowning, his son's disembowelling by a mastiff while out hunting? Yes, yes, of course they could – *but they weren't.* Broda had been severely traumatized by the things that she'd witnessed, not by a childishly overactive imagination, and although Claudia hadn't been on top form herself after that fall down the steps, there was no mistaking what happened to Raspor. The cold sweats in the night testified to that; the nightmares about his heels drumming impotently . . .

No, dammit, Nosferatu was out there. The plan to eliminate the King and his bloodline was unmistakably real. The fog inside Claudia's head started to clear. Someone close to

Mazares was preparing a new order for this country, and they would stop at nothing to achieve it. Suggesting that Rosmerta had seen, or heard, something that linked the killer to these horrible crimes, the significance of which she probably didn't even realize – but the knowledge of which had almost cost her her life.

Claudia grabbed the nearest frock and stuffed her hair into pins. Suddenly she couldn't afford *not* to attend the victory banquet, but first, she had to make sure that Histria's answer to the Vestal Virgins had round-the-clock protection and then she needed to have a long, frank discussion with Mazares. The only question was, exactly how large a slice of humble pie was she prepared to swallow?

A mistake had been made.

The first, admittedly, but one that Nosferatu needed to rectify.

Fast.

'My dear Claudia, you don't have to apologize to me. It was a perfectly honest mistake.'

There had been no chance to talk in the dining hall, and quite right, too. The banquet was to honour the winners of today's games, and to deny them even one small moment of their hour of triumph would have been shallow and lacking in respect. So Claudia had sat at the top table alongside Mazares and, as garlands of violas and parsley, symbolizing victory and strength, were hung around the necks of each champion, she had smiled and applauded, and all the time reflected on the man sitting beside her.

A man who had, with one short revelation, suddenly turned into a stranger. She had thought she knew Mazares, but she didn't. She didn't know a damn thing about him.

The King's greatest strength is that he trusts people, Drilo had said, *and perversely his greatest weakness is also that he trusts people.*

He had talked of the innate sense of justice, too, of the

integrity and responsibility that weighed heavily on the King's shoulders. Of a refusal to delegate, taking on everything himself, and yet she had seen so many examples of that, even to pitching in at the ferry when the ropes had been cut, and not realized.

His Majesty has only one aim, Drilo had added, *and that is for his people to prosper.*

Whereas she had only seen him as a pirate, selfish and exploiting, killing for his own vile ends . . .

If you look at the King, see how he's sacrificed his own happiness in the name of duty, you can see why I steer clear of politics, Kažan had said just this morning in the graveyard.

Obviously Claudia hadn't realized he'd been referring to his own brother, but, piece by piece, a new Mazares began to emerge.

It's wearing him out, Drilo had confided. *Slowly, his pride is killing him.*

And it was true. From the age of sixteen, when, still stricken by grief, he'd been forced to marry his brother's widow, right through the current political tug-of-war that kept Histria a kingdom of two separate halves, Mazares had relinquished all hopes of a normal life. No act could be spontaneous any more. Everything had to be thought through. He had been propelled to a life of public scrutiny, to juggling responsibilities, setting priorities, meting justice, and all the while having to continually look over his shoulder. No wonder he lost himself in the affection of his Molossan hounds. Dogs are loyal, obedient and totally without cunning. With his children cold in their graves, Elki and Saber's was the only unconditional love he would get.

Who could blame him for turning everything he did into an act?

How else could he hope to survive?

Claudia rubbed at the throbbing at her temples. Sweet Janus, it was Histria that was the puppet-master, not Mazares. Mazares was the most subservient puppet of all.

So now, with the honours and the speeches delivered and after a meal at which Elki and Saber had eaten everything their master had had on his plate, the King and his bride-to-be retired from the festivities to the quiet of his private office, where, perched on the edge of his desk, swinging one long, booted leg with what she now knew to be studied nonchalance, he was telling her that there was no need to apologize, it was a perfectly honest mistake.

'After all,' he added, stroking his beard, 'dozens of people must receive missives from royalty every day and not bother to read them, just skip through to the end.'

Ouch.

'Did I really call you a pompous old windbag?'

'Several times,' he said, laughing, 'though if there's one lesson I've learned, it's to abandon all attempts at diplomacy.'

'I embarrassed you in front of the tavern keeper.'

'My Lady, you sell yourself short,' he drawled, his catkin-green eyes twinkling. 'I beg you not to confine yourself to single figures on that score.'

Double ouch.

Suddenly, he jumped off the table, clicked his heels and bowed.

'I'm sorry, too,' he said crisply. 'It was the poorest of manners to keep the joke rolling so long, but once I realized you hadn't read my request properly, I felt it better you should learn about Histria from the outside, rather than by anything I might say to colour your judgement.'

'Then we've both learned lessons about diplomacy the hard way.'

Indeed, the bruises would last far longer than those she'd sustained from her fall.

'As for the tavern keeper, seriously, Claudia, you must realize by now that I'm a man of my people, and the only way I can fully understand them is to mingle among them, be part of them, and listen to what they have to say. Hand on my heart, My Lady, you have not offended me once.'

He was lying. Now that she knew him better, understood

more of this strange and complicated man, she knew this was just one more act. Maybe on the surface it was true – that she hadn't caused actual offence. But Claudia knew in her heart she had hurt him, and a small piece of her died at that moment.

'Claudia.'

He drew a deep breath, held it for a beat of three, then exhaled. He looked older, she thought. Lined. And that terrible pallor on his face . . .

We're tired of burning rapists around here, he had said on the night he bumped into Salome.

It's wearing him out, Drilo had told her. *Slowly, his pride is killing him.*

Oh, Mazares. Wolves are supposed to be strong . . .

'Claudia, you know that tomorrow we hold the annual marriage auctions?'

The job was burning him out and now he wasn't eating properly and . . .

And . . .

'*What did you say?*'

'An ancient tradition, quite barbarous, I agree, with girls of marriageable age gathering in a group and the men circled around. The auctioneer calls the prettiest to stand up and the richest men start to bid for her hand, then the second pret-tiest goes under the hammer and so on.'

Incredibly, that wasn't the worst.

'Peasants consider themselves to have no use for looks in a wife, so they hang around, because often they're paid by the fathers to take the ugly ones that nobody wants and, finally, the crippled – or, as we say here, misshapen – girls are offered to whoever will take them. However, we do have some scruples. No man can take a girl home without a backer to guarantee his intentions and it's illegal for a father to marry his daughter to anyone he happens to fancy, and I know what you're thinking, but my people won't hear of any other system,' he said shrugging.

'*Auction?*'

214

'Yes, Marcus did warn me that you might, shall we say, heat up at the prospect.'

Heat?

'Mazares, you could smelt gold on me at the moment.'

'I tried to prepare the ground the day the ferry rope broke, but then, when I found I was needed, I passed the buck to Pavan, and not, I might add –' there was a twitch beneath that swirling moustache – 'without a certain amount of relief.'

'This is indefensible, you know that?'

'Actually, My Lady, I beg to differ.'

He plucked a stylus from his desk and began tapping it against the palm of his hand.

'Histria has witnessed huge changes over recent years and my people are adapting, believe me. But marriage auctions go back centuries, and you find them from here to Liburnia, right over Illyria and all the way down Dalmatia, Pannonia . . .'

'Mazares, you aren't seriously telling me that you, Mr Upright and Conscientious himself, stand by while women are sold to the highest bidder like . . . like goats?'

This has to be another wind-up.

'That once a year the Histri send their women to *market*?'

'I didn't say I condone it, only that I am powerless to change it. Claudia, Rome has stripped our lands from us and foreigners are farming our soil with slave labour instead of giving employment to local people.'

The passion in his voice was rising.

'We pay taxes to Rome, we live by Roman decrees, we are slaves in our own bloody land.'

'We?'

'Yes, Claudia, *we!*'

He hurled the stylus into the corner.

'Whatever my personal opinions, remember that I repre-sent the Histrian people. I cannot, and will not, force them to change at a pace they are unable to cope with, and if that means once a year having to preside over a bunch of grown men squabbling over women like drunks at a cockfight, then it's just one more unpalatable job among many, but, goddammit, someone has to do it and that someone is me.'

The throbbing behind her eyes intensified. At a time when metalled roads stretched to every outpost, no matter how far-flung, and literally hundreds of miles of aqueducts fetched sweet water to wherever it was needed most, and when ramshackle towns were rebuilt all the way round the world in marble and stone and ships can navigate every sea, Histria was still bogged down in this monstrous archaic ritual?

'My people have been pushed quite far enough,' he maintained. 'Even your Emperor is wise enough to keep out of this—'

'*My* Emperor?'

'Very well, *our* Emperor, now, dammit, woman, will you ever stop breaking my balls?'

Mazares turned his fiery green eyes on her and she watched as they softened. Several seconds passed before he finally took a deep breath and stepped towards her. He smelled of cool mountain forests, perhaps a hint of wine, and something sweet that she couldn't identify.

'Marcus said you had fire in your belly,' he said. 'He was a little loose on the amount, I grant you, but . . . I do desperately need an heir.'

Claudia thought about the faithless Kažan, his feckless sons waiting in line, and nodded.

'Yes, you do,' she replied, and something lurched under her ribcage.

'This kingdom needs fresh blood in its veins,' he said quietly. 'We can't keep intermarrying among neighbouring tribesmen, but more than that, Claudia. More than that, I want children who can stand up for themselves. Who can stand up for Histria. Children who are able to fight their corner against Rome, but equally against their own people, children who are free-thinkers, freewheelers, who are unburdened by old conventions and hidebound traditions. You possess those qualities, Claudia, and tomorrow all new marriages will be announced, so I need to know.'

Catkin-green eyes bored into hers as he enveloped her hands in his.

'Will you marry me?'

Would she? Croesus, this was everything she'd ever wanted!

Claudia resisted the urge to punch the air with her fist and dipped into what she hoped was a suitably reverent curtsy. Originally, she'd hoped to put sons in the Senate, an ambition that died with her husband, since he'd left her childless. Now, though, those sons would be princes! Governing a whole country, not just casting one paltry vote among hundreds! And god knows, it might be a loveless marriage, but it would not be one without passion! Also, it wasn't as though neither of them had any idea what they were in for.

Mazares hadn't loved Delmi, but he had done right by her.

Claudia hadn't loved Gaius, but she had done right by him.

Each would fulfil their side of the bargain, and in exchange for the healthy, strong-willed heirs he was so desperate for, a girl from the slums would be crowned Queen, showered with riches beyond imagination *and*, goddammit, have her sons on the Histrian throne!

'Mazares.'

It was as though the sun had suddenly risen over the landscape, shining light where light had never shone. Bringing warmth where there had only been coldness.

'I know you needed to ask the question formally,' she said, and there was a wobble to her voice, which was only natural, because her heart was bucking like a stallion inside a horsebox. 'But I'm pretty sure you know the answer.'

There was a flash of something in his eyes, but the emotion was fleeting and he bowed deeply to cover it.

'You are . . . certain?'

'Absolutely.'

Smoky eyes held hers for what seemed like eternity, and

217

she wondered if he could actually hear her knees knocking. Finally, he spoke.

'So the answer is no, then?'

'It is,' she replied. 'The answer is no.' And she whirled out of the office before she changed her damned mind.

Twenty-Five

Out across the hills, Dawn rose from her slumbers, draped her crimson nightshift over the horizon and slipped naked into the bed of her husband, the Sun God. As bats folded their wings and badgers skulked back to their setts, the joy of this celestial union was celebrated in song in a million tree tops while, below, coneys scampered out of their burrows, their white tails bobbing over the lush, dew-covered grass as vees of cormorants flapped over the waters towards their feeding grounds.

Claudia saw none of these things.

Face down on her pillow and still fully dressed, she saw only triumphant frescoes painted on an office wall. A helmet perched on a stand. Scrolls piled knee-deep in a corner. Inkstands. Quills. A plate of food left untouched. And a man's lined, grey-pallored face. She saw the hunting trophies that surrounded his desk, or, more accurately, hunting *atrophies*, because, from the mounted boar's head to the bearskin spread over the floor, every exhibit was moth-eaten and dry, dating back to a time when a young prince in jaunty tunic would jog off into the woods with his brothers, his friends and his dogs, a quiver on his back and a dagger in his belt, his aureole of glossy curls shining in the sun and without so much as a care in the world. That joyous young hunter was long gone. A quarter of a century on, he had turned into a grief-stricken monarch, bent by the weight of responsibility and reduced to hiding his rebellious emotions, since the only happiness he had ever known came from two children who lay dead in their graves . . .

In the banqueting hall, exhausted musicians strummed to the last of the revellers, much of whose dense, drunken laughter was absorbed by walls of thick island stone.

How could she? How could she, Claudia Seferius, deny him another shot at that happiness?

She climbed off the bed frame, blinked the tears from her eyes and set the pleats of her robe into knife edges.

When she was born, it was into the slums. When she was ten, her father marched off to war and never came home, and when she was fourteen, she found her alcoholic mother had slashed her own wrists. At which point, she realized that all she owned were the clothes on her back, her mother's good looks and her father's grit – and that it wasn't much of an inheritance. Which was why she vowed that, if she was forced to prostitute her body, it would bloody well be through marriage. Finding a husband became her career. Quite frankly, if someone had said then, *I can make you rich, I can make you the mother of princes*, she would have bitten their hand off. As it happened, Gaius Seferius offered her wealth, social standing and respect – all the things her upbringing hadn't – and she'd been grateful for that. So why not now? Why not now, when the stakes were that much higher?

Picking up a mirror, the same mirror Mazares had sent her, the bronze one whose handle was shaped like a cat, Claudia studied her reflection. Make no mistake, it was still beautiful, but she did not kid herself. The assets she'd had to trade at seventeen were very different from those she possessed today, and she could not rely on looks for much longer. Also, women in trade were anathema in Roman society, and although that might be offset by the perception of wealth, any half-decent audit would soon uncover a welter of financial mismanagement. So then; if age was against her, being in trade was against her and she was broke, why, oh why, did she turn Mazares down?

'Ye can still change your mind,' a gravelly voice rumbled behind her. 'It's a woman's prerogative.'

Claudia spun round. He looked older, she thought, and he was tired. She could tell from the way the thong round his pony-tail had slid down to his shoulderblades. Had he the energy, he would have tied it up tight, but perhaps he was drunk, because there was a strange glint in his eyes that seemed almost feral.

'Pavan, it's late—'

'Correction, ma'am, it's early.'

The scent of leather was like an invasion.

'Late, early, I'd still prefer to be alone, if you don't mind.'

His reply was to advance into her room, close the door and brace his backbone against it.

'Why?' he asked thickly. 'Isn't the King of Histria good enough for ye?'

There was nowhere to go. The shutters were bolted, and even if she managed to undo them in time, the drop from the window would break both her legs . . .

'My reasons are none of your business.'

'That's where ye're wrong,' he growled. 'Histria is my business, and it might only be small, this country of ours, but we're a progressive society and one that looks set to rise with considerable speed.'

'You shouldn't take it so personally when people tell you size matters, Pavan.'

Something rumbled deep in his throat, and she didn't think it was phlegm.

'God knows, woman, this kingdom's crying out for an heir.' He patted the point on his belt where his dagger would normally hang. 'Why would ye not give him that?'

Perhaps she could fob him off with some cock-and-bull tale about being barren?

'After all,' the gravel voice rasped, as he ran his displaced hand along his ponytail instead. 'Mazares is no a bad-looking chap.'

He was certainly no Gaius, she'd give him that. He was handsome, debonair, clever and fair, and not many men in their forties could wear skin-tight pantaloons and still turn heads for all the right reasons.

'Why?' she retorted. 'How bad do you think a man would need to be, before I refused to bed him?'

Pavan's face turned a deep red. 'I didna mean it like that.'

Claudia flung open the shutters, admitting fresh air and sunlight into her room whilst releasing the strong scent of leather into the wild. Down on the foreshore, she was surprised to see Orbilio sitting alone, nursing a goblet of wine in both hands as dawn broke over the landscape.

'It's just that I was wondering,' the general persisted, 'could it be for a different reason that ye refused him? Something money can't buy?'

She tore her eyes away from the still, silent figure and turned to Pavan, trusting that by clenching her fists behind her back it would not show how much they were shaking.

'I don't understand you,' she said.

Like everything else in this bloody country, Pavan was another study in contrasts. What *is* it with these wretched people?

'From the outset, you were against me marrying the King and now suddenly, here you are, telling me there's still time to change my mind.'

The oak tree strode across the mosaic to tower above her.

'As commander of the King's army, it's my duty to see Histria's interests are looked after, but, hell, I've grown up with that laddie.'

Hard grey eyes shifted to the horizon.

'I've watched his brother die, then his father. I've seen his wife betray him and I stood beside him when he buried his children.'

The eyes dropped to Claudia and bored right through her skull.

'To serve one is to serve the other, ma'am, so I'll ask ye again. Why did ye refuse him?'

To her credit, she didn't flinch, and when she finally spoke, icicles could have formed on her tongue.

'Like I said, Pavan, it's none of your business. Now get the hell out of my bedroom before I scream rape.'

'Aye,' he rumbled. 'I reckon ye would at that, but I just hope ye know what ye're doing.'

In four paces, he was at the door and jerking it wide.

'Because, if a marriage isn't announced today, there canna be one announced for a year. Remember that. *Ma'am.*'

As the hinges reverberated, the trepidation inside her retreated. She listened to the fall of his boots on the marble. Waited until the corridor had fallen into silence once more. Then breathed out. Down on the foreshore, Orbilio was still cradling his goblet as he stared across to the islands. He needed a shave, she decided, and wondered what thoughts could be preoccupying him so intensely that he didn't swipe away the fringe that had flopped over his forehead or stop to drink from his glass.

Isn't the King of Histria good enough for ye?

Pavan's questions pummelled her weary brain.

This Kingdom's crying out for an heir. Why would ye not give him that?

He didn't understand. Pavan was like a wounded bull, kicking out in his frustration and anger, for the simple reason that he did not understand. But Mazares did. Mazares understood. Hence that flicker of emotion in his smoky green eyes, which he'd covered by bowing. But not before Claudia recognized that the emotion had been relief . . .

Could it be for a different reason that ye refused him? Something money can't buy?

Suddenly, there was a lump in her throat the size of a wagon and the sea must be carrying salt on the breeze because her eyes were stinging and her vision was blurred. A picture flashed in her mind of her husband on their wedding day. He was in a spotless white toga and about to place his distinctive signature on their marriage contract – status and wealth in return for a trophy wife. The day had been mild and fair, she recalled, and on the whole, it had been a pretty good party. On the whole it had been a pretty good pact . . .

'It's what I wanted,' she murmured aloud. 'It's what I gave and it's what I received.'

223

But at some stage between that day and this, she had changed.

She watched as Orbilio stood up, stretched the stiffness out of his muscles and spiked his wayward mop into place. The rosiness in the sky had deepened, she noticed, a sure sign of impending storms. Perhaps that explained the turmoil inside? But instead of turning away, her gaze remained fixed as he drained his goblet, shook out the drips and walked slowly back to the house.

Isn't the King of Histria good enough for ye?

Claudia placed the flat of her hands on the windowsill and absorbed the warmth of the stone through her palms.

Could it be for a different reason that ye refused him? Something money can't buy?

Sweet Janus, she had already condemned one man to a loveless second marriage. She was damned if she'd do the same to another.

What she couldn't understand, though, was why it bloody well hurt.

Orbilio was halfway back to the house when the cry rang out from the harbour. Considering today was the day when marriages were pledged in this kingdom, it was hardly surprising that boats were materializing from every direction, and rumour had it that the ferryman was also braced for a record number of crossings. Therefore Marcus didn't give the shout a great deal of thought, other than to curse it for interrupting his train of thought.

So many strands, so many deaths, so much terrible waste . . .

He had spent half the night trying to make sense of it all and finding that, when dawn finally broke, all he could think about was how he was going to break the news to the Cretan girl's mother – a slave in his own household, goddammit – that he had sent her daughter to certain death. How could he face that poor woman? *How could he face himself?* It was only when one of the women let loose a mourning wail that his attention was fully drawn.

One of the fishing boats was signalling frantically, and a crowd was gathering down on the jetty. Their expressions were grim.

'What is it?' he asked, pushing his way through to Kažan, who was ordering that the high priest be sent for. 'What's happened?'

Kažan's handsome features distorted into a grimace.

'Bodies,' he said sourly. 'The fishermen have been picking bones out of their nets all bleeding morning.'

He indicated the channel separating island from mainland with his thumb.

'Looks like they were flushed out in the night. It happens from time to time around here, something to do with storms and equinoxes and the Ionian Sea, someone was saying, but it's not a pretty sight, I can tell you. See her?'

He pointed to a woman sobbing uncontrollably as she clutched a small child with long, raven-dark hair that fell to her waist.

'That's her uncle they've just fished out, the poor bitch. He used to build boats on this island. Bloody fine craftsman at that.'

As it happened, Orbilio was already aware of who Broda's mother was. He had spoken to both her and the child, and at length. He knew who Broda's uncle was, too. *And* her father.

'The same boat builder who Nosferatu was supposed to have murdered?' he murmured.

Kažan adjusted the headband round hair that was identical to his daughter's in every respect.

'That's the chap.'

His mouth turned down in distaste.

'Not much left of the poor bugger, though, and look – people are already making the sign of the horns.'

Orbilio had never really understood this business about 'evil eyes', but he knew enough about superstition in Histria, and everywhere else for that matter, to know that the gesture they

225

were making was no automatic response to folklore. These people genuinely believed they were in peril.

'You can practically read their minds,' Kažan said. 'That it was Nosferatu himself the girl saw, and when he'd finished gorging on his victim's warm flesh, he tossed the bones in the channel like rubbish.'

'Someone certainly did,' Orbilio murmured, but his words were cut short by the arrival of another slimy corpse being slapped down on the cobbles. Bloated and mutilated as one would expect after a week in the water, the halo of dark curls surrounding the little plump face remained unmistakable.

'Sweet Svarog!'

The gasp of the high priest took Orbilio by surprise.

'It's true, then! Raspor *is* dead!'

His shock appeared genuine, Marcus thought. Except he'd seen too many grieving husbands/fathers/wives who'd turned out to be cold-blooded killers, that one could never take these things for granted.

'I'm really sorry, Drilo,' Kažan said, laying his hand on the taller man's shoulder. 'He was a conscientious little feller, too.'

'One of the best,' Drilo nodded, then stopped short. 'But good grief, man, what am I doing? It's me who should be comforting you!'

'Me?' Kažan frowned. 'Why me?'

'Heavens, has nobody told you?'

Orbilio's blood suddenly ran cold.

'Told him what?' he asked gently.

'Rosmerta,' Drilo said. 'She took an extra dose of her sleeping draught by mistake, and now, of all times, would you believe, that young physician's disappeared into thin air, we can't find the idle hound anywhere, so the King's had to call in the same mule doctor as tended the Lady Claudia after her fall the first night she arrived here and—'

'And what?' Kažan prompted quietly.

'I'm so sorry, my boy.'

226

Drilo's shoulders slumped.

'The mule doctor is adamant that your wife will – well, that Rosmerta will not last the day.'

Nosferatu was feeling a whole lot better, now, thank you.

Twenty-Six

Orbilio wasn't the only person whose blood turned to ice in their veins. The flurry of panic that swept round the house told Claudia that something was seriously wrong, and that it wasn't purely the gruesome haul in the fishermen's nets. This apparently was not an uncommon occurrence, something to do with storms down in Greece creating currents that could, in extreme conditions, carry ships off their course, but which either way flushed out any remains lodged in Vinja's den. It was how families knew whom to honour with red ribbons in the shrine to the fire-breathing monster. As always, the sea gives up its dead.

And, in a way, it was a relief to discover Raspor's corpse among the grisly finds. Not because Claudia's story would be vindicated. She'd never had doubts on that score, and whether anyone else believed her or not was irrelevant. No, she was glad, because at last the little priest got what he deserved. She might not have been able to save his life, but she could take comfort in knowing he'd receive a fitting burial in accordance with his beliefs and that his bones would rest with his ancestors, protected by gargoyles in empty black robes and safe in the knowledge that his sacrifice had not been in vain.

But right now, Raspor was low on the list of priorities. The dead were dead, it was time to protect the living and, as her footsteps reverberated along the marble corridor, there was only one thought in her brain.

Pavan.

I'll give you *gruzi vol*, you callous, unfeeling bastard. And

228

as for that bullshit about how serving Histria was to serve the King, did he really think she'd swallow that? Who laid his massive paw on the doctor's trusting shoulder and led him away? Who insisted Rosmerta be left alone – for her own good, too! And who, my friend, had been so angry that the King's proposal had been refused? Small wonder. It scuppered Nosferatu's plans for whatever little accident he'd been planning for the King and his bride, the one that he had so insidiously persuaded Mazares to invite his good friend Marcus over here to act as an official witness for.

I'll *gruzi* bloody *vol* you with my own bare hands, you devious bloody bastard. No wonder you were so concerned the other night when those rapists clawed at me. Can't afford to have the bait damaged, can you?

Mazares was still in his office when she burst through the doorway, and it looked as though he'd spent the whole night there, since the cushions on the chair were flattened and his clothes were creased and in disarray.

'Claudia!'

He jumped up and reached for where he'd kicked his boots. 'An unexpected honour, I must say.'

There was no time for preambles. 'You've heard about Rosmerta?'

'I have.' His dark curls nodded miserably. 'Poor Kažan, can you imagine what the poor sod's feeling?'

'Are you referring to Vani expecting his child or him not having to pretend that he isn't ashamed of his wife any more?'

Mazares paused from lacing his boot and stared at her thoughtfully.

'I think I'll get that sour-cherry tree axed,' he said slowly. 'The blossoms are beautiful, but the fruit can be awfully acid.'

'If you think this is sharp, I suggest you saddle up now, because you're in for a rough ride, Mazares. There are things that need airing and they won't wait.'

He stooped to finish his lacing. 'So, Kažan's the child's

father and grandfather at the same time? His sons resemble him so closely that no one's likely to suspect, and anyway –' he turned his attentions to the other boot – 'who's going to care? Half the children in Gora are miniature versions of my brother.'

'Sod Kažan! It's your other brother I'm interested in. Brac.'

Mazares straightened up, tucked his shirt into his pants and clipped on his gold torque.

'Do you sleep in a normal bed, like everybody else,' he asked, 'or do you hang upside down in a cave overnight?'

'Mazares, I'm serious. Surely even you can see it now? Rosmerta's death isn't an accident—'

'Well, I'll agree with you there. My sister-in-law is very much alive. Admittedly, she's in what the Greeks call a *koma*, but, unlike certain people in this room, I would at least hesitate before burying her.'

Claudia heard a gnashing sound and thought it might be her teeth. At this rate, she'd be down to the gums, but she had to accept his point, and, goddammit, he looked even worse in broad daylight. The grey pallor to his face had turned waxy from lack of sleep, the lines round his eyes looked like chasms. Exactly what a grieving man would look like, she supposed, when faced with the prospect of no heir for another year at least, while being confronted by the very woman who'd consigned him to that fate.

She shivered, as much out of contrition as guilt. She'd failed Raspor by not taking his claims seriously. She would not fail Mazares by inducing him to do the same.

Drawing a deep breath, she set to ticking off the deaths on her fingers and made no mention of Pavan's betrayal. The King was a good man, who trusted those around him, but, given a choice, he would trust his general above a shrew – especially a Roman shrew. No. Let him find out for himself that, when it came to rodents, there was a rat in his household that was infinitely more dangerous, for while Mazares might be noble, he was anything but stupid. The facts could speak for themselves.

Like strapping young Brac, dead of a fever three days before his twentieth birthday, and Dol, whose weakness of lungs came on surprisingly late in life, yet had him in his grave aged just fifty-two.

However, when it came to relating the drowning of a twelve-year-old child, the clinical reporter found herself unable to look the father in the face when she recounted the circumstances of his daughter's so-called accident, much less when she rehashed the circumstances of his son's death, and may Juno forgive her, she was almost glad to move on to how his wife's 'suicide' was most likely assisted.

'If you know so much about my family,' Mazares said thickly, 'you will also know that Delmi was prone to bouts of depression. She'd tried to kill herself once before, but Rosmerta, for all her faults, stepped in and saved my wife's life. She never forgave herself for not preventing it the second time.'

'Maybe that's why Rosmerta was mur— given that overdose,' Claudia suggested.

It had to be something that had been done, or said, recently that triggered Nosferatu into action. His was a careful, cold-blooded campaign which Rosmerta had somehow tripped up.

'Nonsense,' Mazares said wearily, pouring two goblets of wine. 'A tile slipped, it gave her concussion and, in her confusion, Rosmerta took more than one dose of the poppy draught to ease the pain. We've all done it, but not with such tragic consequences, of course.'

Claudia sipped at the wine, but the heat had soured it, or perhaps it was nothing more than the bad taste in her mouth.

'What would you say if I told you Orbilio has verified that no tile was missing from the house roof?'

There was a glint in his eye as he watched her over the rim of his goblet.

'Has he?'

'Well. No. Not exactly.'

Dammit, it was impossible to lie to this man.

'But I'm sure if you ask him, he'll go up and confirm my theory, and anyway, what about the boat builder? His body bears out Broda's account, Raspor's body has also been washed up, which confirms what I saw, and now the young physician who rode in yesterday has suddenly disappeared off the face of the earth. How convenient, when he'd just announced his findings!'

'You're worried about the young doctor?' Mazares chuckled as he drained his glass. 'Don't. Pavan sent him back to Gora.'

Well done, Pavan. Very neat. Very tidy.

'Don't tell me. It was for the boy's own good?'

Twinkling eyes studied her from lowered brows.

'Actually, he felt there was more need for a physician in a town where the population is greatest, seeing as we have a perfectly competent mule doctor here on the island, who, I'm sure, will prescribe something suitably minty for My Lady's indigestion.'

Claudia was not finished yet.

'Surely, after hearing how your own physician met his end, you can see it?' she asked softly.

The lines round his eyes suddenly became gorges.

'What a waste,' he rasped, and there was no trace of laughter left in his voice. 'What a waste of a life, of a talent, but what you have to bear in mind, my dear Claudia, is that homosexuality is considered unnatural among the Histri. Imagine if a hot-headed tribesman mistook friendliness for a come-on, who knows how he might react? Obviously, I'm not condoning the killing, but I've long accepted that things can be said – and done – in the heat of the moment that are regretted in the cold light of day. Just,' he added with a disarming grin, 'as I have accepted the curse that lies on my family.'

'Which is precisely what I'm trying to drum into your thick skull.'

How the family totem wasn't the mule, she'd never know! Wasn't it Salome who'd called the Histri boneheaded? Stubborn wasn't the word.

'It's not a bloody jinx, it's a campaign to undermine you,

eliminate your bloodline, bring a new order to this kingdom at the expense of everything you and your father have ever worked for and, Croesus, I'm so confused, I don't know whether he's planning to incite Histria to rebel against Rome or bring the kingdom closer to the Empire, but at the moment I don't bloody care. All that matters is that you're next, Mazares. You're top of Nosferatu's hit list, and whether you believe what I've told you or not, for gods' sake, be careful, will you?'

She finally ran out of steam and it was with a weary voice that she added her postscript.

'He'll want it to look like an accident.'

Mazares's tired eyes managed one further dance as he rested both hands on her shoulders.

'Is it just you and Salome, or is it a precondition of Roman citizenship that women bust their men's balls?'

'Which brings us to another point. You do realize that Salome—'

'Claudia.'

He leaned forward and planted a kiss on the top of her head as though she was three years old.

'Claudia, will you please, please, give this poor eunuch some peace? In case you hadn't noticed, I have the mother of all hangovers this morning, and I could really use a few moments to myself to groan quietly while my skin finds its way back to my body and the tingling in my mouth stops spreading up my whole face, because very soon I will have to step outside wearing the broadest of smiles and play king to my people, while, as you so kindly pointed out, Histrian virgins change hands like cooking pots.'

It was all that hair, Claudia supposed. Proof positive that, if left uncut, the follicles invade the brain and destroy it from the inside out.

'However, if it sets your mind at rest,' he added, sucking in his drawn cheeks, 'I will endeavour not to allow myself to be crushed by falling bridegrooms or smothered by auctioneers in the meantime.'

233

'In those pants,' she retorted, 'you're more likely to be mauled to death by rampant matrons.'

But the words did not get past her lips for the lump in her throat and the salt water that coursed down her cheeks.

Twenty-Seven

Nosferatu had to be stopped, the question was, how? How could Claudia possibly hope to stop the carnage that was tearing this kingdom apart without help?

Clouds had begun rolling in from the east, turning the clear azure sea to grey sludge and trapping the heat under their soft, downy blanket, but the mounting excitement meant that nobody on Rovin gave a hoot about any downturn in weather. The noise was deafening, with everyone shouting at once as fathers strutted impatiently, virgins clustered together like newly hatched chicks and bidders inspected the goods. Claudia could only imagine how rich the pickings would be for those light-hands gliding artfully through the throng. The auction had attracted crowds from as far afield as Liburnia, Dalmatia and Venetia, and to jolly things up musicians in fringed jerkins played the pipes, acrobats tumbled and a thickset Illyrian danced a bored-looking bear. Claudia was dressed in keeping with local tradition, because, wouldn't you just know that in a country where men wear pants instead of tunics and have no use for a barber, they'd be contrary to the end and marry in black? Her hair also hung loose down her back and, since jewellery was banned (oh, please! – such baubles must not be allowed to influence a man's choice of bride!), at least she had no fear of being robbed.

But not all contracts today were for marriage. In the shade of the fountain, salt sellers negotiated deal after deal as their assistants hacked lumps off the block. A Phoenician in ruby-red slippers hawked mirrors, an Armenian ivory carver touted bangles and combs and a long queue stretched back for the visiting oculist, who was dispensing the same remedy for night blindness as for eyes that were discharging pus.

'Thought I might find you down here.'

Claudia smelled the sandalwood before she turned. He was back in his long, patrician gown, she noticed, and wore the toga as a mark of respect for the occasion.

'How did you recognize me?'

'Easy,' Marcus breezed. 'Like picking out a horse. First, one discounts distinguishing features, such as blondes, redheads, fat girls, slouchers—'

'*Picking out a horse?*'

'Would you have preferred it if I'd said cows?'

Further along the quayside, a cloth merchant from India rolled bale upon bale of jewel-coloured cottons over the flagstones, drawing gasps with each imaginative dye, and an Arabian sea captain tossed back a flagon of wine. You could always tell the Arabians. They shaved the whole of their head, apart from a circular mop on the top. Tough luck, she supposed, if you were an Arabian who went bald. The captain tossed back another full flagon – he was obviously on for a bet – and now the auctioneers were taking their place on the bench with the King, fortifying themselves with a glass of strong wine before the haggling started in earnest.

'I presume your intention was to mingle unobtrusively?'

Claudia said nothing, since to state the obvious was to waste breath.

'Black suits you,' he said. 'Plus, you don't look half so ballsy with your hair down.'

'Black makes me look like a crow,' she retorted, 'and I look ballsy with my hair up or down. And now that we've dispensed with the flattery, can we cut to the chase, please?'

There was something different about him this morning, she decided. He looked . . . well, not like when he retreated to the house at day break, that's for sure! Then, his brows were knitted tighter than the stitching on a saddle blanket and he seemed bowed by the cares of the world. But now, within the

space of a couple of hours, no prisoner given a last-minute
stay of execution could have a broader grin etched between
his ears. Orbilio seemed younger, happier, taller, lighter – as
though he was floating on air for some reason and, though it
was an odd thing to say about a man built like a gladiator and
towering several inches above her, he looked weightless this
morning. Dear Diana, if she lived to be a hundred, she'd never
understand aristocrats.

'Two things,' he said. 'One, I thought you might be interested in hearing Orbilio's Great Hypothesis concerning the
young physician and Rosmerta's encounter with a roof tile.'

'You thought wrong.'

'No, please, I beg you to curb your impatience, madam!
But before I let you prise my conclusions out of me—'

'Prize conclusions from the Security Police is a contradic-
tion in terms.'

'—I want to talk about something you said when you were
declining the King's proposal last night.'

'News travels fast.'

'Not as fast as it travels when one listens at keyholes, but
that's not the point. I—'

'Attention, please.'

The order was amplified thanks to a bronze trumpet which
had been sawn off half a cubit up from its mouth.

'Would all remaining brides gather in the area outlined in
chalk.'

Claudia snorted. Whatever you call it, it was still a cattle
pen.

'That means you, dear,' the trumpet added.

Claudia looked over her shoulder.

'Yes, you, miss. Come along.'

She still couldn't see who they meant. Then her shoulderblades received a jolt.

'Don't be shy, dearie,' an old hag cackled, shoving her
forward. 'Yer a pretty gal, someone'll soon snap yer up.'

'*Me?*'

She spun round, but there was no spotless white toga in

sight, and now she was being propelled through the crowd at such speed that her feet were barely touching the ground.

'Let go of me, you son-of-a-bi—'

'Mistress Seferius.'

Mazares's smile was more wolfish than ever.

'I hadn't expected you to indulge so wholeheartedly in our customs, but since you've decided to join us, perhaps we could start the bidding this morning with you?'

'Dammit,' she hissed. 'He put me up to this.'

Twin fireballs scorched the spotless patrician tunic sitting beside him. Orbilio grinned happily while the girl who had been deemed the prettiest of the prospective brides glowered daggers at the interloper who was now setting off the auction instead of her, snapping up the richest husband for herself, the scheming bitch.

The auctioneer's hammer tapped twice. 'Any bids?'

'Three thousand sesterces,' Orbilio said, as the steward dragged Claudia into the arena and paraded her like a prize bull.

'Three thousand?' the crowd gasped.

They were used to dealing in hundreds.

'*Three thousand?*' Claudia protested.

Sweet Janus, his tailoring bill cost less than that.

'Quite right,' Marcus told the auctioneer. 'Make it two thousand five hundred.'

The crowd laughed.

'So help me, Orbilio, I will kill you,' she vowed under her breath.

'Believe me, it's for your own safety,' he hissed back through his grin.

'This is degrading, humiliating and utterly outrageous.'

'Agreed, but not dangerous. Oh, very well,' he called across to the auctioneer. 'Two thousand, but that's my final offer.'

The whole quayside had doubled up and were wiping their eyes.

'*Stop!*'

The laughter stopped abruptly and all heads turned towards the woman who had grabbed the trumpet from the unsuspecting flunky's hand and was marching purposefully into the square.

'*Mazares, I insist you stop this monstrous ritual at once!*'

The speaker was dressed head to foot in white robes, but it wasn't her protest that made people draw breath. Rather that her features were elfin and her hair fell down her back in walnut cascades.

'*Lora!*'

Mazares was off the podium and into the plaza in the blink of an eye.

'Lora, how are you, my dear? Are you well? Are you happy?'

His reaction completely wrong-footed his daughter-in-law. The set of her chin suggested she'd been expecting anger and reproach, a fight to avoid the armed guards, yet the King's sole concern was for Lora's welfare, and it occurred to Claudia that, for all her rantings against him, what that girl wanted to do was throw her arms around Mazares and hug him. But rebels have an obligation to their cause and, behind her, a whole swarm of women in white were pushing their way through the astonished crowd. Plump smiling Naim was among them, Claudia noticed, and freckle-faced Mo, and the Nordic beauty was there, too. Bonni, the girl with white hair and black fingers, which Claudia now knew to be ink stains, thus making her the forger in Salome's racket. And amazingly, surging forward with purpose, there was Jarna, the tanner's wife, the fresh bruising round her eye clearly the catalyst for her change of heart. Noting the frowns of uncertainty which had begun to ripple over her followers' faces, Lora cleared her throat and spoke authoritatively into the trumpet.

'These archaic auctions cannot go on,' she announced. 'It's time we women had a say in our own future and I say, it's up to *us*, who we choose for our husbands. It's *us* who decide who's good enough to sire our sons . . .'

In the riot that erupted, Claudia found it very easy to slip back into the crowd as Lora urged women to stop being doormats, to accept that they had rights equal to their menfolk, and to damn well start using them.

'*Don't* let yourselves be sold off to useless lumps of gristle and fat, just because they happen to be rich! *Don't* sacrifice love because it's what your mothers did and their mothers before them! Now is the time to stand up for yourselves, girls! Take what's yours by right and say *no* to this abomination that passes for marriage!'

'*Hisssssss.*'

'*Hurrah!*'

'*Booooo.*'

'And what might a young grieving widow's opinion of those sentiments be, I wonder?' a baritone rumbled in Claudia's ear.

'I condemn them entirely,' she replied tartly, because he was still the Security Police, and the Security Police, as everyone knows, never sleep.

'Just as I thought.'

Mazares was doing his best to calm the upsurge that had gripped both sexes with passion, but, King or no King, he lacked the tactical advantage of Lora's metal trumpet, meaning it was his daughter-in-law's exhortations that rang over the crowd.

'I say *no* to being sold off like cattle! *No* to being herded like sheep!'

'It's a funny thing,' Orbilio murmured, 'but I could have sworn I saw a flash of lemon cotton beneath the black when you bit that steward back there.'

'Tch, and you'd think the aristocracy would teach their children not to swear.'

'I would do more than swear, if I thought you were trying to sneak off the island.' He stepped in front, blocking her progress. 'This is a dangerous game being played.'

'Really? Because last time it was all in my mind.'

'You intend going to Amazonia, don't you?'

With Pavan, Kažan and Drilo stuck here for the auction, a ritual that not even the Terrible Twosome, Marek and Mir, would dare miss, there was no better time to go visiting, and

240

although Claudia's money was still on Pavan as Salome's accomplice (or vice versa), she couldn't take chances at this stage. If she was to confront the lioness in her den, now was the moment – an opportunity made even more attractive, seeing that Lora had depleted the Amazonian workforce.

'Certainly not!' she retorted. 'It was a long night, I'm tired and I just want to lie down.'

Something came from his throat that sounded like *hrrumph*.

'Honestly, Marcus,' she said, and there was enough honey in her voice to drain a beehive. 'The combination of that fall down the stairs, the run-in with thugs at Salome's farm, and now Raspor's body washing up, has given me a terrible headache.'

He might be lighter than air this morning, but his scepticism remained firmly rooted.

'I have no intention of doing anything more strenuous than resting for a couple of hours in my bedroom,' she persisted smoothly. 'And since Mazares insisted on posting an armed guard at my door, I'm quite safe, and frankly, Marcus, the best place for you to be is at the King's side. He's in far more danger than I am.'

Another hrrumph, but at least this one seemed to be in a mood of concession.

'You promise?'

'Cross my heart.'

'Very well,' he said grudgingly. 'I'll stick with Mazares.' He turned, then turned back. 'But you give me your word?'

Claudia shot him her most radiant smile.

'Would I lie about something as serious as this?' she asked, frantically signalling behind her back for the ferryman on the other side of the channel to cross over.

The third hrrumph was somewhat reluctant, but finally, urging her to take care and trust no one, Orbilio fought his way back to the King, leaving Claudia to marvel at the aristocracy's ability to dish out advice which they themselves had no intention of taking.

* * *

Amazonia was eerily quiet, but the riot of perfume and colour was as explosive as ever. Herbs for remedies, flowers for market, trees for fruit, vegetables for the table. The fecundity of the farm bounced off in waves, and again she was struck by the deep sense of serenity that pervaded the land. They say it's a woman's touch that turns a house into a home. Imagine, then, the effect of several hundred women. Happiness and harmony pulsed from the soil and dripped from the blossoming trees. Claudia checked the dagger hidden deep in the folds of her pale lemon gown and the thin blade strapped to her calf.

Tethering her horse at the gate, she worked her way round to the farmhouse. Several fields were horribly blackened, the crops all but wiped out, but the majority of the land was remarkably unscathed, proving that Salome's Amazons had been well trained in their fire drill, and although the thatches on many of the storehouses had burned through, Tobias was busy sawing timbers to make a framework for tiles, not thatch, thus ensuring the buildings could not be destroyed so easily in the future.

He was, of course, assuming that this farm had a future.

She watched him, stripped to the waist, scowling as his saw rasped through the wood, and the muscles in his arms were corded and strong, and the flesh on his back tight and tanned. He would probably be handsome if he only smiled, and she moved on before he turned round to measure the next section of timber.

The thatch on the pigsty hadn't been touched. It lay where it had collapsed, but the black spotted sow didn't mind. She had used the scorched grass for her bedding and lay sprawled on her side, oinking away as five tiny pink piglets suckled and squeaked, blissfully unaware of the dark clouds that gathered above.

'Clever girl,' Claudia whispered, and suddenly she was gripped by an uncontrollable shuddering as images of that night came surging back.

Screams. Flames. The sow crashing against the walls of her

242

sty in blind panic, resulting in stillborn piglets that she would have eaten the minute she'd birthed them, and rage shot through every inch of Claudia's body. How dare they? How dare they set fire to crops, destroy buildings, rape virgins, for no motive other than bigotry? Inflicting pain and destruction simply to exert some kind of control? The rapists were dead, the arsonists shunned, but their chauvinism had not been erased, and no wonder Lora fought so passionately for what she believed in. Rosmerta said Lora had loved Delmi like a mother. Claudia gave an affectionate tweak to the pig's ear and patted her spotted rump. Lora and Delmi. Two women who had been contracted into loveless alliances would have much in common, and if Lora picked up that baton when Delmi died, her zeal would have been further fuelled by Salome's obsessive commitment to equality. This would have escalated into contempt for the King's tolerance of what she considered cold, heartless practices, firing a desire to turn the situation about.

'What it is to be young,' Claudia murmured to the donkeys grazing the lush grass in the orchard. 'To have ideals you still believe are worth fighting for.'

Even if elfin-faced Lora didn't understand the finer points of anarchy! Such as how the King and Mazares are one. Bound by duty, the two are inseparable, and if Lora had loved Delmi, it was obvious that, in spite of herself, she adored Mazares as well.

'Ah, but the passion,' Claudia told the geese dabbling on the fringes of the pond. 'What passion beats in young hearts!'

Croesus.

She stopped short, watching bees buzz round the yellow iris on the margins, listening to the frogs croak in the shallows.

That was it!

Passion!

Passion was the key to this mystery.

Passion was at the heart of it all.

Her instinct had been to assume the killings were in aid of an uprising against Rome, but this was wrong. She saw now that this carefully planned elimination of anything and anyone who stood in Nosferatu's way was because Histria wasn't Roman *enough*. Stuff independence! Nosferatu was after closer links with the Empire, not fewer, and although the arch-ghoul would probably call it 'siding wholeheartedly', it was only by sucking up to Augustus that the country's influence and supremacy could grow at the speed Nosferatu was after.

Passion.

Passion for glory, passion for control, passion for Rome and all things Roman, like law, like trade, like progress.

But most especially, passion for power . . .

Oh, yes, Nosferatu sighed, it was passion all right. Passion for glory, passion for control, passion for Rome and all things Roman.

Like law.

Like trade.

Like progress.

But especially passion for power.

Sweet Janus, it was just a hair's breadth away, too . . .

Twenty-Eight

The treatment room looked exactly as Claudia had left it. Neat piles of petals and roots stood lined up on the table, seeds of celery, mustard and dill had been set aside in mortars to be pulverized later, while infusions of dewcup, soapwort and chamomile bubbled gently in cauldrons that dangled over red, glowing charcoals. On the workbench, in between a dish of grated horseradish and a jar marked agrimony tea, sat a heap of dried myrtle berries and, on the shelves, papyrus labels proclaimed decoctions of everything from rosemary to oak bark. Cloves and nutmeg fragranced the warm, healing air, enhanced by oils of juniper, peppermint, jasmine and ginger, and the instruments that hung from the wall gleamed.

'I had a feeling you'd come,' Salome said without turning.

Even the black tomcat was snoozing on the same wooden stool.

'Has the balm helped?'

She was referring to the white alabaster pot that had appeared in Claudia's bedroom yesterday evening. The pot had been tied round the middle with straw, into which a small posy of chive flowers and forget-me-nots had been artfully arranged.

'Enormously,' Claudia assured her. She hadn't touched it.

'Good, because it contains basil, cypress and marjoram, and if you rub it in twice a day, morning and night, as I instructed, the stiffness in your muscles will be gone in no time and it will help the bruises to fade.'

Deft hands continued to mould the macerated remains of horehound, aniseed and cardamom into a paste.

245

'I . . .'

Salome paused in her task and looked round. The glint in her eyes was too bright, Claudia thought. As though she'd been laughing or crying, or something else she wanted to hide, and the smile on her face wasn't right.

'I didn't thank you for saving my pig the other night,' Salome said. 'It was a brave thing you did, my dear, and, great Marduk, you had a lucky escape. Pavan told me what nearly happened.'

Did he indeed?

'Are you all right?'

'After tumbling down a flight of stone steps, I barely noticed the extra bruises,' Claudia said.

'I meant mentally.' Salome returned to her paste, rolling it into a long sausage. 'Psychological bruises take longer to heal and they are much harder to cure,' she said quietly, cutting the sausage into tiny pastilles to counteract the coughs that would unquestionably result from the change from dry to wet weather. 'It's the emotional scarring I'm worried about.'

Claudia didn't doubt it, and she pictured an eight-year-old girl with raven-black hair, traumatized by what she had seen. Who better to keep an eye on the witness than the owner of the shadow whose murderous hands had throttled the life out of her uncle? Who better to pop in with healing herbs, to check that Broda didn't know more than she was letting on?

'Your emotional scarring or mine?' she asked, and something jolted inside.

This wasn't right.

Dammit, this *wasn't* right.

She pushed the tomcat off the stool and sank on to the warm wooden seat. Sure, the evidence pointed to Salome – but her gut said the evidence was wrong. It was, she thought, as the cat jumped back up and began to knead dough on her lap, a question of exactly what evidence they were talking about . . .

Salome stopped slicing the cough-mixture paste, wiped her hands on her apron and pushed her long, red hair out of her face.

'I *was* fond of him, you know. My husband, I mean.'

She drew up a stool next to Claudia and the cat immediately transferred itself to her knees.

'In fact, I thought I loved him until . . .' her voice trailed off.

The pieces fell into place with a click so loud Claudia wondered the whole world couldn't hear it.

'Until you met Mazares.'

Pain clouded Salome's eyes. 'How did you know?'

Mazares, Mazares, it was always Mazares. Every question centred round him, and she remembered the Zeltane Feast. With more work on the farm than they could possibly cope with, Salome still made the time to watch him when he wasn't looking. She watched over him, as well. She disguised herself in blue robes to strew healing herbs as he jumped the Fire of Life and, although Salome tended Broda, it was not out of self-preservation. She did it in the same way she tended the tanner's wife and all Mazares's people, because she cared for him most of all. If his people were healthy, his heart was content. His happiness was all that she wanted.

Shit.

'Does it matter?' Claudia replied.

Suddenly she understood why Salome hadn't married again. Such were her feelings, she couldn't face sleeping with any man other than Mazares. It's why she was so reckless with the numbers of slaves she helped to escape. With no heirs to this land, she had nothing to lose. Claudia swore softly again.

'We need to destroy the evidence, Salome, and there's no time to lose.'

'What evidence?'

'Oh, for heaven's sake, you know damn well that Rome's on to you,' she snapped. 'What on earth are you hoping to achieve? The chance to smuggle another couple of slaves out before the troops close your operation down?'

'Claudia, I won't turn away a single soul who asks for refuge, and when it comes to numbers, my dear, you can't begin to imagine how many poor wretches have been brutalized by

247

their owners. Whipped, beaten, raped, it's horrendous, but thanks to our Freedom Trail, these people can have new papers and start a new life.'

It explains why there are so many women, Claudia thought dully. It's always the women who end up as victims, and only those young enough and brave enough can run off, because the older ones would have babies, and no one can hope to flee 300 miles with children in tow and the slave catchers not hunt them down.

'I'm not questioning the morality of your actions, Salome.'

Although frankly she doubted that even a quarter of the hard-luck tales were true. Once word got out that there was a rabbit run open, it's surprising how slick a lie can become when you have 300 miles to practise it.

'It's the legality that concerns me, and the consequences, which will ruin far more lives than you've repaired.'

She had no idea. Dammit, the silly bitch had no *idea* what would happen once Rome got wind of her racket.

'You think I care if this goes to trial?'

Salome tossed her red mane with defiance.

'Great Marduk, the evidence I'll lay before the court will open people's eyes to the realities of enslavement. My Freedom Trail will become an inspiration for others. Next year, there'll be twenty such organizations, the year after that fifty . . .'

Sweet Janus, she honestly believed it would reach *trial*.

'Salome, we don't have time to argue,' Claudia told her.

Orbilio had already sent off his dispatches. The rider left at first light. The damage was already done.

'Start a bonfire in the yard, burn all the forgeries, destroy every testimony you've kept and anything that connects this place with runaways, because once word reaches Augustus, you can forget about justice and martyrdom. The army will have you put down like a dog, and it's not just a case of Bonni, Mo, Silas and Tobias being sacrificed to the cause. Not even Lora's exalted status will save her. The Emperor will have everyone on this farm executed whether they were participating or not.'

'They can't!'

'They can and they will, and you might be able to carry that on your conscience, but I certainly can't, now get going.'

There wasn't even a pause. Salome might have shoved reality to the back of her mind in the name of righteousness, but she knew enough about Roman reprisals to remember that examples were always made. She knew enough about slavery, too. The rules were straightforward. If a slave killed his master and didn't confess, then the whole household was deemed guilty and put to death. Ashen and shaking, she piled logs on the cobbles as Claudia used the coals from the treatment room to get the bonfire burning. How long before the rider reached Pula? How long before the soldiers marched north? They would be here tomorrow, she calculated, turning this farm upside down . . . but another fire on top of the damage already done would not be questioned. She was fanning the flames with her skirt when a hand clamped over her wrist.

'What the hell's going on?' Tobias snarled.

Claudia told him.

'Oh.'

She wrenched her hand away, but his scowling eyes pierced her for several long seconds.

'I thought you were a spy,' he said at length. 'I thought Rome had sent you, masquerading as the King's bride, because it was obvious you'd never marry Mazares.'

Oh, was it! She was tempted to take him to task over this, but her mind had already flashed back to the night of the attack, when she'd overheard him and the others at the feast. Silas had suggested it was too far-fetched for Claudia to be a spy, arguing that if Rome wanted to send one, surely they'd have sent one undercover. With icy clarity, Claudia recalled Naim's reply.

They've already tried that once, me lovely, she'd said. *Remember that little Cretan girl, the one with the squint?*

Silas had buried his head in his hands. *We shouldn't have let our guards down,* he'd said. *We should have sent her back.*

He knew. The old man was wise to the ways of the authorities.

He knew what would happen to the farm and the workers, if word of the Freedom Trail got back. And Tobias knew, too. Claudia recalled how the hairs on her neck had started to prickle when he gave his chilling response.

Well, we didn't, and that's one spy they won't be seeing again.

At the time, and in light of Orbilio's account, she'd feared the worst. But look at the man! Look at them all! These people weren't slogging their guts out day in and day out for money, or glory, or power. The farm just about ticked over, because all the profits of their hard labour were being ploughed back to give runaways a new life and a new identity. The masters were working harder than any slave and they were doing it out of love, not for greed. Idealists the lot of them, and Claudia shook her head in despair at their naïvety and ignorance. Love, she thought, as Salome came running back with pells of parchment stuffed under her arms, has much to answer for.

'Where is she?' she asked. 'Where's the little Cretan girl, the one with a squint?'

Salome slanted a glance at Tobias. 'Athens, isn't it?'

His springy curls nodded as he tossed the statements into the flames. 'Running a brothel the last we heard.'

'And making more than us, that's for sure,' Salome laughed, pushing her hair out of her eyes with the back of her hand. 'But Lora – dear me, Lora was furious, wasn't she, Tobi? "Another example of the exploitation of women!"' she mimicked.

Tobias, of course, didn't smile.

'I don't know why she was so insistent that I shouldn't go with her this morning,' he muttered. 'It's bound to turn ugly, a bunch of women rising up against the establishment and disrupting the marriage auction. I should have been there for her, Salome. Stepped in and helped her escape.'

'Well, my dear, there are two things,' Salome said. 'Firstly, Lora doesn't want to escape. She intends to meet Mazares head on in this matter, and the other, of course, is that she doesn't want you rotting in jail.'

Her nose was black from smuts.

'Don't you see, Tobi? Don't you understand why Lora refuses to return to Histrian society?'

'She was worried she'd be palmed off with Mazares, just like her mother-in-law. She's said so many times.'

Salome rolled her cat-like green eyes. 'Yes, but *why* do you think she's so passionate about women marrying who they want, not who they're told to? It's because of *you*, you bonehead!'

'Me? Salome, I swear I've never given that girl any encouragement.'

'Then it's about time you bloody well did, because Lora's no fool. She's seen how you look at her – which reminds me.'

She turned to Claudia.

'How did Mazares take the news when you declined his proposal?'

Mazares, Mazares, always Mazares. Claudia felt the world spin. How on earth was she going to tell this poor woman, who had already seen one ideal crushed, that it was Mazares all along . . . ?

But tell her she would have to. How it was Mazares who was looking to create new out of old and eliminate the stale bloodline. No one was better placed to be more Roman than Mazares and no one, as Claudia had said many times, had greater opportunity and motive. Killers like Nosferatu don't have the same thought processes as everyone else, she would have to explain. He'd have viewed the murder of his own wife and kids as nothing more than eliminating obstacles in his path, and how easy – oh how easy – to make these things appear accidents.

The trouble was, Salome was so in love with Mazares that although she could grapple with the imperial stance on her Freedom Trail, hearing monstrous accusations levelled against the man who, in her mind, was purer than pure, meant that Claudia would have to tread carefully. So, as the next batch of incriminating documents were piled on the flames, she outlined the plot that was poised to tip Histria over its finely balanced edge, and thanked Jupiter that Orbilio was by the King's side, making certain that no more innocent lives could be taken.

When she finished, the silence was almost interminable and, surprisingly, it was Tobias who broke it.

'Funnily enough, Lora suspected as much,' he said. 'She told me that she believed her husband had been murdered, and she never accepted that her mother-in-law committed suicide. That's why she sought refuge here in the first place. She feared she was next.'

'Delmi not take her own life?' Salome tutted, her lovely brows drawn in a frown. 'Lora loved her dearly, I know, so I can see how she might want to believe that, but, dear me, her husband murdered by *dog*? Anyway, our Lora's never been a girl for not speaking her mind. If she feared there was a killer on the loose, she would have broadcast the fact.'

'Not necessarily,' Claudia said. 'She already believed that her presence here was the cause of the farm's rape and pillage, yet she stayed on. Now, Lora doesn't strike me as a coward. If she thought she could stop the destruction, she would have left. There had to be another, more compelling reason to keep her here.'

'Yes. Tobias was one, and her commitment to the Freedom Trail was another.'

'Actually, Salome, there might be a third.' Tobias looked troubled. 'She did say–' he gulped and looked from one woman to the other and back – 'Lora did say that she wondered, well, if Mazares himself wasn't behind it.'

Claudia could have kissed him.

Not so Salome.

'I have never heard such nonsense in my entire life! The King is a good man, Tobias. He is honest and fair and does right by his people, the notion is utterly ridiculous.'

She bundled her loose hair into a bun to calm herself down.

'Now then, Claudia, you never did tell me how he took the news of your refusal.' Green eyes glared daggers at Tobias's betrayal. 'How is he, poor man?'

This was going to be tougher than Claudia thought.

'Don't you worry about Mazares,' she said, forcing a smile. 'If you must know, he got horribly drunk and I left him trying to nail his eyeballs back into focus and stop the tingling in his mouth from spreading any further over his face. Tobias, did Lora voice her suspicions to anyone else?'

'Yes, I think she told Pavan—'

'Tingling?' Salome grabbed hold of both Claudia's wrists and the grip was stronger than steel. *'Did you say he had tingling in his mouth that had spread to his face?'*

'Yes,' she winced. 'But he—'

She tried to shake free, but Salome was like a woman possessed.

'It's monkshood, you ninny! The King's being poisoned, and if the symptoms have reached this stage . . .'

She was racing to the treatment room before she'd even finished the sentence.

For the first time, Nosferatu experienced a ripple of unease.

Nothing definite.

Nothing that one could put one's finger on and say, *That's the thing, that's the cause of this unrest, let's get rid of it.*

Only a vague fear that something was starting to unravel.

Twenty-Nine

Claudia's footsteps echoed through the maze of marble corridors, and as she ran, the censure of every strange beast sculpted out of bronze or painted on the wall bored into her – dragons, griffons, serpent-tailed giants – and their anger was boundless. In the distance came a rumble of thunder. The storm had been building, yet Claudia could not shake off the notion that Perun's enmity had been stirred and that his wrath was to follow as surely as dusk follows day.

'Long before the tingling that starts in the mouth and spreads up the face', Salome had said, hurriedly packing a basket of remedies, 'Mazares would have experienced a general feeling of fatigue, of not being right.'

Something dropped in Claudia's stomach, as she remembered the pallor, the hollows under his eyes, the deeper than usual lines in his face . . .

'That would have been followed by chills and sweating.'

Which, of course, with the island in uproar, he'd have shrugged aside.

'He'd have had vomiting, a crushing feeling of anxiety . . .' Salome blinked, but her voice was calm as she announced that death would result from respiratory failure with the victim fully conscious.

'Weak lungs,' Claudia said bleakly. 'Everyone knows it's hereditary.'

She thought of the wine. Its sour taste. The way he'd pushed his food round his plate.

He was dying and she hadn't noticed.

He was dying and she'd accused him of betraying the one thing he loved above all.

Histria.

Thunder rumbled closer this time. Perun was closing in on his foe. Claudia could not outrun the god's wrath, but she could run like the wind down this hall.

'You must not blame yourself,' Salome had said. 'I knew he was ill. I should have insisted . . .'

It was as close as she came to breaking down. Recriminations could come later. Right now, she had a fight on her hands, but hers wasn't the only one. The streets of Rovin were in chaos, with fist fights and cat fights on every corner, name calling, scuffles, brides in tears, mothers of brides in tears, bridegrooms incandescent, merchants bemoaning too much unsold stock and soldiers caught up in the riot. Because that was the point. Everyone had an opinion and everyone voiced it at once. Master or servant, rich man or poor, this was no time to stand by. History was being challenged this day. History might even be changed. People demanded a say in their future. They were entitled to be part of the change.

Quite what had happened to Lora and her white-robed Amazons, Claudia had no idea. Tobias had accompanied her and Salome, his scowls so transformed by the notion of Lora reciprocating his feelings that Claudia feared he would try to carry them both across the channel on his back, he seemed so confident of walking on water. Love, she tutted ruefully, and wondered why the face of a tall patrician should suddenly intrude on her thoughts. The walking on water bit, she supposed. That was exactly how he'd looked this morning.

As it happened, she hadn't been able to find him in the commotion, even though you'd think his white toga would stand out a mile, but no. Orbilio had vanished into thin air and she only prayed that Mazares was with him. There were other prayers she sent, too. Most were to Apollo, god of light and healing, that he might spread his rays over Mazares. Some were to Fortune, because luck is fickle, and a couple to Carna, who presides over a man's vital organs, but quite a few were aimed at Minerva. Heaven knows, the bitch had always had it in for Claudia, but can't she let bygones be bygones? And, as goddess of wisdom, give her the nous to look beyond her blinkered vision next time? Mazares shouldn't suffer for Claudia's stupidity, and whether it was too late to reverse the damage, not even Salome could tell. Her last view of the Syrian girl and her horticulturist had been of the two of them pushing their way through the crowd with an urgency that was painful to watch, but Claudia had had no doubt they would find him. The King would be down there somewhere. Among his people. To the end . . .

Guilt ripped at her innards and clawed at her heart. What she wouldn't give now to turn back the clock! First Raspor, then Mazares and now there was no chance to redress the balance. No one to save, no one to protect – oh, but wait. Two attempts had been made on Rosmerta's life. The least she could do was sit by her bedside and, while she waited, pray to Luna, goddess of the moon, to shine her light of truth on this land and bring peace to this kingdom once and for all.

Contrition gave speed to Claudia's heels, but reproach made it seem like the ground was hardly covered. Sweet Janus, would this nightmare never come to an end? At Rosmerta's door, she paused. Calm. Must be calm. Must be calm for the patient. As her hand reached for the door, she heard a soft scuffle. Could the miracle have happened? Could Rosmerta actually have come out of her *koma*? Pushing open the door, she gasped.

Yes, Rosmerta was out of her *koma*. Her hands were pummelling Pavan's massive shoulders and her feet kicked beneath his oaken frame. But the scream that came from her mouth was muffled by the pillow the King's general was pressing over her face.

Nosferatu saw only that a dam was breaking, a dam that must be shored up.

* * *

It could have been a scene from any of the frescoes. Time stood still. Frozen. And as though it was someone else she was watching, Claudia felt completely detached from the setting as she picked up the high-backed chair from beneath the window, hefted it up by its legs and swung it with every ounce of her might.

With a low moan, the spell was broken.

The human oak tree was felled.

'Is he dead?'

Rosmerta was coughing and gasping for breath, but she was strong. She would recover, and though she'd be weak from the combination of pain and painkiller, not to mention a third attempt on her life, thank Jupiter she'd pulled out of her *koma*. One less victim for this pitiless bastard.

'No.' Claudia looked at the bloodied hulk sprawled across the bedroom floor. 'The general will be fit enough to stand trial for treason.'

'Treason?' Rosmerta studied Pavan as though he was an oversized cockroach. 'Did you say treason, my dear?'

Through the pain and fog, Nosferatu saw a chink appearing in the armour of years of meticulous planning. There was no light from this chink, only the blackness that comes from an abyss in which there is a destiny but no control.

This cannot be.

The dam must be shored up.

The dam *must* be shored up.

Pavan groaned, shook his bloodied head and rolled on to his stomach.

'We have to get the hell out of here,' Claudia told Rosmerta.

Janus, this freak was unstoppable. The bastard son of a bastard son, the ghoul couldn't die. Nosferatu was immortal, after all.

'Not at all, Lady Claudia.' Rosmerta patted her shoulder as she heaved herself out of bed and waddled across to her clothes chest. 'I know how to deal with this.'

Claudia's heart was racing, her palms sweaty.

'Forget the heroics, Rosmerta. Let's lock him in and leave someone else to deal with this fiend.' They'd done their bit. Time to cut and run while Nosferatu slipped and slithered in his own blood. 'Come on, let's go!'

She heard a soft click behind her. The sort of sound, she thought, that a key might make when it turns in the lock.

Pavan's grey eyes skewered Claudia through the runnels of blood. '*No!*' he roared. '*No-o-o-o!*'

'He's quite right,' Nosferatu said, and her voice had a harsh edge. 'You're not going anywhere, Lady Claudia, and neither for that matter is Pavan.'

Sweet Janus. *Rosmerta?* It can't be. Not Rosmerta. She was bossy and vain, not an ounce of dress sense, she was shallow and snobbish, the victim of a selfish philandering husband, but, if anything, she looked after people rather than harm them. Hadn't Vani said she was like a tigress with those she protected. And yet, and yet . . .

'Vani said you were Histri through to your marrow.'

'So I am, my dear, so I am. What you have to remember is that Histria is part of Rome.'

A flash of steel caught Claudia's eye before she realized what was happening. She leapt forward, but the blade was already deep in Pavan's back. Horrified, she could only watch as, with a wheeze, the King's general collapsed onto the tiles.

'I should have listened to Lora earlier,' he gasped, every syllable wracking his lungs. 'I should . . . have seen . . . from the start that it was ye, not bad luck, that . . . wiped out the King's family.'

'And anyone who got in my way,' Rosmerta sneered. Drops of bright red blood dribbled down the blade in her hand and pooled on the floor at her feet.

'Ye'll not get away with this.'

She laughed. 'But I already have, Pavan, I already have! I presume it was you who sent that young doctor away?'

He nodded grimly. 'Knew . . . ye'd try to stop the lad . . . giving . . . evidence. Sent him . . . back . . . to Gora.'

'Waste of time. Who's going to listen to one lone voice, when the King's dead and the kingdom's in chaos? And that's assuming the boy lives long enough to speak in the first place!'

Pavan clutched at his chest.

'I . . . should have . . . silenced ye . . . as ye slept, ye evil bitch . . .'

'Never underestimate the ineptitude of a local mule doctor.' Rosmerta wiped the knife on the counterpane. 'One only needs to look at the Lady Claudia to see that any man who diagnoses all manner of complications after a fall in which she sustained nothing more than a few bruises, and who couldn't recognize the King being poisoned right under his nose, was not to be trusted with the correct dosage of painkiller.' She snorted. '*Koma* be damned. All he did was put me into a sleep that restored my strength. In fact, you could say that it was his incompetence that killed you.'

'I . . . am not . . . dead.'

'Yes, you are, Pavan. Oh, yes, you are.'

Something flashed, but before Claudia could prevent her, the blade was in his back up to its hilt. His huge frame convulsed twice then fell still. She gasped. Rosmerta smiled. It was the sort of smile a crocodile wears when it spots a wounded gazelle in the river.

'This is how it is,' she announced, and her voice seemed to come from the end of a long tunnel. 'Pavan is Nosferatu and the Lady Claudia realized this, which is why she came running. To protect me. Luckily, she caught him in the act of smothering me and saved my life.'

Claudia's body was ice. If only she'd *walked* through the corridors. If only, if only, if only . . . !

'You clubbed him, my dear, but not hard enough. Enraged, Nosferatu strangled you, while I, too weak from the overdose, could only watch helplessly as he crushed the life out of you. But then, when the beast came at me again, I reached for my dagger with the last ounce of strength before I relapsed. Though you do understand, don't you, my dear, that this was not how it was meant to be?'

259

Claudia said nothing, because there was nothing to say.

'The dog,' she muttered at last. 'How do you murder a man with a dog?'

She must be insane. Here they were, standing in a pool of Pavan's blood with Rosmerta flexing her fingers – the same fingers that had closed round the neck of the boat builder, the royal physician and heaven knows how many more – and all Claudia could think about was *death by dog*. Perhaps this is why people are said not to fear death? Their heads become light at the end. Nothing matters. Only trivia. Only ridiculous, useless trivia . . .

'One of my better pieces, I think,' Rosmerta replied. 'Took some organizing, but I had a man train one of the hunting dogs by taunting it with the lad's tunic until the poor beast associated cruelty and hunger with that shirt. My sons are good boys. They'll make fine senators one day, providing they do as I tell them. Like keeping the trained mastiff on a tight leash until it was just my sons alone in the clearing with their cousin, at which point, of course, they released it. When it had, er, fulfilled its duty, I had them hack it so badly that no one would recognize that it wasn't part of the usual pack and then, while the hunting party bewailed the terrible accident that befell the King's son, Marek and Mir killed another mastiff, burying the body to ensure there were no "extra" dogs in the count. Exquisitely executed, even if I say so myself.'

The room was beginning to swim. So callous, so cold. *And so strong.*

'All your accidents were clever,' Claudia said. 'Even the one you fixed for yourself.'

'This?'

Very gingerly, Rosmerta prodded the bandage wrapped round her forehead.

'No, my dear, this is proof that the gods smile on my venture. This wasn't my doing – no need, after all. No one suspected me. Why should I harm myself? But you can rest assured I shall penalize *very* heavily the idiot who cannot maintain his own roof properly!'

'Why senators?' Claudia asked dully. 'Marek and Mir could be princes. Kings, even.'

'Bless you, child, they'll be both. Can't you just picture the New Order in your mind? You have to remember, Lady Claudia, just what a bunch of uneducated losers these Histri are. Half want to go back to the old ways – I mean, as if *that* will help them! – so, I say no more of this ridiculous shillyshallying. Move the capital back to Pula, integrate, become part of Rome, and then we have everything, don't you see?'

Rosmerta cracked her knuckles.

'Best of both worlds. We'll become a family of rich royal merchants, with all the luxuries that Rome can bring as well as total control over the Histri – and tell me, dear, what could be more *perfect* than that?'

'Rome and all things Roman,' Claudia echoed.

She had been thinking of higher issues, like law and justice and peace, but in Rosmerta's eyes, Rome also meant fashion. Including curly blonde wigs that distorted shadows on house walls in the moonlight, to leave impressionable young girls conjuring up the name Nosferatu.

'That's why you speak such perfect Latin, I suppose?'

'Oh, don't *you* start!'

The nerve was red raw.

'You sound like that other little bitch! Delmi was nag-nag-nag, too, calling me lazy for not even *trying* to fit in with Histrian ways. Well, why should I? I'm Roman! Then she'd castigate me for ignoring my sons' education, their religious upbringing, their social skills – like none of this was Kažan's fault! Their father was never around, but she didn't nag *him*, now, did she? Oh, no! And I did *not* pander to my boys when they skipped lessons, and I didn't *always* condone their behaviour when they contrived to get their tutors sacked. Boys will be boys, as I kept telling Delmi, and then I discovered that all the time she'd been criticizing me – *me!* – the hypocritical cow had been warming my husband's bed.'

'Yes, but you didn't tell Mazares.' There had to be a soft side to appeal to. 'At least you spared him that pain.'

'Like there was any point!'

Rosmerta swatted any thoughts of soft sides away like a fly.

'She was his Queen and, really my dear, who would suffer from such a disclosure? Not Delmi. No, no, it would be my Kažan who'd be sent away, which would mean me going too, so there was only one way to end *that* situation. My, if you'd only seen the life drain out of her when I told her that her little girl was dead. Suddenly it was a case of, *Oh, so no more criticism, then, Delmi . . . ?*'

'You saved her life, Rosmerta. She tried to commit suicide, but you brought her back.'

'Only because I hadn't finished with her.' Rosmerta snorted as she advanced across the room. 'If that little bitch thought she could escape me that easily, she had another think coming.'

Claudia's head was pounding.

'But me. Why me? I'm Roman.'

'Yes, dear, and truly I have grown as fond of you as I have of my own darling Vani. Heavens, I'm so proud my son's made her with child, you have no idea how happy it makes me, so don't think it gives me pleasure to do what I have to now. It's just that you leave me no choice.'

The dagger Claudia kept concealed in her gown suddenly flashed in her hand.

'Is that a fact?'

'Yes, my dear, it is a fact,' Rosmerta said, and instead of flinching, jumping back or even feinting as the weapon lunged forward, Nosferatu once again outsmarted the enemy.

She punched Claudia square on the jaw.

The blade had clattered uselessly into the corner. Claudia knew that much, but, blinded by white light, she couldn't see it. She couldn't see anything but the light, and when the light faded, pain took its place. Ferocious, juddering, all-encompassing pain, and a feeling of total stupidity. Once again, she'd tried to make a straight move complicated and once again, she'd paid the price. It was the same as that night at Salome's, when she should have drugged the guards and run off instead of playing mind games, and here, she should have just charged. Head down, knife in the belly, bull-in-the-potter's-yard charge. But no. Stupid bitch, you try to outwit her. The woman who's outwitted everybody for years, and you think you can do better. You can't.

There was little time for self-pity. Although her thoughts had flashed by in a fraction of a second, a hand had already clamped round her throat.

'Maybe not strangled,' Rosmerta boomed, as she slammed Claudia's head against the stone wall.

Jupiter, no. Not like this.

'I think you deserve a heroine's death.'

Something wet was running down Claudia's face, but there was only one thought in her brain and that thought wasn't survival. It was to kill the fiend that was Nosferatu. This monster must not slaughter more innocent victims. Her evil had to be stopped . . .

'I want people to see that you fought Nosferatu like a true Roman.'

Rosmerta thumped her victim's head against the stonework with just the right amount of force.

'Let's have your blood establish your heroism.'

'Yes, let's,' Claudia gurgled, and this time there was no mistake. The stiletto she kept strapped to her calf embedded itself in Rosmerta's neck.

'*Yeeeeeee!*' The wail was unearthly, but either Claudia was too weak or Rosmerta was too strong. Or Nosferatu really could not die . . . 'You –' *slam* – 'bitch –' *slam*

Claudia lashed back. She kicked, brought her knees into Rosmerta's stomach, clawed at her skin, tried to gouge, but there was no strength in her swings, no power behind her punches, and each time her head connected with stone, co-ordination grew that little bit weaker. How many more? How many more could she take before she passed out?

'I'll see you in hell –' *slam* – 'for this.'

And would he know? she asked herself. Would Marcus ever know that she—

'No, Rosmerta,' a male voice growled, and miraculously the grip round her neck fell away. 'It's ye who's going to hell.'

There was a scuffle. A scream. Then a pause. A terrible pause in which Claudia could see nothing but redness and clouds, and she tried to get up, to reach for the statuette that sat in the niche, to bring it down on Rosmerta's head, but she kept slipping in something sticky and warm, and the world seemed to be falling away at her feet. Then a voice broke the silence.

'Bastard!' Rosmerta screamed. 'You bastard, you bastard!'

The bastard ignored her and suddenly Claudia was lifted on to the bed and a sheet was wiping the blood from her eyes.

'Next time ye throw furniture,' a gravel voice rumbled, 'would ye have a mind to use a wee stool, please?'

Nosferatu couldn't stop screaming.

Bastard! He was wearing a cuirass, the bastard! Beneath his shirt, that fat oaf had been wearing a thick leather cuirass, and now he was binding her wrists in irons – irons, if you please – and tying her legs at the ankles, and all that lazy Roman cow was doing was sitting on the bed holding a bedsheet to her head. *My* bedsheet at that.

'Lady Claudia, I insist you stop this farce at once!'

Nosferatu might not have spoken. Did the chit not understand?

'I've always been looking out for your best interests, my dear, surely you realize that?'

Just how many times must she tell the wretched girl how fond she was of her? Why, when Mazares said he'd be bringing a bride here from Rome, Nosferatu had been delighted. Such a vibrant young creature, as well! The King would be dead – oh, and on the very day his marriage was announced, too – but what a bonus. Nosferatu had been perfectly willing to take the girl under her wing. She was funny and witty, and she'd be part of the family, *plus* she was rich and in trade. Dear me, she could guide them through the minefield of commercial wheeling and dealing in Rome, and she'd know *all* the latest fashions, of course. Yes, indeed. A very *precious* part of the family.

'I don't think you understand what I can do for you, girl.'

What on earth did the ungrateful minx mean, she wasn't a pet? *Pet?* Hadn't she just tried to pass her off as a heroine? The saviour of Histria's hour? And what's this nonsense about facing judgment?

'I am Rosmerta!' Nosferatu pronounced 'Wife of Kažan, mother of Marek and Mir, grandmother of a child yet to be named. The King is dead, long live the King, therefore, I am the Queen – and queens, you imbeciles, do not face judgment.'

We *are* judgment.

Don't you see?

Thirty

Clouds had closed in to swallow the hills, trapping heat that you could cut with a woodsaw. Thunder rumbled like the bellowing of the Minotaur imprisoned in the bowels of its labyrinth – half man, half bull, all cannibal – and the growls were relentless, rolling from island to island and back. With each roar, the night sky turned a deeper shade of purple and crackled with bolts of white lightning.

'Hrrrowwl.'

In the dark, Drusilla's crossed eyes glowed like diamonds.

'Yes, I know, poppet.'

The rasp of cicadas was grating on Claudia's nerves, too, as she paced the cool marble floor of her bedroom. Salome had treated her head wound with tincture of birthwort and applied a poultice of marsh mallow to Claudia's jaw, and as much as she would have liked Salome to stay, Salome had other, more pressing matters, to attend to.

'Yowwwwl.'

As another silver shaft splintered the heavens, Claudia was gripped by a feeling of impending finality and she shivered. Surely the news must come soon? She shivered again, dreading the news, dreading the lack of news. She wanted nothing to change. Everything to remain suspended in time just as it was. Frozen. Preserved in this limbo for ever.

So, she washed down the exact number of flower buds of meadowsweet, honeysuckle – and something she couldn't identify – as Salome prescribed with the oregano tea she had left, then swallowed another handful because the pain wasn't

266

dulling, though it wasn't the throbbing in her head that concerned her.

'I can't stand this,' she told Drusilla. 'I can't stand this interminable waiting.'

Salome had ordered her to stay in bed. She had lost a lot of blood, she insisted, and on top of her previous injuries, it would be foolish to risk infection. But who could sit twiddling their thumbs while the Grim Reaper's sickle swishes back and forth over Mazares's head? Except the pacing only added to the sense of impotence, and the desolation in her heart was as cold as the Arctic.

She heard boots in the corridor. Hurrying. Scurrying. But they passed on, and the hall fell silent once more.

Time passed.

The sky turned black, as black as the Thunder Maker's face, whose bolts split the heavens. She thought of Raspor. Of the arrowheads that hung round his neck.

'Oh, Perun,' she whispered. 'Mazares is a good man. Don't let him die.'

Fear turned to anger. How could he do this? How could he not realize he was so ill? Damn you, Mazares! Would it have been so hard to delegate a few tasks here and there, so you could at least tell the difference between burden and poison? *It is killing him*, Drilo had said. *His pride is killing him*, and he was right. Rosmerta couldn't have woven her evil if Mazares hadn't shown her the way!

Claudia continued to pace. She'd only be in the way in his sick room, and in any case, Mazares was weak enough at the moment, he needed strength pulsed into his body, not fear. Right now, the King needed calm. He needed the soothing touch of a woman who loved, but didn't panic. A woman, moreover, who never doubted . . .

An old proverb twisted its way into Claudia's head. It was a favourite of her father's, she remembered. That there was a remedy for everything except death. Oh, but if there was even a remote chance of saving Mazares, Salome could do it. On willpower alone she'd win through, and she possessed a knowledge of herbs that had been passed down through the years, each generation adding her own bank of learning. The trouble was, the answer to whether Salome's blend of courage, willpower and healing was strong enough would not be known for some time, and Claudia couldn't keep prowling this room. She had to do something.

There was only one thing to do.

Island funerals are lonely rituals for someone who isn't a native. For priests, in particular, they lack not only the grandeur of their urban counterparts – the professional musicians, hired mourners, orators, acolytes, sacrifice, augury – but also the warmth and companionship that accompanies the deceased on that final farewell as friends and relatives line the streets, rather than strangers merely nodding to pay their respects.

To be fair, the people of Rovin had done their best for Raspor, but even assuming his corpse had been in any fit state to travel to Gora – which, in this heat, it was not – there was no escort available to accompany him on that last, lonely journey.

The riots that had interrupted the auction intensified once news of Rosmerta's conspiracy filtered out, and the King's illness had done little to quell it. The Histrian people were in turmoil. They would not leave Rovin, they couldn't; never before was Mazares needed so much. Despite some protection by his leather cuirass, Pavan was too weak from blood loss to take charge, Orbilio far too Roman and Kažan too close to the source of their pain. Nor was Drilo up to the task, but they took their high priest's advice when he pointed out the urgency of burying the grisly haul that had been dredged up by the current. Sadly, this meant Raspor was but one of several hastily prepared burials, denied the dignity of even a personalized service.

And because order had broken down, or perhaps because he'd needed something to focus on, the ferryman hadn't closed up after dark. Naturally, he protested when he saw his passenger's injuries, but recognized in her the same need to be busy and unhooked the rope without speaking.

Around the archipelago, Perun's anger crackled and spat, and the Kingdom of Histria trembled under his boot. Claudia averted her eyes from the heavens, staring into the deep, silent waters, and her knuckles clenched white round her torch.

Another torch already flickered in the tree-lined graveyard.

She had watched it wind its way down the twisting, narrow street from the house to the ferry, and she'd followed its progress across to the mainland, watching the light getting smaller and smaller as it receded into the blackness. What she hadn't been able to work out was what glistened in the torch-bearer's free hand. But then, how could she possibly have guessed he'd be carrying a spade?

The shovelling stopped when he saw her approach, and he wiped his brow with the back of his wrist. It left behind streaks of red mud, like the battle paint worn by certain Teutonic warriors to frighten the enemy, but Claudia wasn't frightened. Not of Kažan.

'Raspor, I presume?' His liquid dark eyes indicated the chaplet of flowers brimming over her basket.

'I owe him this much.'

She had brought other things, too. Spelt, black beans and laurel leaves to strew on his grave, as well as a small bough of cypress. These might be Roman, but then so was she. Raspor would understand.

'You'll find him over there, second mound down on your right,' Kažan said, returning to his digging.

Claudia thanked him. It was too early for top stones to have been laid on the graves, and as she scattered her offerings, she thought how fitting it was that the thunder god whom Raspor had served was so active tonight. The little priest would appreciate that.

'Is it rude to enquire who you're digging up?' she asked, as another sheet of lightning ripped through the sky. 'Or is this another local custom I'm not aware of?'

Kažan grinned. 'I'm doing the *bajuks*' work for them,' he

said. 'I'm keeping evil spirits out of the cemetery and, since you ask, it's the boat builder's body facing eviction. I won't have his dirty bones contaminating sacred soil, Claudia. He isn't fit to lie here.'

She glanced across to the hideous masks nailed to the tree trunk. It was impossible to make out the *bajuks'* expressions in the darkness, but the empty black robes that flapped in the wind like sinister pennants gave their position away.

'I didn't realize you felt so passionately about homosexuality.'

'I feel passionately about blackmailing bastards,' Kažan said bitterly. 'Rosmerta told me why she had killed him – oh, and before you ask, no. Murderers aren't allowed to lie in sacred ground, either. Their souls are thrown to the shroud-eaters. They will never find rest.'

Claudia looked across to where Dol the Just rested. In peace . . . ?

'I'm not sure how much of the story will come out,' he continued, 'but I'm betting this bastard's role won't be aired. The court will want to protect Broda as much as they can.'

He paused to wipe the sweat off his face with the hem of his tunic and sighed deeply. 'I don't expect people will believe that I knew nothing of my wife's plans, but it's true.'

'On the contrary, Kažan. I think they'll understand very well.'

It was common knowledge that the couple rarely spent time together. Never talked, because he was never around. Hunting, fishing and women were his only interests, Pavan said, and he was bloody good at all three. Claudia watched while the earth piled up around him. Rosmerta might be a monster, but it was Kažan who had made her one. Charming, handsome, witty and fun, it was his neglect that turned her into what she was . . .

Claudia swallowed, and the wind hissed like snakes in the trees.

'You know she killed your father?'

Kažan pinched his lips together, but didn't stop digging.

'She poisoned Mazares,' she said, 'she poisoned Delmi, she murdered their children, the boat builder, the royal physician . . .'

The pain on his face was pitiful to watch.

'. . . Raspor, of course, and these crimes go back many years. But you know what troubles me, Kažan? Brac. Rosmerta wasn't even on the scene when your brother died.'

She laid her basket on the path.

'His death doesn't fit the picture.'

'Perhaps that's what gave her the idea,' he said, pausing. 'Fevers are unpredictable and death is indiscriminate.'

'Yes. I would accept that.' The heat twisted the night air like a coil. 'Except I saw Pavan hold a pillow over Rosmerta's face.'

'Fine fellow, our general. He saw a way to solve the problem and avoid public scandal at the same time, and he'd have succeeded, too, if you hadn't brained him with an armchair.'

'Yes, I would accept that, as well,' Claudia said. 'In fact, if we put it all together, we have the whole picture, don't you agree? That Brac was murdered for the noblest of reasons?'

'Brac?' The spade didn't falter. 'I told you – hell, everyone knows – it was a fever that carried him off.'

Brac be nimble, Brac be quick, Brac jump over the candlestick.

'Fit young man, newly married? It happens.' Far too often, unfortunately. 'But then, I got to thinking.'

Brac jump long, Brac jump high, Or Brac fall into a fever and die.

'Mazares said your brother was confident to the point of cocky, and he talked of how the elders hoped Brac would grow into the kind of king that your father was. Would grow into, you note. Hoped.'

'If you're implying what I think you're implying –' Kažan flashed her his famous little-boy-lost smile – 'just remember who releases flocks of finches on the anniversary of his brother's death.'

'Like you release roof tiles, you mean?'

Like an inflated pig's bladder when it suddenly ruptures, Kažan shrank before her eyes. The spade fell from his hand but Claudia felt no satisfaction. No satisfaction at all in the knowledge that no tile was missing from any rooftop.

The islanders were proud of their burgeoning heritage. Rovin, if you don't mind, was the island beloved of the King, and they were fiercely proud of their king. Therefore, they were desperate to make him proud of them in return. Witness the perfect order this town was kept in. No litter. No graffiti. Everything spotless and tidy.

'You have no idea.'

Kažan slumped against the side of the pit as the first hot raindrops started to fall.

'You have no idea what it's like to have a brother strutting around like some puffed-up cockerel, telling me how he's got the best of this, the biggest of that, while pointing out how worthless and useless I was, an unwanted afterthought, nothing but the runt of the litter.'

As droplets became heavier, Claudia grasped a new side to Dol. One in which duty came first as he oversaw everything himself, leaving his sons to grow up without him. The eldest compensated by becoming a braggart and a bully, leaving the youngest to be overindulged by his mother. Only the middle son learned by avoiding their mistakes – then made one of his own by following his father's example.

'It was a good way to go,' Kažan said.

The rain was drumming, turning the red mud to orange sludge.

'Fevers creep up, until all sense of logic is lost. Brac died in his sleep. Crumbs, it was obvious to me, even at the tender age of fourteen, that Mazares was head and shoulders the best man to take over from Father. Brac didn't want the job. He didn't give a stuff about Histria, all he was bothered about were his pecker and his belly. No, Mazares was the caring one. He was the best-looking of us, too, clever at schooling, and Brac's bride wasn't just a stunner, Delmi was a princess. As a mere second son, Mazares would only have qualified for a chieftain's daughter, same as me, so, if you like, you could say I was doing both my brothers a favour.'

An interesting viewpoint, but one which Claudia doubted many would share, and Brac least of all.

'What about Rosmerta?' she asked.

'Yes, well, knowing what I know now, I'm doubly sorry that wig was so thick, and as for that incompetent idiot of a mule doctor . . .'

Another one who'd underestimated the doctor's abilities, it seemed, because when Kažan slipped what he believed to be an overdose of painkiller down his wife's throat, he was merely putting her into that recuperative sleep.

'I hate her, Claudia, I've always hated the bitch. The look of her, the touch of her, it's revolting, and can you imagine how much I ground my teeth doing what I had to, until I'd sired those boys?'

His sodden hair shuddered.

'She stifled me. One sniffle and she'd have me covered in mustard poultices. She was bossy, domineering, always made me feel less of a man and, sure, I made light of our separate lives, but hell, that isn't marriage.'

No, it isn't, Claudia thought. But it takes two to settle into that kind of arrangement.

'Then Vani told me she was pregnant and that changed everything. Mir knows full well it isn't his, he hasn't touched her in months, and it's not as if she loves the lad.'

So it was Mir the athletic Vani was married to, was it? Claudia tried to picture which of the two sons had restrained the mastiff on its short leash and which one then released it. Either way, both were guilty of murder, and this time they wouldn't escape the smell of roasted man-meat. The flesh on the fire would be theirs.

'So, you wanted Rosmerta out of the way to marry Vani?'

Oh, Kažan. Don't you listen to any of your women? Don't you understand a single one? For better or worse, Vani had nailed her colours to the marital mast. Adultery was one thing, but divorce was out of the question. She tried not to think how it was for Delmi, lost in grief and looking for consolation in the handsome lover with the slow hand, only to find emptiness in both.

'Vani and I are good for each other, you've seen that, but more importantly, that's my *child* she's carrying.'

Love, protection, affection, Claudia could understand all that. But . . .

'Why didn't you divorce Rosmerta?'

The puzzlement in his eyes was her answer and Claudia instinctively edged back a pace. He'd stifled his brother and got away with it. With his wife, it hadn't occurred to him to do anything else, and no wonder there had been a look of such deep concern on his face when he realized the assault hadn't proved fatal. He was worried Rosmerta had seen him, so he tried to finish her off with the poppy draught. Like a rogue tiger, she thought, he'd acquired the taste. Kažan had become a rogue male . . .

'What are you going to do?' he asked quietly.

Claudia drew a deep breath.

'Nothing.'

She lifted the last remaining item from her basket and balanced it on the edge of the boat builder's grave. It was a small phial of green glass that, until this morning, had sat on the shelf in Salome's treatment room. The papyrus label proclaimed it as hemlock.

'We must each take responsibility for our own destiny, Kažan.'

Murderers weren't allowed to rest in this holy precinct, but that was presuming somebody knew.

'Only you can decide whether you want your soul at the mercy of shroud-eaters and to never find rest, or whether you would rather lie here, with your brother and father.'

The rain drummed out Kažan's reply.

Thirty-One

The boat-thronged harbour ebbed away into the distance. Slowly, the scent of the islands was replaced by the tang of the ocean, and the white hill that was Rovin, rising out of the foam like Venus, Goddess of Love, grew smaller and smaller until it was no more than a spot on the horizon.

The great striped sail billowed and shook as Claudia rested her elbows on the red-painted rail and rested her chin in her hands. Strange, but she would miss these crystal-clear waters, the pebbly beaches and golden coves, the eternal beauty of this evergreen archipelago. Histria was not at all how she'd imagined, but the biggest surprise was how hard it had been to say goodbye to this heavenly oasis of pines and vines, a land full of contrasts, of ancient secrets and wisdom. She would never return. Too much had happened, but there was an emptiness at knowing she'd never inhale the herbal aromas of Salome's treatment room again, or watch fleeces being combed instead of shorn, or listen to the Amazons squabble and sing as they worked in the fields, their skirts kilted up to their knees. Nor would she know how Broda's emotional scars would affect her as she grew into adulthood, or whether Raspor would be re-buried in Gora or left in peace where he was.

'Copper quadran for your thoughts,' a baritone murmured in her ear, and suddenly sandalwood was blotting out the smell of pitch and salt. With just a hint of the rosemary that his patrician tunic had been rinsed in.

Claudia turned. What could she say? That she had been

275

gazing at the land as it blurred into blue on the horizon, conjuring up Nymphs of the West singing lullabies in gardens full of apples of gold, which had been walled by mighty Atlas himself . . . before she remembered how Histria was a land of two halves. That werewolves roamed the dark side of the collective imagination, as well, alongside shroud-eaters, vampires and fire-breathing monsters, and that arch-ghoul with the lolling head, Nosferatu.

'I was just thinking how a girl can't even catch a boat nowadays without it swarming with Security Police.'

Orbilio grinned. In fact, now she came to think of it, he'd been grinning like an idiot since he boarded this ship.

'You have to agree, though, that when it comes to swarming, I'm up there with the best of them.'

'No, Marcus, that's smarming, and you owe me a quadran.'

'I owe you an apology, too.' His expression became grim. 'I ought to have taken your concerns seriously, only, so many deaths seemed . . . well, absurd.'

Also, she thought, he was too close. He'd known Mazares a long time, and if Mazares himself was convinced that his family was jinxed, that conviction would have no trouble transferring itself to others. Orbilio couldn't have changed one damn thing. But she would let him work that out in his own time, not hers. She hadn't forgotten who'd palmed her off like an old vase in the first place!

'You realize you've ruined my hundred per cent detection record?' His strong, patrician nose wrinkled. 'The runaways racket's closed down, but I've no conviction, and, since I wrote in dispatches that my prime suspect was all but in irons, the only credit I'll be getting is a bollocking for aiding a Cretan girl to escape. Also, I see no point in reporting Rosmerta's plot to Rome or they'll send a flurry of governors by return post, and that will be utter disaster.'

'Into every life a little rain must fall, Orbilio. I'm sure someone will dream up a luscious attempt on the Emperor's life to redress the balance.'

Steaming in with the navy, charging up with the cavalry,

legging it in with the legionaries, his career wouldn't remain in the shadows for long. Marcus Cornelius was far too ambitious for that – except, now that Claudia was returning home without a royal ring on her finger or a contract to supply Histria with her wine, she could only pray that the tentacles of his ambition didn't stretch in her direction. She would have to be even more inventive with her finances from now on.

'Yes, and talking of rain,' he said, 'that storm was a monster, but, praise be to Juno, it didn't last long.' He slanted her a quizzical glance. 'What chance, do you think, of the calm lasting?'

Claudia thought carefully before she answered.

'Fair,' she said. 'Maybe even good, if Mazares continues to flourish.'

The relief – oh, the relief – when Salome told her that the cold sweats were gone and the tingling had subsided completely.

'Why didn't you accept his proposal?' she'd asked, placing a parsley poultice on Claudia's swollen jaw.

'Because I'm not the right woman for him,' she'd replied bluntly.

The right woman doesn't question her man's integrity. The right woman's trust doesn't falter. The Syrian girl pushed her foxy mane behind her ears in a way that would scandalize the matrons of Rome, where society decreed that women must tie their hair up.

'Maybe,' Salome conceded. 'But then again, my dear, have you considered the possibility that it was because Mazares is not the right man for you?'

Not at all, she thought, pushing aside images of dark, wavy mops, and anyway dawn was starting to break. Admittedly, it was cold, grey and damp, but it was still dawn – which meant there was still time.

'Come with me,' she ordered Salome.

Mazares sat propped up in bed, his curls lank, his skin yellow and with purple caverns under his eyes, but to Claudia

277

he'd never looked better, and, on the rug by the window, his two Molossan hounds snored contentedly.

'That woman's a witch,' he drawled, shaking his finger at Salome. 'She fed me the most abominable potions you can imagine. As if I wasn't in enough discomfort!'

'Console yourself that she won't need to resort to such drastic tactics when you're married,' Claudia replied crisply. 'Pavan, do you still have the papers?'

'Aye.'

One arm in a sling, he passed the scroll across with the other. Here was another one who should be in bed, she reflected, but it seems you can't keep these three-headed gorillas down.

'What are you talking about?' Salome and Mazares chorused at once.

'There's still time,' Claudia said, 'if you hurry, because in a few minutes it will be morning.'

The King and the widow exchanged puzzled glances.

'The morning of the day *after* marriages can be announced,' Claudia explained.

'Yes, but—'

'But nothing, Mazares. She loves you, you love her, now put your damned seal on the contract.'

She should have realized. That jolt of electricity when they bumped into each other. The way his jaw dropped as the blue nymph consigned her herbs to the Fire of Life. The pig he'd sent her, the spotted kind she'd always wanted. The way he'd watched the farm from his window, which was how he was able to raise the alarm so quickly. But, most of all, it was the fact that he suspected what was going on regarding her Freedom Trail and sought a friend's advice, rather than the tribune in Gora . . .

There would be ructions, of course. Salome's views on equality of the sexes alone would produce enough fire to heat the palace throughout the winter, but then, in those pants, marriage to Mazares was never going to be lacking in passion! And she would give him the kind of heirs that he wanted.

Children who'd stand up for what they believed in, free-thinkers, free-wheelers, he'd said, unburdened by conventions and hidebound traditions. Yes, indeed. With Salome around, he'd never go short of those!

'Mazares, you have three minutes of today remaining.'

Dancing catkins swivelled towards his redheaded healer. 'Just what drugs did you feed this poor wretch?'

But, instead of laughing, Salome threw her hands into the air. 'What *is* it with you boneheaded Histri? Can't you *ever* see what's under your noses?'

He blenched. 'You mean it's true?'

'Great Marduk, I've loved you since the first day I met you, now will you please, please do as Claudia asks, and no, this has nothing to do with time running out. It's so the bride can bloody well kiss you.'

His reply sounded like, 'Why am I cursed with women breaking my balls?' but Claudia couldn't be certain, because, for one thing, Pavan was rustling the parchment in her ear, and for another, the King's mouth had been completely covered by a ravishing redhead. Well, well, well. Who said you can't be a dutiful monarch and still be happy?

'Claudia!' he called out. 'Wait. I haven't thanked you for, well, for everything, and look at you! You're black and blue . . .'

'Mazares, there are thirty seconds left to announce your marriage. We can make small talk later.'

Except she knew it wouldn't happen. That she must take the next boat off the island. Be gone before he found out. But, by all that was holy, she'd miss that velvety drawl, that lazy sparkle behind his eyes, even, dammit, those ridiculous pants, and, who knows, maybe Mazares would even miss her? Although, if Salome's fervour was anything to go by, he'd have little time to dwell on the past. Soon Histria would be invested with so many heirs, he probably wouldn't be able to move for the blasted things, and her heart swelled with happiness for him.

Kažan's suicide would come as a blow, but on top of so

many shocks, it would be that much easier to absorb, she supposed. Later, of course, the pain of his loss would sink in, but then again, later, Mazares would be stronger, and with Salome at his side, he would be more able to cope with his grief.

Strangely, it was Kažan's death that finally made the man. When Claudia returned to sprinkle hyssop on Raspor's mound, you wouldn't know the boat builder's grave had been touched.

But now the island of Rovin was gone. The green archipelago with it. Even the coast of the peninsula had faded to nothing . . .

'There's one thing I don't understand,' she said, as Orbilio rested his foot on a coil of rope and leaned his face into the wind.

'Only one? You must be slipping.'

She ignored that.

'How is it that two people can be so much in love and not see it?' she asked.

His response was to laugh and toss her a mirror.

'Beats me,' he said.